MUSCLE AND BONE

MARY CALMES

Muscle and Bone

Copyright ©2021 Mary Calmes

http://marycalmes.com

All rights reserved. No part of this book may be reproduced or transmitted in any form or by any means, electronic or mechanical, including photocopying, recording, or by any information storage and retrieval system without the written permission of the author, except for the use of brief quotations in a book review.

This is a work of fiction. Names, characters, places and incidents either are the products of author imagination or used fictitiously. Any resemblance to actual persons, living or dead, business establishments, events, or locales is entirely coincidental.

Cover content is for illustrative purposes only. Any person depicted on the cover is a model.

Cover art Copyright © 2021 Reese Dante

http://reesedante.com

Edit by Lisa Horan

Proof Edit by Brian Holliday and Will Parkinson

❀ Created with Vellum

First off, I have to thank Lisa Horan for the amazing work she did on this book. She made certain that what was in my head actually appears on the page and that was no mean feat. I love world-building but she kept me from falling too far down the rabbit hole.

Brian Holliday and Will Parkinson are much appreciated for their questions and comments that prodded me to think about the why of things and not just the how.

Thank you all, my wonderful readers, for your continued support and I hope you enjoy my new world.

MUSCLE AND BONE

You belong to me and I know it down deep, in muscle and bone, where my wolf lives.

Avery Rhine isn't an average homicide detective with the Chicago PD. In fact, Avery isn't an average anything. Sure, as an omega he knows he's at the bottom of the food chain, but that's never slowed him down. He's got a great life, complete with a loving family and a best friend who'd take a bullet for him, so what more could he possibly want or need? Except, maybe, for the world to change. And to find someone to spend more than one night with, but that isn't high on his list of priorities. He's never been one to believe in destiny or whatever else the fantasies sell about there being someone special out there meant just for him.

Then a chance encounter at a party changes everything.

Graeme Davenport has no delusions about finding his true mate. The consensus is that if an alpha doesn't find their other half by the time they're thirty, the chances of it ever happening go from slim to none. He's not a mere alpha, though; Graeme is a *cyne* who sits at the pinnacle of lupine hierarchy, so he's obligated by tradition and duty to choose an omega now, sign a contract, and bond with him. Love is not part of the equation.

When Graeme and Avery meet, their fierce attraction to each other flies in the face of reason and logic. Avery's intense physical reaction to the alpha is something he's never experienced before, while Graeme, who has always been the soul of discretion, loses all his inhibitions to desire for the man he wants to possess. They are two very different men trying to navigate expectations, separate reason from innate primal drive, and do it while working together to solve a murder.

It will take everything they are to find a middle ground, and to learn to trust in a fated kind of love.

1

AVERY

Without question, the gatherings were the worst part of being an omega.

If the guys at work could see me dressed in my black tailcoat and matching dress pants, the wing-collared shirt with studs and cufflinks, white piqué waistcoat and white bow tie, along with the black silk socks and the patent leather cap toe dress shoes...they would laugh themselves into a coma. The good news was, they never would.

It wasn't that I was hiding anything. They all knew I was a lupine, and therefore only part human. My ancestors were not fully homo sapiens but homo canum as well, because, to put it simply, I was part wolf. It was a mutation that gained a foothold at the same time humans were evolving from apes, and instead of us going extinct, like a million other species that blipped in and out of the fossil record, lupines stuck. And even though both species moved through the centuries together, one was hidden in darkness and one lived in the light.

A hundred years ago, the species were segregated, not

allowed to marry, barely even permitted to be friends, but like progress of any kind, there were reformers and radicals and people fighting for change and equality and inclusion.

Seventy-five years ago the courts ruled that humans and lupines were equal, and if a human being could be a police officer, then so could a lupine. I was lucky, because I grew up in a time where me wanting to go into law enforcement had never been the pipe dream it was for my grandfather. Even if it did mean I was still somewhat of an anomaly. He was very proud the day I graduated from the academy, as was my mother. My father, on the other hand, had explained to me, ad nauseum, that the occupation was both beneath me and not something that would, or could, even be tolerated once I was mated. He changed his tune a bit when it was written into my contract, but assured me that a smart alpha could work around any clause, no matter how ironclad the language. I would give him the indulgent nod at that point, which would bring about a quick end to our conversation.

As the son of one of the richest lupine families in Chicago, I was part of the *jarl*, the upper class, the elite, and was supposed to concern myself with only the glitterati of the city. That had never interested me in the least. And while my father had insisted I join the family business, as only he would—I was an omega after all, good for very little—and my brother tried guilt to get me to come on board, and my sister threatened me with bodily harm, my mother had always been on my side. She taught middle school in the inner city; I was a police detective. We were the rebels in our family, two peas in a pod, each of us following our dreams.

"You're late, Avery," my parents' housekeeper, Corvina, informed me tersely as I walked through the kitchen. She was there supervising the caterers, snapping out orders, something she loved doing.

"Good evening, Corvie," I called out cheerfully, grinning wide.

"You, with the face and the dimples," she fumed at me, but couldn't help smiling. I was her favorite after all, had been since birth. "You're not eating enough!"

"You always say that," I teased her, breezing through the swinging kitchen door and out into the short hall.

From there I went to the closet, hung up my coat, and then slipped into the meandering crowd, moving through the ten thousand square foot limestone mansion in Chicago's Gold Coast area. I was hoping to fly under the radar until I could locate the sanctuary that was my mother. I just needed to keep my head down,

"Avery." My brother, Ambrose, called out my name.

Normally, I was able to get the lay of the land first, but he'd spotted me before I could avoid him. Someone, probably my brother, had gotten wise to me climbing up the side of the house on the rose trellis to my old bedroom. That maneuver would dump me out on the second floor and allow me to make sure I looked presentable before I walked out my door and peered over the balustrade and down to the level below to check and see where everyone was. But tonight, when I was about to start my climb, I saw one of Ambrose's many assistants standing on my old balcony, clocking me and talking on his cell phone at the same time. No doubt he was reporting my position to Ambrose. My partner, Wade Massey, would have asked how I knew he was one of my brother's flunkies. And I would have told him it was because they all looked the same, like little clones from a *GQ* photoshoot, sycophants with their two-thousand-dollar suits, polished wingtips, and three-hundred-dollar haircuts.

"Come here!" Ambrose ordered, actually yelling, which he never did. I would have told him it was gauche and stood there in mock horror, trying my best to look aghast, but I knew he was thinking it to himself as he looked around, appalled at his own behavior. I'd hear about it later, what I'd "forced him to do," but I didn't care, and had no idea if it was the volume or his spontaneous action he was so chagrined over. Either way, I continued with the pretense that I hadn't heard him over the din of conversation, and said *excuse me* and *pardon me* a hundred times as I moved through the crowd to evade him.

"Avery!" my sister, Andrea, bellowed, which was in just as bad form as Ambrose, but I spun around and headed the other way through the press of people, moving under one of the arches in the cavernous living room of the house I'd grown up in.

"Avery," Sandor Graves, our butler, a man who had served our family for as long as I could remember, barked, hoping to get me to stop so he could deliver me to my father.

I turned and waved at him like I was on the jumbotron at the United Center, but didn't alter my course in the least because, really, did he think that was going to work? Had it ever? He was not my father, and if I wouldn't stop for the patriarch of our family, did Sandor honestly think I would stop for him?

Being a wolf, I could feel everyone closing in on me, and worse, because I was an omega, there was always that extra layer of hardwired, genetically engrained trepidation that came from being at the bottom of the food chain. My brother and sister were both alphas. My mother had impressively birthed two, which was a feat that not many betas, as she was, could boast of. When she had me, she'd received hundreds of condolences. The odds were—in scrutinizing the members of her family tree, as well as my father's—that I'd be a beta, or at least a gamma like many of my cousins. It was just bad luck I turned out to be that which another family could claim for their own.

"Avery," Sandor growled, closer than I'd thought, and I had that moment of fear, of dread, and I hated that even after all the years of police training, and the fact I had a Glock 22 strapped to my calf under my pants, still, I was responding like an animal and not a man. It was one of the many reasons my wolf and I did *not* get along.

I felt our butler's hand on my shoulder, slowing my momentum toward the salvation I could now see, and because I didn't want to deal with him, or any of them, I cheated.

"Mom," I yelled, shrugging off his hand, and I made sure my voice carried like it did when I used it on suspects to *freeze* or *get on the ground*.

People turned and stared, which would have mortified any other member of my family but not my warm, down-to-earth mother.

Elira Rhine Huntington snorted and quickly abandoned the circle of fawning admirers she was constantly at the center of at any party she, or anyone else, had ever thrown. "My baby," she gushed, rushing over, her movement made possible because people cleared a hole for the golden-haired goddess that was my mother. "How are you, love?"

I lifted my arms, walking toward her, and she filled them, wrapping around me tight. "I'm good, Mom. How're you?"

She pulled back to look up at my face, her own lighting up with a smile that made her charcoal eyes, several shades darker than my own, crinkle in half. "I'm wonderful, and so far I've got the winning bid in the silent auction for Chicago Blackhawks tickets," she informed me gleefully, rubbing her hands together.

"That's creepy as hell," I assured her, pointing at her hands, which she instantly dropped to her sides.

"Pardon me?"

"You and blood." I shook my head in seemingly solemn judgement.

"I'm sorry?" she replied, affronted.

"Action movies, MMA fights, hockey, documentaries about the mob, boxing, you're all about blood and gore, lady. Back in the day I bet you would have gone to the coliseum and watched the gladiators."

"Who?" She feigned shock, clutching her chest. "Me?"

I tsked at her, curling a piece of hair that had come loose from her long, thick side-braid, around her ear. "I can tell I've insulted you deeply."

"To the quick," she agreed, cackling as my father, Alexander Huntington, owner and chairman of the board of Huntington, one of the biggest builders in the country, stepped in front of us, scowling.

"Hello, darling," she cheerfully greeted the man she loved, reaching for his hand, which he instantly clasped.

"Hey there, old man," I taunted, giving him a quick clap on the shoulder.

I didn't think his scowl could get any darker, but with those blue-black eyes of his, made somehow even more foreboding with his black hair and silver sideburns, it was possible.

"When your brother calls you," he admonished through clenched teeth, "you treat that the same as if *I* were calling you."

"Oh yeah?"

"I'm serious, Avery."

"No, I know. But how many times in my life would you guess you've said that to me? Throw out a number."

He rubbed the bridge of his nose. "Avery."

My name was always uttered with the same mix of exasperation and resignation by the man who'd carried me around on his shoulders when I was a child. He loved me and wanted to throttle me in equal measure.

"C'mon, let's quantify it," I baited him, pushing like I always did.

"I'm certain I have no earthly idea."

"Let's say a million, just to be in the ballpark." I snickered and turned so I was beside him, draping my arm across his shoulders. "Tell me, and be truthful."

"You––"

"Has telling me to listen to Ambrose ever worked out for you?"

"This," he growled at my mother, gesturing to all of me, "is your fault."

"Well, yes, I should hope so," she agreed, beaming at him, completely unfazed.

He sighed deeply, clearly resigned, long-suffering, and then turned to me, pulling me into a tight hug, nuzzling his face into my hair and inhaling deeply. That maneuver was all wolf and left his scent on me, which marked me as his offspring, his child, his son. His own.

"Oh!" My mother whimpered in delight at seeing us together.

When he leaned out of the embrace, I noticed his furrowed brows were back. "You couldn't have shaved?"

"I was in a hurry," I assured him, drawing out the last

word. "I work out of the Eighteenth District, old man. Do you know how far that is, in traffic, from here?"

"Yes, but—"

"And you wanted me here at six?" I scrunched up my face and shook my head at him. "You're lucky the monkey suit is clean."

He was about to say something when my bicep was grabbed and I was spun around to face my brother. Ambrose's deep, dark midnight blue eyes, the same as our father's, were trained on me, along with the familiar glower perfected by Alexander Huntington. Only the silver at the temples was missing from my brother's hair. What was different, what softened his face, were the laugh lines. Ambrose Huntington was a serious man, but his wife never let him get away with anything, and she made him smile often. I was grateful for her every day and thankfully she was there, slipping between us, a sliver of joy in a scarlet crushed-silk gown.

Dove Huntington lifted her arms, and I bent and hugged her, lifting her off her feet for a moment, making her giggle with delight.

"Can you two please not," Ambrose groused at me as she kissed my cheek.

"How are you, you gorgeous thing?" she purred as I set her back down on her feet, gazing up at me in absolute adoration, waiting for my answer.

"I'm good," I told her, taking her hand as she slipped it into mine. "We caught the guy wanted in those acid attacks on the models."

She gasped. "Was it who you and your partner thought?"

I nodded. "It was, fortunately, and we caught him before he hurt anyone else."

"You know what he's doing?" my brother asked her.

"You don't follow the crime in this city?" Andrea Donahue, my sister, appeared beside my father. "My God, Ambrose, how can you not?"

He threw up his hands in defeat as Andrea stepped into the small family circle we made and opened her arms for me.

I greeted her just as I had Dove, lifting her off her feet and squeezing tight.

She laughed, even though I knew she didn't want to. She never did. In her mind, anything that *she* considered feminine or girly was bad. Wolves, on the whole, were a sexist, misogynistic lot. Had she been born into any number of other families, she would never have been allowed to work in whatever business made them their fortune, even having been born an alpha. But Andrea was my father's daughter, and he saw no difference between her and my brother, even with my brother being his heir. For my father, whoever was the smartest and most capable would take over from him when he retired, sex be damned. At the moment, my brother was CEO and my sister was CFO, so it was a crapshoot, unless you knew them. For me, my money was on Drea, because she could think outside the box, and Ambrose only saw four corners. I also secretly hoped Ambrose would throw caution to the wind and return to his real love, which was painting, but thus far that had not happened.

"Don't shake her too much," my brother-in-law, Crawford Donahue, ordered me when he reached us. "Your sister's pregnant."

"What?" I put her down gently to take her chin in my hand. "Poppet, you're gonna be a mommy?"

She snorted out a laugh, and then, seconds later, uncharacteristic tears filled her eyes as she nodded.

I grabbed her again, and she melted against me, shivering, unable, it seemed, with the new hormones coursing through her body, to resist the pull of my warmth. Omegas were like candy to alphas, betas, and gammas, all ranks falling under their spell pretty quickly. It was why we were both loved and hated so fiercely. History was filled with stories of evil omegas twisting poor unsuspecting wolves, especially alphas, around their fingers and forcing them to commit abominations. To me, the omegas in the stories had always seemed like easy scapegoats.

"Let her go," Ambrose ordered me, and once I did, after giving her a kiss on the forehead, he stepped in front of me. "Did you hear me yelling?"

"You yelled?" My mother gasped dramatically.

"For the love of God, Mother," he grumbled, letting his head fall back on his shoulders in total defeat. I chuckled as he slowly lifted it to look at me in utter dejection as Crawford leaned in to give me a hug and kiss, the only one, apart from his wife, that he was ever so touchy-feely with. Again, him being a beta, he couldn't resist me.

"You're supposed to come when I call you," my brother muttered belligerently.

"I think you have me confused with Cosmo," I countered. "I'm not your beagle, I'm your brother, in case you got us mixed up again."

"Avery––"

"Don't be a dick, all right? Just gimme a hug," I placated him, holding my arms open.

His sigh was as deep and resigned as my father's had been, because I exhausted them both equally, but he took a step forward and leaned into me anyway. He didn't even protest when I squeezed a grunt out of him. His wife made the *awww* noise when he pushed his face down into my shoulder, needing me just for a moment.

"I'll try and listen to you next time," I soothed him.
"See that you do," he mumbled.

I WAS MAKING the rounds of the room, greeting people I only saw at these frou-frou gatherings, when I was yanked sideways into an alcove. Rounding on my attacker, I found Linden Van Doren, who was both one of my oldest friends and enemies. He was loyal to a fault, while still prone to throwing me under a bus at any given opportunity. It had been particularly bad when we were younger, doing everything from smoking weed to sleeping with boys. I was always the one grounded, and he was the one sneaking pizza to me.

"What are you doing?" I groused at him, noting that he'd curled his strawberry-blond mane rather than pulling it back into the normal queue.

"It should be perfectly obvious that I'm hiding," he snapped back.

I crossed my arms, going for bored.

"I have some admirers—don't bat my hands away," he chastised me. "You're a mess."

I made sure to sigh like I was dying, but he wasn't fazed in the least. Instead, he fussed with my bow tie, my shirt, my cuffs, smoothed a hand down the lapels of my jacket, and tugged and patted until he looked me up and down, shrugged like that was as good as it got, and leaned back against the wall.

"Seriously, why're you hiding?"

"Because Daw, Tyne, and Colby are looking for me."

"Those are people's names?"

"You *know* they are," he scolded.

"And which ones are they, again?" It was hard to keep up

with all his suitors.

"Steel, oil, and venture capital."

"Ah," I said, recalling the last party a couple months back.

As an omega, no matter whose son I was, and probably more so because I was a rich man's progeny, I was required to attend all gatherings where unmated alphas would be in attendance to see if any of them wanted to lay claim to me.

It was an antiquated custom that wasn't going away anytime soon.

When I had moved out of the house and got my own place downtown, I had tried to skip the mandatory social interactions, and my father had threatened to make such a scene in front of everyone I worked with—which was a fate worse than death, with me trying to make detective—that I quickly gave in. But now, years later, at thirty-two, I understood how unconcerned I should have been from day one. No alpha in their right mind, no matter how rich my father was and how fat my dowry would be, wanted me. I was by no means a typical omega.

If an alpha hadn't found their fated beta or gamma, usually between eighteen and thirty, then it became, statistically, a crapshoot that they ever would. There was a pull thing that went on, this overwhelming draw. I didn't fully understand it, even when Ambrose tried to explain, but if they had not discovered their one true mate, who would somehow magically appear, then they would decide to settle down comfortably with an omega. A beta or gamma was a soulmate for an alpha, like my mother was to my father. There was a shared sense of building a life together, forging a path and a future. An omega, on the other hand, was an ornament.

When an alpha was in the market for an omega, they

were looking first for someone to bear their children or, if the alpha and omega were of the same sex, parent the alpha's offspring from a surrogate. Second, an alpha wanted someone with exquisite taste and style who would oversee their staff, and host as well as arrange to attend all society engagements and, of course, run their household. An omega was expected to be immaculate and represent their alpha with grace, poise and beauty. If the alpha was a member of the *jarl*, the whole perfect omega thing was even worse. It was all completely beyond me and always had been. My interest in being anyone's 1950s housewife was utterly nonexistent. I had friends, though, who had been training to be perfection-in-the-flesh their entire lives.

Linden, among others, was the epitome of delicate omega beauty. Me, on the other hand, who showed up with black eyes, various cuts and contusions, and smiling with a split lip, was no one's idea of genteel, ephemeral loveliness. I was too muscular as well. Omegas were supposed to be lithe and lean, fragile. I was the exact opposite of that. The only fun part of attending the parties was seeing the alphas recoil in horror when they met me.

"Are you listening to me?" Linden snapped his fingers in my face. "I said that the whale is here."

"No, I was checked out. Sorry."

He groaned miserably.

"Whale?"

"Yes. There's a *cyne* here tonight, and you know you can't find an unmated one here in the States anymore. You have to travel abroad to land one."

"You are aware that a whale isn't a fish, aren't you?"

"What?"

"I mean, you land a marlin, you don't land a whale," I

instructed, winking at him. "I feel like you should be watching more Discovery Channel."

"God, I hate you."

"I know," I agreed with a smirk, "but tell me who you're looking to catch."

"Graeme Whitaker Davenport *the Fifth*."

"Okay." Linden spoke the name like I should know who this alpha was. I didn't, of course, and was not at all impressed by the suffix he made sure to emphasize.

He sighed deeply, utterly beleaguered. "He's the Earl of Wakefield and Muir."

My scoff was fast. "You're making that up," I baited him. "We don't have earls in this country. Maybe you need to watch the History Channel too."

"Listen––"

"It all started with the Mayflower and––"

"Can you just be serious for five minutes?"

"I dunno, let's find out. Start the timer."

His growl was loud in the small alcove. "Graeme's family is from England, but he was raised here in America and then went to college abroad," he explained to me. "Apparently his father died when Graeme was very young, and then, tragically, his mother, who was an omega, succumbed to grief, as you know some do. His grandparents, who lived here, raised him and his brother."

"Sounds reasonable."

"They have real estate investments all over the world."

"Like my family."

"No," he assured me, the patronizing tone not lost on me. "They make your family's company look positively bougie by comparison. They do ten times the business your father does. He's worth billions."

"What's bougie mean again?"

"Avery." He said my name like a curse word.

"So he's super rich."

"Yes," he replied irritably.

"Cool" was all I could think of to say.

"For heaven's sake, Avery, you need to take this seriously."

"Why do I?"

"Because at some point, as an omega, your own body is going to force you to bond. The pull can't stay dormant forever."

But I was betting the "omegas were slaves to their need to be bonded to an alpha" panic was a good story, same as Santa and the Easter Bunny. I had done my research, as well as talked to many older omegas who'd never bonded, who had regrets, same as anyone else, but none of them had gone mad because they remained single. In the wild, yes, a lone wolf was in danger. The pack took care of all its members, and everyone got fed and stayed warm. But in the world around us, a lone wolf went to Costco and ordered Grubhub and shopped on Amazon. This whole terror about being unbonded was exhausting. This wasn't the 1850s, or even the 1950s. Being single needed to stop being the worst thing anyone could think of.

"Are you listening to me?"

"Yes," I lied, because when I heard his voice go up I tuned back in, figuring he was asking a question.

"I don't care what all those unbonded omegas told you," he stated, the irritation thick in his voice. "They either don't remember or didn't want to scare you. But I've seen omegas go into heat after having sex with an alpha who didn't offer for them, and it's horrifying to watch. They lose all sense of themselves."

I rolled my eyes.

"Avery!" he nearly yelled. "The facts are indisputable. You sleep with an alpha and he casts you aside, you go into heat, calling all-comers until it subsides. Some omegas find mates, but most of them just go insane."

"Insane?" I parried. "Really?"

"Avery, you––"

"Tell me, Lin, where are these hundreds and hundreds of crazed omegas kept?"

"They're thrown out onto the street, Avery. You know that."

"This whole thing is perpetuated by––"

"Heat happens to an omega when the alpha they trust with their body doesn't claim them," Linden replied flatly. "That's crushing for an omega."

But that part I knew for certain was bullshit. I'd slept with many alphas and betas, gammas, and more than a few humans, and fucking the alphas was the same as fucking the others.

Did omegas go into heat? Yes. Without question. But heat, for all intents and purposes, was an omega pumping out a ridiculous amount of pheromones to lure a mate, basically drowning the other wolf in their scent, and that, I suspected, could be overwhelming for the omega as well as for anyone in their vicinity. But did I think the omega lost control during any of that? Hell no. That was ridiculous.

"You need to form a bond," Linden declared, "and so do I. And since I know what I need to be happy, which includes exorbitant amounts of money, my strategy for happiness is to seduce the earl, marry him, and live like a queen."

"Sounds like a plan," I agreed, because it was not my place to judge him. We were different people, raised in vastly different circumstances. He was a commodity to his family, nothing more. He had been polished like a priceless jewel his entire life. Every moment he wasn't with me when we were younger had been filled with etiquette, grooming, and diction. I remembered watching him learn how to walk into a room, hold a cup, and to be the embodiment of beauty and sophistication and good breeding.

His father had nothing at all to do with him. His mother was merciless in his preparation for his debut, at eighteen, into society. As far as I knew, me and my mother were the only ones who ever hugged him. It always made me sad to see him look up for approval and never receive a smile from anyone. Most omegas were just like him. They fell into one of two categories: either their family was interested in using them as a bargaining chip to merge with a another, equally affluent family, or the omega was flat-out sold to the highest bidder.

I annoyed the crap out of my family, but they loved me, and I knew that with absolute conviction because my childhood had been completely and utterly normal. Usually omegas were sequestered. In my family I was treated the same as my siblings; all of us were hugged and kissed, scolded and grounded, and told we were unique and smart and funny. Beauty, how we looked, wasn't all that important to either of my parents. They were much more concerned with what kind of people we were.

Being born into my family was a blessing. If I never bonded, it didn't matter; my family wasn't dependent on me making a match. Linden's was. I had no right to criticize him or his motives.

"No one here is more beautiful than me," he stated without a hint of self-doubt. "The earl is mine for the taking."

I gave him a quick pat on the cheek. "I one hundred percent agree with you," I conceded. "Except for Bridget."

"Oh, Avery," Bridget cooed as she swept into the alcove that was suddenly a bit tight with three of us in there. "You're so right."

"Get out," Linden demanded icily.

"Calm down," she tutted at him, leaning into me as I put an arm around her. "If the earl is into men, then you win. You're the prettiest one I know."

I never understood why there wasn't some list that was given out before these things: this alpha likes girls, this one likes boys, this one loves every color of the rainbow. It only made good sense not to waste everyone's time. Why, even now, every alpha had to meet every omega was beyond me. There were so many antiquated customs.

"I'm the most beautiful person you know, period," he corrected her, bringing me back to the conversation.

She cocked her head sideways to look up at me. "You're the most handsome, though," she murmured, reaching up to touch my jawline. "But would it kill you to shave?"

"You sound like my father."

"Honestly, Avery, I can barely see your gorgeous dimples." I chuckled as she squinted and tipped my head to the side. "Why are you covered in lipstick?"

"My mother, my sister, my sister-in-law, they were all over me. You know how it is."

"It's because we're like catnip to all the others—alphas, betas, and gammas. They can barely keep their hands off of us," she said, using her fingers to try and clean me up. "And you especially, because your family loves and wants to smother you in equal measure."

"Who, me?"

"Ugh," she groaned, pulling a handkerchief from her tiny clutch to get the rest of the lipstick off before she turned to Linden with accusing eyes. "You were just going to let him go out there with lipstick all over him?"

"It made him look like a lothario, and I understand the earl is quite the prude."

"I see," she said sourly. "So you thought, 'Let's make Avery even less appealing just to be on the safe side.'"

"Something like that."

"Even less appealing?" I repeated, pouting. "Was that nice?"

"Dearheart, we both know that as omegas go, you're far too––"

"Rugged, rough, unkempt," Linden offered in quick succession. "Stubbled?"

"––capable," Bridget finished, completely ignoring him, "to have an alpha offer for you."

She wasn't wrong, and I'd come to count on that.

"Omegas, as you know, are supposed to be cared for, lavished with attention and tokens of affection, as well as opulence and wealth. We are not something a poor man could ever hope to possess, but with you having a job—and a scary one at that—you don't need an alpha. You can provide for yourself."

"Without question," I affirmed happily.

"You'd make an alpha feel positively impotent, and not one of them has the intestinal fortitude to be able to deal with that. They're actually quite vulnerable and needy, and you know this because you have not one but three in your immediate family."

"Again, I'm in total agreement with you."

"Well, for those of us who want to live in the lap of luxury, it's showtime, because look"—Linden pointed—"I think he's arrived. All the others are lining up under the arch to the living room."

I just needed out of the alcove; the reason wasn't important. It was getting hot, and I had layers of clothes on.

As we stepped out into the crowd of onlookers, Linden bumped into a woman. At first I thought she was a server, but upon closer inspection, I realized she was wearing a black suit, not a uniform, and her white shirt and patent heels were expensive, so I knew she was a guest. Her hair was a deep, rich brown, a shade just a touch lighter than her suit. I loved the messy pixie cut and her enormous brown eyes.

"Be careful," he snarled at her.

She tipped her head in acknowledgment of him, but before she could walk away, I interrupted her exodus. "Are you all right?"

"Oh yes, perfectly," she replied smoothly.

"I'm sorry about him. He's an ass."

Her eyes narrowed as she scrutinized me. "It's to be expected from a spoiled, rich omega."

I laughed softly. "I promise you we're not all douchebags."

She smiled then, and it was kind, and she offered me her hand. "I'm Kat Holt, and you are?"

"Avery Rhine," I replied, taking her hand. "It's a pleasure."

"The pleasure is all mine, I assure you."

"Will you stop with the help, already," Linden grumbled, coming up beside me. "Look at the earl over there."

"Excuse me," I said to Miss Holt, "I need to murder my friend."

She chuckled, and it was a good sound. I slid my hand from hers so I could whack Linden in the abdomen,

"Ow," he groaned, bending over just a bit.

"Dear God, what is that on his face?" Bridget gasped,

suddenly breathless. "Is it—is that some kind of scar?"

"Yes, I noticed it when I walked by him earlier," Miss Holt answered, and we all turned to her. "It begins high on his left cheek, crosses through a portion of his lips, and runs down to his chin."

"He's disfigured," Bridget whispered with a shudder. "That's why he's not mated. No beta or gamma would have him, so he's decided to claim an omega."

"What does it matter? He's rich," Linden announced like this was news. "He can get his face fixed if his omega insists upon it."

"It depends," I reminded him. "If the scar was given to him while he was in his wolf form, then it can't be altered. You know that."

He shivered. "How can we find out before we go over there?"

"I think you just have to roll the dice," Bridget whispered, squaring her shoulders. "But when all is said and done, it doesn't matter. Only the manner in which you'd be kept does."

"Yes, true," he admitted, nodding. "Though how are you supposed to look at that for the rest of your life? It's gruesome."

"No," I disagreed, looking the man up and down. "It's nothing."

"Nothing?" Bridget croaked out. "Are you looking at him?"

"Yeah, I am. He's got a great face," I replied sincerely. I had no idea what Linden and Bridget were seeing. The man was stunning. "And the scar's sexy as hell."

"You're deluded," Linden declared patronizingly.

"Not this time," I assured him with a wink.

"You're just trying to get a rise out of me, because yes, that scar is hideous."

But to me, the scar was such a small part of what made up the man.

The earl's hair was chestnut brown with streaks of silver, which he wore in a combed back undercut, but I suspected he was graying prematurely, as he couldn't have been a day over thirty-five. He was tall, easily six-four, built like a swimmer with wide shoulders, a broad chest, narrow hips and long legs. The suit he wore, complete with tails, like the rest of us, fit him like a second skin. He was a designer's wet dream, and the man could have walked off the cover of any fashion magazine. But it wasn't the body that was truly mesmerizing; it was, in fact, his face. The scar made him seem dangerous and deadly, and the primal part of me I worked hard to quash each and every day, responded to the strength and raw power that rolled off him even at a distance.

I felt it then, the throb of arousal that came only when I lured an alpha—not a beta, gamma, or human, but an alpha—to my bed. One part of being an omega was absolutely true: we craved submission, and that, only that, got us off. Only an alpha could make me submit, so I had to either get drunk enough to let someone else control me or find the real deal and bed an alpha. With the others, the pretense of succumbing to the power of another was short-lived. Most times I didn't get off; I sobered up too quickly, or the guy offered to bottom. I could top as well as anyone, but there was no way to climax doing that. With an alpha, I could come, but I lost interest as soon as the passion faded, because no one I'd met could ever sustain the dominance I needed. It was an act they put on, and that simply wouldn't do. I had to surrender, had to be *made* to do so, and staring across the room at Graeme Davenport, I saw a man who could take what he wanted. I nearly gasped with the yearning that rushed through me.

My wolf would accept a bite from his, and to the man, I would submit. As both reactions were terrifying, I remained rooted to the spot and tried to breathe through my desire.

"Really, though, the scar's not important, and maybe he'd be open to sharing his omega with others," Linden said, breaking the trance I found myself in as I stared. "I don't have to fuck him every night, and I certainly don't have to look at him when I do. That's what a light switch is for, after all."

But what a pity it would be to have him in the darkness. Even from across the room I could see that the man's eyes were a lovely, warm, peaty brown. Having those on me, watching me, heating as he stared...I couldn't think of anything I would want more.

His chiseled features were perfect, even his nose, long and aquiline, his high, sharp cheekbones, and his full, lush mouth that I wanted all over—

"Bridget, you whore," Linden hissed under his breath as she slipped around him to get into line behind the other omegas who were there to meet first the *cyne*, and then, if that failed, all the other alphas in the room.

"You better go," I told Linden, bumping him with my elbow.

"Aren't you coming?"

"I'm too capable, remember?"

"I didn't mean that you shouldn't—"

"I'm not the omega an earl is looking for," I reminded him. "You know that."

He grunted and then left me, getting in line several people behind Bridget.

"Watch this," I said to Miss Holt, leaning close to her, my interest in the man ebbing with every second that I didn't go to him. Always, this was how things worked for me. If I could hold off acting on my impulses, slowly, steadily, my logic kicked in. Because clearly, I was out of my league. He was there to find an omega to wait on him hand and foot, to breed with, and to make his house a home. Nothing wrong with that; I just didn't have time. "Keep an eye on Linden."

"Why? What are we—oh." She chuckled. "How is he managing that?"

One by one, the omegas in front of Linden saw him and surrendered their place in line, letting him creep up to Bridget.

"His family is one of the richest in these here parts," I teased her, giving my voice a ridiculous twang, and she grinned back. "And because all those guys and girls know he's a vindictive asshole, they're gonna let him cut in line until he gets to Bridge."

"But she won't let him go in front of her, will she?"

"No way," I replied as she slipped her arm into mine. "They've been rivals way too long for her to let him get away with that shit."

"And you're friends with both of them?"

"Friends is a *strong* word," I apprised her playfully as she leaned into me. "We grew up together, and I think because I can't, and don't, compete with either one of them, they don't see me as a threat. They both treat me better than they do most people."

"What do you mean you can't compete with them?"

I snickered and turned to her. "You can't tell me that even though he was a prick to you, you could deny, empirically, that Linden Van Doren is the most beautiful man you've ever seen in your life. That hair is natural, you know."

She nodded slowly. "I've traveled all over the world with my boss, Avery Rhine, and I've met more than my fair share of drop-dead gorgeous men"—one eyebrow lifted mischievously—"but you know the one man I've never come across before tonight?"

"No, who?"

"One who thinks my boss's scar is, and I quote, 'Sexy as hell.'"

2

GRAEME

I was hiding.

It was childish, and I knew that, but still. Going to parties was tedious, and I would have preferred to gargle glass. I knew if I could avoid being where I was supposed to be for another twenty minutes, I could send a courier with a note telling my host I had been, unfortunately and quite thoroughly, detained, so I had left my office early and gone home. Now I just had to hope that Kat, my personal assistant and bodyguard, was not as tenacious as she typically was about making sure I didn't miss an opportunity to offer for an omega who caught my eye. Of course, to do that I had to show up at excruciatingly uncomfortable social gatherings where I felt more like a sacrificial lamb than the alpha I was.

Every three months, all across the country, one of the rich and powerful lupine families in every city hosted what was called a gathering, but everyone knew it to be an omega party, where omegas were presented. It had to be as insufferable for them as it was for me, and I could state, unequivocally, that the practice was untenable. They were complete and utter horror shows of vapid conversation where, somehow, the champagne was always warm and time moved at a glacial speed. I'd never been to one where I didn't pause as the overly-coiffed, perfumed, and swaddled-in-couture creatures were paraded up to me and wonder why they all looked malnourished and in need of sustenance.

"That's because they're all looking for a bonding," my sister-in-law, Georgiana—Gigi—had apprised me with a knowing nod and a smirk over dinner the night before. Being an alpha herself, she'd been through it as well. "Believe me, I remember when I had to stand in front of all those preening peacocks myself. All omegas give me hives."

Her husband, my brother, Stone, snorted out a laugh.

"Come on," she snapped at him, one of her gorgeous copper color brows lifting, "don't you remember what's his name, Dabney—what was it?"

"Gilroy," my brother and I said at the same time.

"Yes, Dabney Gilroy," she echoed with a shudder, "with the handkerchief and the mascara and that perfume that used to make me sneeze."

"You like mascara," Stone reminded her with a salacious grin. "You've had me in lip gloss and mascara and some very scary eyeliner many times."

I heard her breath catch as she responded to a memory combined with his pheromones and the smile that made his eyes glint. "Yes," she murmured, swallowing hard, "I have."

The things they did in their bedroom were not, I was certain, for the faint of heart, and I didn't need to know. I gagged at my end of the table. Loudly.

She cleared her throat, sat up straight, and scowled. "You look stunning when I make you up, and of course I like it on me, but Stone, there are roses in the garden with more fortitude than that man ever thought of having."

He shrugged in agreement.

"And when you dress up and let me take things off you--"

"I *will* vomit," I threatened her, and my brother, the ass, snickered.

She grunted. "You know, someone told me once that the omegas don't eat the entire day before those stupid parties. The grayish pallor is supposed to be attractive."

"Why?" Stone asked her.

"From what I gathered, the alpha is supposed to feel like if they claimed that certain omega, then they could provide for them so they'd never go hungry again."

"How very *Gone with the Wind*," he groaned. "That's practically primeval. What kind of thinking is that?"

"It's how they're raised," she reminded him. "From the time they're very young, they're made to feel small and helpless. They're groomed to be on the hunt for an alpha to make them whole."

Stone shivered, returning to his meal. "Just watching that debacle always gave me the creeps."

I put up my hands in a gesture of agreement.

Gigi gasped suddenly, startling both me and my brother. "Oh dear God, I'm so sorry."

I glanced at Stone, who shrugged, clearly just as confused as I was by her outburst.

"I...I spoke out of turn, when your dear, departed mother was an omega herself," she rushed out, her silverware clattering noisily to her plate as she shoved her chair back and leapt to her feet, turning toward my brother. "Stone, I--"

"Stop," he urged her gently, holding out his hand, which she grasped quickly. "My mother being an omega has absolutely no bearing on this conversation at all."

She grimaced as she lifted her welling blue eyes to me. "Graeme, I never meant to insinuate that she was less than or—"

"Yes, dear, I know," I soothed her. "It didn't even cross my mind to think of her."

She nodded fast rather than trusting her voice and a few long, stray auburn curls came loose from her messy bun.

Stone got up then, retrieved his wife's napkin from the floor, leaned in and kissed her on the temple, then the cheek, and whispered something in her ear that allowed her to take a breath.

"Gigi," I crooned, "love, I know your heart."

"You do?" she whispered roughly, still on the verge of breaking down.

"Of course I do," I assured her.

She sniffled once and then lifted her chin and squared her shoulders, regaining her composure before wiping under each eye with a quick flick of her fingers. Retaking her seat, she accepted her napkin from her husband, placing it back in her lap before raising her crystal goblet and taking a sip of sparkling water.

"Look at me, please," Stone murmured, his tone coaxing.

Slowly, she gave my brother her attention.

"Darling, I don't remember anything about my mother. Do you understand?"

She nodded and I noted how pale she looked.

"Your mother is the only one I've ever known, and I'm thrilled she adores me so completely that I've basically eclipsed you, both your brothers, and your sister."

He was teasing, laying it on thick, and it had the desired effect as she chuckled and then smiled, the devotion obvious in her gaze. "She does love you dearly and thinks of you as one of her own. God help the others when they bring home mates."

He waggled his eyebrows at her, and when he reached over, cupping her cheek, I watched as she leaned into his touch, her sigh deep as she released all the tension of the last few moments.

"Now, tell me what you were going to say," I insisted, taking a sip of the Merlot we'd paired with our beef bourguignon. If we were all home for dinner, we ate together. It was one of the best parts, in my estimation, of us living under the same roof.

She cleared her throat softly. "I was going to remind you that things are different for you. You're the *cyne*, you *have* to either find a mate––"

"Which, let's face it," Stone said, wincing, "at this point probably isn't in the cards."

"Stop that," Gigi scolded him. "That's a terrible thing to––"

"But true," Stone reminded her.

"It is," I agreed.

"Yes, but––"

"Finish," I ordered her, then gestured at my brother. "Ignore the rabble."

She hmphed in his general direction and returned her focus to me. "As you have not found your fated beta or gamma, it's in your best interest to bond with an omega you meet at one of these horrible parties."

"In my best interest?" I eyed her, one eyebrow lifted.

"Fine. In the best interest of the family," she amended.

That was more like it.

"We both know that even if Stone had never found me, or technically, if I'd never found him, being unmated wouldn't be a problem for him or the house of Davenport or the Estate of Wakefield and Muir, because *he's* not the heir. But for you…" She trailed off, biting her bottom lip, giving me a look of sympathy. "You don't have a choice."

She wasn't wrong. My grandfather, during his last trip to Chicago, had put me on notice. Thirty-four was pushing the envelope of acceptability. All the other *cynes*, meaning alphas who led *holts*, were already married with children. I was the only alpha he knew of who hadn't tied the knot. I was sure I could look up others around the world who were just as unattached as I was, but in our circle, I was currently the odd man out. It didn't help that his peers and subordinates constantly brought it up to him.

"It's too bad Stone wasn't born first," I muttered irritably. "This would all be moot."

Stone grinned at me. "I would have made a terrible alpha, Graeme. I don't have your patience or your care for the estate and the people, and trying to make heads or tails of that investment portfolio of yours is––" He thought a moment and then turned to his wife for help.

"Impossible," she offered instead of trying to come up with something clever. "You're the brains, Graeme. We're simply your scrappy backup."

"Oh yes, scrappy backup," Stone agreed, chuckling. "I like that."

She beamed at him, as smitten as she'd been from the beginning, and he smiled in return, the love tangible and warm between them.

I was equal parts happy for and jealous of my brother. Stone, being second born, as well as being a beta, was able to not only pick who he wanted but had never, ever had his choices be the concern of the entire family, both immediate and extended.

We lost our father young. I was four and Stone was two,

and my mother was far more fragile than anyone could have ever imagined, even as omegas went. It was true an omega suffered difficulties beyond grief if they lost their alpha, but Fiona Davenport was dangerously delicate. After Graeme Davenport the fourth died, she fell quickly into the bottle, then turned to pills, and was dead a scant three months later. I didn't remember grieving her; she had never been particularly attentive and was often absent. If I concentrated, I could recall what I thought was the sound of her singing, but I was never certain if that was an actual memory or something I'd been told.

My father was different. His face I could conjure without looking at pictures on walls or on pages in albums. He was the one I missed, both then and now. I could easily bring to mind his booming laughter, his dark brown gaze, and the warmth of his hugs, which had been both grounding and enveloping. The world was colder once he was gone. If not for my grandparents, I might have turned inward and become silent and brooding, and Stone, neglected by me, might have become selfish or bitter. The two of us could have become self-entitled and cruel, as many alphas and betas in our circle were, but my father had been an anomaly—born into a wealthy family but raised by doting parents—and so too were Stone and I; we were brought up the same way. My grandparents had a son who was kind, wise and loving, and they saw no reason to change any part of their parenting style when they raised my brother and I.

When I turned fifteen, my grandfather asked me the question posed to all alphas at that milestone, the same one he'd asked my father all those years ago. "Will it be a female, or male, or you're not sure yet, or neither for you, Graeme?"

I remembered being scared of what he would think, but

as his hazel eyes met mine, I found the courage to reply, "Male."

"All right," he answered like he could not have cared less, got up from the table on the other side of his den, walked back to his desk, hit the intercom and told his assistant to make arrangements for several suitable surrogates to be designated for when I was ready to birth heirs.

"Grandpa."

He lifted his gaze to me from a spreadsheet that had caught his eye.

"It doesn't matter to you that I want a male mate?"

Instantly I got a scowl. "Why on earth should I care who you want to mate with? The only thing your grandmother and I concern ourselves with is that whoever you choose must be from a suitable family."

I smiled at him.

"Don't test me, boy," he warned brusquely, pointing at me. "You try and bring a struggling actor or singer or, dear God, some kind of half-assed painter into this family"—the shiver of revulsion made me snicker—"and I will toss them out of here so fast it will make your head spin!"

"Yessir."

"And I will lock you up until you come to your senses!"

I had no doubt he would have followed through on his threats, but as it turned out, I was harder on others than he ever thought of being. I judged everyone quickly and decisively, and if they couldn't hold my interest, I moved on.

Eight years later, when I returned home from school, first Oxford and then the Sorbonne, and successfully defended my place as *cynehlaford*, or *cyne*, king-alpha of a *holt*—in my case the Davenport *holt*—I was thrust suddenly into the business of finding a mate.

Yes, we were people living in the modern world, and yet

we were bound to ridiculous, antiquated customs that made my stomach churn. It was one of the things I vowed to change with my position as a ruling member on the *Maion*, the council of *holts* that every *cyne* in the US sat on. The council reported to our *dryhten*, our leader in America, who then reported to our *konungr*, our king, who lived on a sprawling estate just outside of Rome.

It was a lot to keep track of, but it was helpful for humans, especially when things needed to get done, to have specific people to speak to about laws, regulations, and things like education and policy, diversity and the differences and similarities between shifters and non-shifters. That part of being on the council, I liked. Being a part of educational opportunities, cross-cultural appreciation and understanding, that was enjoyable. Going to parties, because as not only an alpha but a *cyne* I was supposed to be actively searching for a mate or offering for an omega, that part I hated. And then it got worse.

It was bad enough being forced to attend events where I was trotted out like a prize bull for the omegas to gawk at *before* I'd been disfigured, but when I nearly lost my left eye defending my cousin Remington in an altercation with another family and was left with a particularly horrific scar, the whole thing went from annoying to downright agonizing while all the pretty, preening, insipid, gold digging omegas who wanted to be kept in wealth and splendor, aspiring to little else, not only had to pretend to find me attractive but also had to try not to stare in open revulsion and sometimes outright fear.

It wasn't easy. The scar was a canyon. The other alpha had grabbed my muzzle in his powerful jaws, held me down with his claws near my eye, and then ripped forward with his teeth. It was fortunate that he'd been so focused on trying to tear my head off that he didn't notice when I got both my front paws up under his throat until it was too late. He drowned in his own blood, but even with my shift, the damage was done. Irreversible. The greatest plastic surgeons in the world could remake my visage, but the first shift would return the mutilated skin. It was one of those tricky peculiarities about being a shifter.

So I was now forced to stand there, with my ravaged face, to meet these vacuous omegas who did nothing for me. I knew I had a type, I preferred my men strong and virile, but there was a reason two alphas were never seen together, at least not for long. One of them had to submit, and that was not in the nature of an alpha. It wasn't that I wanted to fight a bed partner, but having to exert power to hold another man down got me off like few other things could or did. The issue was that only other alphas caught my eye and earned a second look. All other wolves were hardwired to defer to me, and that quick submission left me cold.

Yes, I had taken many betas and gammas to my bed over the years, but the temperament of a beta was so gentle and docile, a peacemaker, like my brother, that I was not, as a rule, drawn to them. A gamma was similar, though with a somewhat wilder streak, but both always succumbed. And while I enjoyed humans, they were not a long-term option. I'd shared my bed with more than a few, especially during my undergraduate years, but as they couldn't heal damage like a shifter could, I ran the risk of biting and clawing, of mauling, or of outright killing them. The last time I took a human to bed, I got so caught up in a frenzy of arousal and bloodlust while my partner begged me for harder and faster that I nearly eviscerated the man. I had tried to be careful after that, but tepid lovemaking for a shifter was not sustainable. There were only two times a wolf could be fully free:

during a shift and in bed. I wasn't about to sacrifice either, no matter how beautiful I found the human. Being alone seemed to be my destiny.

"Graeme."

I groaned, returning myself to the present as Miss Holt, Kat to me, came into the kitchen. She was dressed not in yoga pants or threadbare jeans, an old T-shirt or a sweatshirt with a butchered neckline, but instead in a suit and heels, looking crisp and terribly polished. I girded for what I knew was coming.

"Did we forget that we have a gathering to attend at the home of Alexander and Elira Huntington? They are this quarter's hosts of the presentation of the omegas."

Her patronizing singsong voice wasn't helping in the least.

"Well?" she demanded.

I regretted giving her so much leeway to bait me, but even though I'd given keeping her at arm's length my very best shot, her warmth and caring and sarcasm and loyalty had won me over years ago. Now we both knew she would never be fired, even though I threatened her with it on a daily basis.

"Are you listening to me?"

I must have winced.

"Why are you fighting this? You know you have to go."

I knew I did, but that didn't mean I had to like it. Any of it. Because beyond my irritation with having to deal with the parties, I felt sorry for the omegas themselves.

An omega was not considered an equal partner in the eyes of human or lupine law and was not permitted to marry, so by that same law, there was no divorce. An alpha could send an omega away to live alone for the rest of their lives, though, only allowing them to see their children if the alpha saw fit. In short, an alpha owned their omega. It was a bonding. Marriage was something humans engaged in, as well as alphas and betas and gammas, in whatever configuration worked. Omegas were excluded from marriage, as they had no rights beyond what was designated in their contract. It wasn't fair, and since the laws were made by alphas, change was slow in coming. The truth was, alphas were always on the prowl for a shiny new omega to claim.

"Graeme?" Kat increased the thread of urgency in her tone.

"You know," I began solemnly, "I have this tickle in the back of my——"

"You missed the last two gatherings," she informed me curtly, crossing her arms, "and you told me *back in August* to remind you *in November* that you should probably attend since there would be several young alphas from your *holt* there attending for the first time, as well as your cousin Remy."

I had a vague recollection of that.

"As *cyne*, as the heir and leader, you have right of first refusal and must decline an omega any of the other alphas want to offer for."

It was a protocol older than Rome, the city our king lived in, antiquated and outdated, and yet everyone complied because it affected omegas, and no one cared enough to ratify the laws. Of course, some of this could be placed on the omegas themselves, and their families, and everyone getting paid. When exacting change affected income streams, it was like trying to alter the course of a barge.

"Remy certainly could call me," I suggested to Kat. "He has my number."

"And the others?"

"They're all so young, Kat. Should they be offering for an

omega this quickly when they haven't even given the whole *finding your true mate* thing a try? Perhaps me not being there would be a blessing of sorts."

She sighed in a way that let me know I was terribly vexing.

"We could go to dinner instead," I threw out hopefully.

She rubbed her forehead and then looked up at me as I continued to pick at the snack I'd pulled from my refrigerator, some sliced cheese and jamón ibérico.

"If you don't go, you will receive a slew of emails—and by slew, I mean a flood from everyone here in Chicago, and across the country, and in England—accusing you of not taking your commitment to the family seriously, and then we will *both* receive a phone call, maybe even a Skype session, from your grandfather."

I grunted.

"I don't know about you"—her voice dripped with sarcasm—"but I do *not* enjoy being browbeaten by a man in his pajamas and a fuzzy robe at three o'clock in the morning!"

He did have a habit of waking us up.

"And then he'll come here and set up those horrible individual meetings, and then we'll have to visit the matchmaker again, and she'll ask me why I'm not married and what kind of girl am I looking for and—"

"Fine," I growled at her, taking a gulp of the bourbon I was having along with the snack before I called our cook to have her prepare me a steak. "We'll go. But if anyone faints again looking at my scar, we're stopping for pizza on the way home, and you're buying." I was adamant.

"Agreed." If she was any more smug, she'd be preening. "Now, shower and shave. Your tuxedo is in your closet; I've had the tailcoat and trousers freshly steamed. The lapel pin with your family crest is on your dresser."

Once more into the breach.

As I suspected, on the way in, one after another after another, a vapid creature paled as they took in my scar. Or worse, pretended to ignore it and tried to make conversation as I moved, far too slowly because people kept stopping me, through the crowd.

Yes, I was actually an earl.

Yes, dual citizenship was a real thing, and yes, *so* fun.

Yes, lots of property, in America and England. All over the globe, actually. Loads of it, acres and miles of it.

No, it was a sapphire in my lapel pin, not a blue topaz. One was darker; might want to look that up.

"Mind the sarcasm, please," Kat reprimanded under her breath.

Yes, born a *cyne*; it was that pesky birth-order bit.

"Really?" she asked, sounding pained.

I could feel my right eye start to twitch.

Yes, yes, actually an earl—again with that one. I had the paperwork and everything.

"Don't be glib," Kat warned, shoulder-checking me.

"I need a super-secret earl decoder ring to show everyone."

Her groan was long-suffering. "Just c'mon," she prodded. "They want you to stand in a certain place."

Of course they did.

"Don't grind your teeth," Kat reminded me. "It's a terrible sound, like nails on a chalkboard, and it scares the omegas."

"What about me, pray tell, does not scare the omegas?

Perhaps make that list instead, as I'm certain it would prove shorter and easier to compile."

"And stop growling," she stated painfully. "They faint when you do that."

I would do my best.

More omegas stopped me to chat. A few of them were so young. One girl swooned when she met my eyes. Her chaperone shot me a dirty look, as though I glared on purpose to see if they'd run. That didn't even sound like something I'd do. It would have been naughty.

And now there was a line and...and...

I was cold. I was never cold. What in the world?

The hair on the back of my neck stood up; then there was a prickly flush of heat on my skin that unsettled me because I was shivering just moments before. I glanced around for Kat, but she was nowhere in sight.

Gentle throat clearing, and I focused on the woman in front of me, with her platinum blond hair and long-lashed blue eyes. She bowed low, and when she straightened and offered me her hand, I took it quickly because there was a scent, a flutter of something in the air that was...different. Since anything different could only be qualified as good, as in the opposite of this crushing boredom, I was intrigued.

"And you are?" I stared at her, inhaling deeply, trying to catch the scent again, the faintest trace of agarwood? Sandalwood? It was like the still-smoking embers of a fire, of oud and vetiver and musk.

It was sublime. I wanted it all over me.

"Bridget Mills," she announced herself, smiling at me, lashes fluttering, eyes downcast before lifting, releasing pheromones at the same moment and filling the air with apricot and vanilla, caramel and a rush of fresh strawberry.

I dropped her hand and took an instinctive step back. I

didn't want her smell to have a chance to replace the faint trace of the other alluring, tantalizing aroma.

"Sir? Are you well?"

I would be as soon as I found the origin of the scent I wanted to roll in, or on. It was lingering on her clothes or in her hair and was released when she moved.

"I'm...fine," I managed in response. "Where did you—"

"Sir, may I—"

"I'm sorry; there's quite a line," I explained, calming, collecting myself and my thoughts. Clearly, I was confused. There were too many layers of perfume in the room, even as large as it was. What I needed was some fresh air to clear my head and nose, but to do that I had to greet and dismiss all the waiting omegas, and this one was standing in my way. "If you'll excuse me."

Her eyes widened, and I saw the flare of anger but couldn't have cared less. Then I turned and suddenly found myself face-to-face with a truly stunning man. His rose-gold hair and jade-colored eyes were a remarkable combination. Along with his flawless porcelain skin, he was nearly blinding. He was perfection, and for a moment I was enthralled... because the smell, it was his. It had been coming from him. His scent was heavenly. It was warm cedar and wild black spruce, and the musk was back, with the aged leather and that same vetiver smoke. It was rugged and wild and—

The disappointment was crushing, almost painful, and it took everything in me not to reel as though from a blow. My chest tightened with defeat even as I faced perhaps the most beautiful omega I had ever seen in my life. He was grace and beauty incarnate, a man who should have been kept under glass to remain forever immaculate and untouched. But all of that radiant perfection was completely and utterly wasted on me, because I realized, beneath the rugged and wild, he smelled of uncut roses in a lush garden, honey, brown sugar, and a hint of jasmine blooming under a boiling midday sun.

What I wanted was muscles under sweaty, salty skin, evergreen woods at dawn, and a ride in the country with the windows down on a hot summer night.

Every omega gave off a scent meant to entice an alpha. I'd seen men I'd known my whole life catch just a whisper of something in the air and be consumed with finding the source, to the exclusion of all else. I had no idea that would ever, or could ever, be me until this very second.

"Where," I began, but my voice went out on me.

"Have I been all your life?" he taunted me.

"No," I rumbled hoarsely, and I realized I was probably glowering when he appeared startled. There was no doubt most people fawned over him, but I needed answers. "Have you and Miss Mills perhaps been running in a field?"

His face scrunched up as he recoiled from the mere suggestion. "A well-bred omega would never run," he informed me. "That's simply not done."

I tried to keep the disappointment out of my voice. "Yes. I mean, no, of course not. Forgive me, I meant no offense. I would never wish to imply that you weren't a gentleman."

"Whatever would make you think that I—oh," he groaned, sounding pained, as he breathed in. "I must have Avery's scent on me. That's horrifying."

It was anything but, and I nearly gasped as I caught a hint of the spoor again when he ran his hand through his hair.

"He always comes to these things right from work. It's totally barbaric."

An omega who worked at all was unheard of, but the most important part of the explanation was that what I'd hoped was now confirmed—Avery was a man. A man I needed to meet as quickly as possible.

"If I've told him once, I've told him a million times that he needs to take these events more seriously, and now he's stinking up me and Bridget, and that's just vile."

It was incredible, and dear God, if Avery smelled this good on others, the scent would be even better all over me. I wanted that. Even more, I wanted mine on him. "Avery who?" I asked nonchalantly, masking my interest with a bored tone.

"Rhine," he replied with a roll of his eyes. "He's Mr. Huntington's son, your host for this event. I'm sure he's around here somewhere."

And I would spend the rest of my evening hunting him down, because nothing else mattered but finding the man and claiming him as mine.

3

AVERY

She tugged on my arm.

I planted my feet.

"I can move you, you know."

"Lady, I'm a cop," I explained to Miss Holt, smirking at her.

Her eyes narrowed to slits.

"Okay, wait, wait, wait," I directed, taking hold of her hand, still in the crook of my elbow. I knew that look on a beta, and I didn't want to tempt fate. They liked balance and peace, yes, but they were stubborn as hell too. Challenging her was a bad idea. "Before this escalates and we get into some weird pissing contest, I know you mean well by wanting me to go over there and meet the man who I now know is your boss, but c'mon, lookit me. I'm a mess, right? I'm not the kind of omega that would best...serve..."

"Avery?"

What was I thinking? I was smarter than this.

"Avery?"

"Sorry, sorry," I said quickly, gesturing toward her boss. "You know what? I'm being an idiot. Let's go."

She was quiet, unmoving, studying my face.

"What? C'mon, let's do this."

"Most omegas," she began, "meet alphas with a fair amount of excitement, yes? But also trepidation, and even fear, because they know if they're chosen their lives will never be their own again."

"Sure."

"But you—how many alphas have you met?"

I had to think. "Let's see, from eighteen to now...fifty-eight? No, fifty-nine. There was an alpha just this past summer who lost his beta; it was really sad, and he got to meet us all, and he wanted Bridge, but her father put the kibosh on that."

She continued to stare at me.

"What?"

"Let me guess, not rich enough?"

I waggled my eyebrows at her.

"All right, so you've met fifty-nine alphas, and not one has ever chosen you?"

I squinted at her. "Did I mention I'm a cop?"

"You did, yes."

"Well, I ain't giving that up, no matter what anyone says, and my father has made that a stipulation of my bonding."

"He has not."

I scoffed.

"You're not serious." She was in awe, eyes wide, staring at me.

"You seem surprised."

"He's written that into your contract?"

"Yes, ma'am."

"How?"

"What do you mean *how*?"

"I mean—I just—I've never heard of such a thing."

"Yeah, no, probably not. But it makes me being counted on as an omega who would take care of a home and raise children and all that kind of a longshot."

"It's more than that," she said, her voice faltering. "I can't imagine an alpha who would be willing to take you on."

"Exactly," I told her smugly.

"Why did your father agree to that?"

I grinned at her. "First, he loves me and wants what I want to matter, and second, he answers to my mother."

"Explain."

"My mother, his true mate, his beta, if *she* insisted—which she would, 'cause she's my mom—he would have caved, even if he'd said no to me at first."

"Why?"

"Whaddya mean *why*? He loves her; he'd do anything to make her happy."

"No, I mean why would your mother agree with you over your father?"

"Oh, she teaches school."

Her eyes got even bigger and wider. Every now and then I was reminded how strange and wonderful my family was. "Your mother works outside the home?"

"She does, yeah."

"Who are you people?"

"I know, it's nuts, right? We're a weird-ass lupine family."

"So you will remain a law enforcement officer?"

"I will indeed."

"But how would that work?"

"How do you mean?"

"I *mean* the pull of the alpha, what he wants, will override your free will."

I shook my head. "Not with me it won't."

"You obviously haven't met any powerful alphas."

"Maybe"—I shrugged—"but I have three in my immediate family."

"You do?"

I nodded.

"Well, I still have to assume that when you meet the one who will claim you, their power will be greater than your own."

I squinted at her. "And yet, all I've ever heard about is omegas twisting their alphas up so tight that they become slaves to them."

"Again, only if you have a weak alpha."

"I'll take your word for it," I placated her.

"It's not up for debate. It's—Avery, surely you understand you're a wolf first, human second. Reason will fly right out the window when faced with the desire of your alpha."

I remained quiet.

"You're an animal before any––"

"Am I, though? Are any of us?"

"Yes," she assured me firmly. "You know that."

"Maybe millions of years ago, when we were running around killing mammoths or whatever. When the first one of us decided to fire up the grill instead of having steak tartare for dinner again, I think the human part took over."

"But you can't fight your nature."

"You don't think so?" I countered.

"No," she insisted, easing her arm free so she could stand in front of me and argue. "You're an omega and are made to make a home for an alpha."

I grimaced, as it was hard to imagine anything worse.

"You doubt this?"

"Do I look like homemaker material?"

"I--"

"Are you homemaker material?"

"I'm a beta," she informed me defensively. "I'm made to be a mate, yes, but if I ever find my mate, if that wolf is an alpha, we'll need a housekeeper, and if she's a beta like me, or a gamma, then we'll have to divvy up the chores."

"Here's the thing. I may be an omega, but the service I've chosen to give is to the city of Chicago. I take care of as many people as I can."

"And you feel no pull to care for and nurture a mate?"

"No, ma'am. And I've never met anyone, besides my partner, who actually needs me."

"Your who?"

"My partner," I told her, grinning. "I'm a police officer," I continued slowly, enunciating the words, goading her. "We solve crimes together."

Quick scowl. "All this charm and banter, it's smoke and mirrors. I can see right through you."

"Is that right?"

"Yes, omega, that's right," she assured me firmly, giving me a pointed stare. "You need to be claimed, and you need a home. Cop or not, you need to be cherished and cared for, and you desperately need an alpha to give you hard limits."

"I might need something hard," I teased, smirking at her.

She groaned disgustedly. "Walk with me."

"Certainly."

But when we turned to go to the earl, he was gone.

"Awww, he left." I feigned sadness. "That's too bad."

"Stay here," she ordered, pointing at the floor. "Right here. Don't move. I'll go find him and be right back."

"Of course, yeah, totally," I agreed with a nod, giving her my super-serious *for sure* face.

She rolled her eyes and left.

"I have never been treated so poorly in my life," Bridget raged, coming up beside me. "You were right not to give that man the time of day."

I smiled at her as Linden reached us, passing me an Old Fashioned, and Bridget the same.

"Could he have *been* more dismissive?" he asked her. "Or acted any more bored?"

"Or conceited or rude?" she added imperiously, chugging the drink down. "My God, what an ass."

"Absolutely," he seconded, draining his as well. "Let's do shots."

"May I speak with you?"

Turning, I found Sandor, looking annoyed as usual. There was a permanent furrow in his brows whenever he looked at me.

"You could," I assured him, "but I gotta do shots with my friends."

"I--"

"He does," Linden told him, taking hold of my bicep and pulling me after him.

"First, I--"

"Please, Sandor," Bridget said, using her sweetest, sexiest voice, looking down and then lifting her baby-blue eyes to him, twirling a long platinum curl around her finger. "I've been treated abominably, and I need solace that only another omega can offer."

He sighed deeply, unaffected because he knew all my friends and they irritated him to no end. "Fine," he agreed, then scowled at me. "But, young man, when your father calls you, you will respond immediately and with--"

"Absolutely," I quipped before allowing Linden to tug me after him. I could hear Sandor huffing in irritation behind me.

I drained my Old Fashioned at the bar, the one usually manned by my brother—who made a damn good Moscow Mule—but was now being run by a professional bartender for the party. We ordered shots of tequila, which were lined up in front of us.

"This is a goddamn Roland Mouret dress that I got just for this party," Bridget informed us. "And do you think this hair just happens?"

"It's lovely," I assured her, poking at her long blond tresses. "The diamond barrettes are a nice touch."

"Right?"

"What about me?" Linden groused loudly. "This bespoke suit is Italian."

"You look pretty too," I conceded, "and your makeup is better than Bridget's."

"Hey," she growled at me.

"C'mon, look at the liner," I ordered, pointing.

His jade-green eyes were accentuated by long, thick lashes, and the black liner made them pop.

"Fine," she conceded. "Your makeup game is on point, Lin."

"Thank you."

"And that suit makes your waist look tiny."

"It's not the suit; it's the corset underneath," he informed us. "And, if I'm being honest, it's getting a bit hard to breathe."

I noticed then that his eyes were glassy, and he appeared paler than usual. With his alabaster skin, not many people would have noticed, but I'd been looking at him since I was five, so I could tell.

"For fuck's sake," I groused at him, putting an arm around his waist and drawing his arm across my shoulders.

"We're going out to the balcony, and you gotta come with us, Bridge, because I'm not leaving you here alone."

Between the ages of eighteen and twenty-four, unbonded female omegas were attended by chaperones. At twenty-five, those chaperones became bodyguards. Male omegas supposedly didn't need chaperones or bodyguards, for the simple reason that they could not be impregnated. Speaking from experience, I would have argued that the amount of trouble Linden and I got into would have been reduced considerably had there been someone there keeping an eye on us.

"Mills," I prodded her, using her last name, which she hated. "Come with––"

"I'll keep her company." A man was there, having stepped in close from the crowd, and as his voice held a slight pulse of power that I felt prickle over my skin, I knew he was an alpha.

"Bridge, just––"

"I'm here, Avery," her bodyguard, Lucas Grant, called over to me from where he was, farther down the bar.

The alpha blanched, because yes, while he was at the top of our hierarchy, Lucas was six-five with bulging muscles and surly attitude and had always been an immovable wall between Bridget and the outside world. I couldn't imagine Lucas wouldn't intimidate any lupine but a *cyne*.

"Perfect," I called over to Lucas and then glanced at the alpha. "Good luck."

His eyes were like saucers as he stared at me. I was chuckling as I walked Linden toward the balcony off the enormous living room.

Leaning him on the balustrade, I flipped up his jacket, unclasped his waistcoat, yanked his dress shirt out of his pants, and went to work on the corset. Once it was loosened,

Muscle and Bone

I plastered myself to his back so I could reach around him and unhook the front.

"I never knew you wanted to put me up against a wall," Linden whispered into my hair as I worked open the corset.

"Shut up."

"I would let you," he said hoarsely. "In fact, I have a small packet of lube in my breast pocket, and it's all warmed up and ready to go. All you have to do is take me up to your bedroom, and you can fuck me right there."

I snatched it from him so he wasn't tempted to use it with anyone else until he got himself together.

"Come on, Avery, you know you want me. Everybody wants me."

It was true; every man he'd ever met wanted him. "We both know you need an alpha to get off, Linny," I reminded him. "If you're not tied up and held down, you're not gonna come."

"Lies. Who told you that?"

"You did," I disclosed, getting the last of the hooks undone and tossing the corset on the chaise closest to us.

"Oh my God," he choked out, taking a big gulp of air as I turned him in my arms to face me and loosened his tie, then removed the studs in the shirt so it was no longer choking him to death.

"Is that better?"

"I thought I was going to pass out," he answered, breathing in the mild early November air. "I don't know what happened."

I took his face in my hands. "The stupid corset happened, and yeah, it's sexy under your clothes, but you didn't have to wear it so tight that it cuts off the oxygen to your brain."

He couldn't meet my gaze.

"You know you're beautiful; why're you trying so fuckin' hard?"

"I'm not getting any younger."

"Then pick one of your *many, many* suitors and settle down," I told him.

His gaze lifted to mine. "I'm a romantic at heart, you know this. I want to be swept off my feet. I want the fairy tale."

"We both know what I'm gonna say."

He groaned. "Make your own fairy tale." The "How?" that followed was morose.

"We could start by talking to my dad about your contract, as I've suggested a million times," I reminded him. "He buys it, you fulfill it by working for him, and you can live with me for free and––"

"Stop," he groaned. "This far-too-familiar conversation always gives me cold sweats."

I shrugged, and suddenly there was a man there, crowding me away from Linden.

"Pardon me, sweetheart, are you not well?"

"Aww." Like the flip of a switch, Linden was in his element again, ready to be worshiped and fawned over by another random alpha. He glanced at me, squinting to let me know that I needed to make myself scarce. "What a knight in shining armor you are to come check on me."

I stifled a groan, barely, and when I turned to go back inside, I was nearly trampled by two other men trying to come out onto the balcony to tend to him.

Checking on Bridget, seeing that she was drinking with three men now as Lucas looked on, watching, ever vigilant, obviously bored out of his mind, I decided I'd done my duty and could call it a night.

Walking around the edge of the room, making my way back toward the kitchen, I waved to my mother, who waved cheerfully back, and was nearing the door when a man stepped in front of me.

Since my reflexes were quick, even with four drinks in me, I didn't walk into him, instead keeping my balance, and I looked up into the face of a handsome man I immediately realized was an alpha. I was going to bow, but he lifted his hand to stop me.

"I need a favor," he announced.

"Sure," I agreed, taking a step back.

"I need the name of the omega you took out to the balcony."

He looked drugged, or drunk, but I knew he was neither. He was drowning in Linden's pheromones, which always smelled like roasted pumpkin to me. Linden hated that description, but I'd assured him, on many occasions, that it was a warm, comforting scent.

"His name's Linden, and he'd love to meet you." Linny *always* liked lots of suitors vying for his attention. If one was good, ten was better in his book.

"Thank you," he said, and made to clap me on the shoulder, but his hand was caught by Miss Holt's boss, Graeme Davenport, earl of something-and-something. I couldn't remember.

"Sir?" The stranger paused, confused, and dropped his hand.

"Leave. Go do whatever it is you're going to do, but do not touch him."

"Certainly," the man agreed, shooting me a look like Graeme was nuts and then pivoting on his heel and wading back into the crowd to make his way toward the balcony.

Watching him go, I turned back to the *cyne* and started to bow; it was what I'd been taught to do, and since I wasn't raised in a barn, it was the natural next step of our interaction. In fact, I would have bowed to the alpha who'd just left us if he hadn't stopped me. I was surprised when the earl caught my bicep so I couldn't bow to him.

"Sir?" What was going on? Most alphas got off on the bowing and scraping.

He cleared his throat, inhaling deeply. "No, please. I don't like all that ridiculous posturing, and never mind calling me *sir*."

"Oh, okay." I liked the resonance of his voice. Neither Linden nor Bridget had reported that when he spoke, it was low and husky and whiskey-smooth. The rumble made my pulse quicken.

He took a step closer, his hand lifting and then falling, returning to rest at his side. "I didn't get to meet you earlier."

"No," I agreed, retreating a step because something was off. He smelled strange. Not bad. Amazing, in fact. But different. I was breathing in leather and incense, pine and smokey musk, and the scent was thick, beckoning, drawing me closer, so instead of following my instincts and lunging at him, I withdrew another foot. "When everyone was in line, I was talking to your charming assistant."

"You found her charming?" he asked, taken off guard but still moving forward into my personal space. "Most find her abrasive or off-putting."

That made no sense, and I squinted at him. "But she's lovely."

"She is lovely," he agreed, looking me slowly up and down before returning his gaze to mine. "And most people miss that entirely."

"I don't see how."

"You're quite perceptive and—you're Avery Rhine, aren't you?"

"I am," I answered, even though it didn't sound as if he was uncertain he knew who I was, but asking so he could address me by my name.

He took another step closer, and when I took one more back, I bumped the wall. "You know, I always thought the idea of the omega going by their mother's maiden name to denote their status, or lack thereof, was something right out of the dark ages. Why can't an omega share the surname of the rest of their family?"

I shrugged. "Well, that way you know who the omega is right off the bat, and there is the matter of lupine law to contend with."

"True," he agreed, staring at my face. "Though no alpha worth a damn can mistake an omega when they see one...or smell one."

"I've been told that." I found my footing, both literally and figuratively, as I stepped around him so he had to turn and face me. I didn't like having my back up against the wall, and now I had the freedom to leave when I wanted to, no longer trapped. "Is it the same way an alpha can tell when they've met their fated beta or gamma?"

"I believe so," he replied gruffly, "but I don't know, and never will."

It hurt me, for some unfathomable reason, imagining this man without a mate. There was a tightness in my chest and a chill lodged in my bones. It was overwhelming, the grief I felt for him and how driven I was to offer comfort. All of it, my reaction, was alien, and what in the world was prompting it?

"Don't say that," I found myself pleading. Why it was important for him to find a loving mate I had no idea, but it was. With my heart in my throat, I attempted to ease his sadness. "I'm sure you'll find your mate."

He smiled then, kindly, warmly, and I inhaled deeply, wobbling a bit, my knees suddenly weak enough that I needed to sit down. His hand slipped around my bicep, bracing me, keeping me steady, turning me until my left shoulder bumped the wall. We'd traded places, and I was once again where I didn't want to be, caged between him and freedom. Even though, without him there holding me, I was fairly certain I would have been on the floor.

"I'm convinced I will as well," he agreed.

"What?" The thread of conversation was beyond me.

"I meant that I don't know how things work with betas and gammas, and never will. Not now."

It was hot in the room, nearly stifling, and I needed air but realized he'd herded me toward the laundry room near the kitchen.

"True mates are rare, don't you agree?" he asked, letting go of my arm, reaching around me to open the door just as I stepped back into it. I would have lost my balance had it been open. He took hold of the knob, stepping in close at the same time.

I closed my eyes, struggling not to press my face to his chest and breathe him in.

He opened the door and moved forward in small increments, like the tick of a clock, an inexorable counting down—tick, step, tick, step—his movement deliberate, until we were both through and he closed the door with a click behind him.

It was quiet in the small room, and somehow cooler, the air moving, which made no sense, and for a moment all I smelled was fabric softener before the warm animal musk was back, along with the scent of fresh, crisp, snow-covered evergreens.

"Well?"

He'd asked me a question. "Yeah," I managed to drag the word from my throat. "But you should never...give up on finding...your mate."

"Avery." He murmured my name, and I lifted my head so I could meet his eyes; up close, they were dark, like currants, but swirled with amber. "I promise you I will not."

"That's good," I croaked out, my voice breaking as I dropped my gaze, thinking about the fact I had never in my entire life been jealous that I wasn't born a beta or gamma. Not until right that second. The man would make a loving and loyal mate, of that I was absolutely certain. I could feel it thrumming under his skin, the promise of nurturing and shelter, of protection and his solid, grounding presence. He could be trusted and leaned on, his strength something my wolf could taste in the air vibrating around us. "Can I ask something?"

"Anything," he answered, his voice a rough, hoarse rumble.

I lifted my head. "Do you always smell like this?"

He grunted. "What do I smell like?"

"Smoke and musk and...fire."

"*To you*," he whispered. "I think that's what I smell like to you."

"That's strange," I husked, working hard to hold myself still and not lick the side of his throat before I bit him. I couldn't remember ever wanting to bite someone; that wasn't me. I didn't do that, either in or out of bed.

"It's not strange at all," he argued, closing the distance between us to mere inches before he slowly, carefully lifted his hand and slipped it around the side of my neck. "Those are my pheromones calling for you, reaching for you, luring you closer so I'll give you what you want."

"What do I want?" I whispered, lost in the sound of his voice.

"My bite."

I jolted against him, and his answering growl, low, deep in his chest, drew a quick whine from me I wasn't proud of. Because yes, I wanted to feel his skin between my teeth, the ache from not acting almost painful. But more than that, so very much more, was the desire to have his fangs in me, deep, and to have my blood on his tongue.

"What the fuck," I cried out, shivering, feeling my throat swell and my eyes burn. I lifted my gaze to his as he gently, with a featherlight touch, pressed his thumb under my chin. "Who are you?"

"You know who I am," he replied, his voice sultry and smooth, curling around me, more temptation than I could possibly resist as he tipped my head up and bent down toward me. "Avery. You know."

"You're Graeme Davenport, and you're a *cyne*, right?"

"I am, but that doesn't matter. I'm something more important to you."

"An earl and––"

"No. Something more important, and more vital."

I shook my head.

"Yes," he whispered thickly, and I could hear the words and feel their heat on my face at the same time. "Tell me. We both know."

I did, and it was terrifying, as well as the freest I'd ever felt in my life. I felt like I could fly even as I was unsure. "My mate," I declared breathlessly. "You're my mate."

"And you're mine," he affirmed. I heard the power

behind his claim, the conviction and certainty and, most of all, the utter possessiveness. "Avery Rhine, you are all mine."

I had things to say, questions to ask, but he took me into his arms and claimed my mouth, and my world exploded as my heart stopped and then started again, beating anew only for him.

4

GRAEME

As an alpha, the promise, always, from the time you were old enough to understand your place in the world, was that someday, if you were blessed, you would find your fated mate. That wolf, whoever they were, would know you inside and out, be attuned to you, even to the beat of your heart, and would stand forever at your side. If, however, an alpha didn't find their soulmate, then they could mate with a friend—a beta or gamma they were truly fond of, which could be risky if their fated alpha ever showed up. Easier than that was to declare for and bond with an omega.

I had always thought the idea of taking an omega, bonding with one, as my father had, making someone a possession, was archaic. But as I devoured Avery's mouth, tasting him, sucking on his tongue, making him open and take every mauling kiss, one after another as he writhed against me, I realized I was at war with myself. Half of me knew owning an omega was wrong, but the other half, the animal part, rejoiced in the idea that not only was the man mine, because he was my mate, but that on paper, in the eyes of all lupine-kind, he would belong solely to me.

I needed to bite him, mark him so everyone would know, even before a contract was signed and filed, that he was claimed. I broke the kiss to breathe, to swallow gulps of air as I panted above him, and I realized, as my brain cleared, he was quickly working open his trousers.

"What are you——"

"Take this," he ordered, passing me a small packet of lube that was warm and so had to have come from somewhere next to his body.

"Why are you carrying lube in the breast pocket of your tailcoat?" I asked gruffly, not liking the implications one bit.

"Because you never know when you're gonna get lucky," he answered with a sexy leer, taking off his jacket and laying it over the washing machine before shoving his pants to his ankles. His hands were all over me in seconds.

I should have been admiring the man's smooth burnished-gold skin, his flat stomach or long, cut cock, and I was, but the words coming out of his mouth were designed to enrage me. "You mean to say you come to these things and have sex?" I nearly yelled.

He shrugged. "I have, not often, but the lube is more for after, if I go to a bar. You'd be surprised how many guys will do you in a bathroom when you're wearing a tuxedo."

I felt the heat flush my face. "Listen to me"——I nearly snarled, the jealousy bitter on my tongue——"I will gut anyone who——"

"Yeah, mate, I get it," he placated, snatching the packet back, kissing me quick and dirty before he dropped to his knees, shucking my pants and underwear down my thighs just far enough to allow my already hard, leaking cock to bounce free. "Baby, lookit you," he murmured appreciatively before he took me down the back of his throat in one fluid motion.

I had to brace myself with a hand on the washing machine, and I tried to get his name out, but it sprang from my lips garbled and slurred. Impossible to even form words with his hot mouth milking my cock, back and forth, the suction perfect, the squeeze and drag, his tongue, his teeth, all of it exquisite and maddening.

Just imagining the amount of practice needed to have such confidence and technique—I'd never had a more skillful blowjob—was enough to make me homicidal. There had to be countless men who had experienced the ecstasy that was Avery Rhine's delicious mouth.

"Fuck" was all that ground out of me as my cock slipped from between his lips. He laved my balls, slurping noisily before returning his attention to my shaft. He took hold of my hand, the one not braced on the washing machine, and put it in his hair.

When I flexed my hand, tangling my fingers in his thick dirty-blond hair, he moaned loud and decadent, and I shoved in deep, fucking his mouth. In moments I was feeding him my dick, again and again, rocking forward, lost in the sensation until he shoved me back, stood up, put the lube packet in his mouth, ripped it open with a practiced ease that made me grind my teeth, and squeezed the entire contents onto my cock, one-handed, cupping the back of my neck with the other to pull me down for a kiss.

I was a good kisser, I knew what I was doing, but Avery was a great kisser, and he explored my mouth, nibbled on my lips, rubbed over my tongue with his sinfully, languorously, all the while stroking me from balls to head, building a need in me that had my body pulled tight like a bow before he turned, pressed my wide head to his pink puckered hole and pushed back against me just enough that I slipped inside his body.

"You're not—I don't want to hurt you," I moaned, not wanting to cause him a moment of pain, knowing I was big, having been told enough times, having more than a few lovers who hesitated before taking all of me inside them.

"You won't hurt me." He whispered the promise, turning his head, offering me his mouth. "Now fuck me."

Hunger and yearning crashed through me, and I yanked his head back, expecting a cry but getting only a low, seductive chuckle.

It hit me hard, like a punch in the gut. I wasn't in control, he was, and I needed to take back the power, dominate him, or stop.

"Please, my alpha." He murmured the words I needed. "Make me yours."

I thought for one terrifying second I was going to shift to my wolf right there as I pinned him over the washing machine with a clawed hand around the back of his neck, while the claws on the other, gripping his left hip, pierced his skin and drew blood.

He whimpered and moaned, lifting his ass for me as I drove forward, thrusting hard and fast, burying myself to the balls, rutting deep, in relentless strokes, using him, taking my pleasure, desperate to make him mine, body and soul.

Slipping from his stretched channel, I manhandled him down to the floor, put him on his hands and knees, and then shoved back inside him, pounding hard, our skin slapping together lewdly as he called my name in a rough, guttural whisper.

"Work your cock," I ordered, curling over his back, slowing my movement, no longer pistoning into him, instead dragging my length almost free of his channel before stuffing him full. "Make yourself come."

The muscles in his ass clamped down around me as I took hold of his silky hair again, and yanked back and sideways, ready to mark him. I wanted to sink my teeth deep into the hollow between his shoulder and neck, but he pulled free and turned his head for a kiss, catching his lip on my canines. I tasted his blood as he savaged my mouth. The moment I took over the kiss, his moan became carnal and decadent and full of longing.

"Graeme," he keened when he broke away for air. "Please, just fuckin' have me."

His words, fractured and aching, rife with longing, pushed me over the edge, and I was rough with him, using him hard, letting myself go as I never allowed or trusted.

He was mine, made for me, so I knew he alone would respond exactly as I would to him. I was precisely what he needed, wanted, had to have, and he was the same for me.

He came hard, spurting over the rug, jolting under me as he collapsed, facedown, only his ass in the air as I buried myself to the hilt, the feel of his muscles working, clenching and unclenching, so tight and perfect, the spasms coming in waves bringing me to climax moments later.

My orgasm wrung me out, and I pumped into him, rutting through the aftershocks of both his and my own, draped over his back after long moments, unmoving, sated and wishing I could wrap him in my arms and fall asleep. The urge to take him home with me and put him in my bed was nearly overwhelming.

"I'll never be able to look my mother in the face again," he groaned, his low chuckle the sexiest sound I'd ever heard in my life. "Holy shit. I can't believe I got cum on the rug in her laundry room."

I licked over the place where I wanted to put my mark, and in that moment I knew he'd saved me from a complete breach of decorum and propriety. An alpha who couldn't contain themselves was considered weak and undeserving of a mate. He'd shielded me from that judgment, and while I was thankful, it was also cause for concern. It meant that in the heat of passion his brain was still working, whereas mine was not. What did that say about my control versus his? I had easily surrendered to my base animal-wolf nature. He had remained utterly human. How was an omega more composed than an alpha?

"I think maybe I should take the rug with me and get it cleaned."

Why in the hell was he talking about a rug? He'd just been claimed by his alpha.

"But first off, we gotta get out of this room without anyone seeing us. I think I should leave first."

Leave? Leave me?

He wasn't going anywhere without me. Not ever. And this, my reaction, was exactly why alphas declared their intentions and contracts were signed before mates were ever left alone together. This. This recklessness. This was what happened when pheromones were released and an alpha took control of a willing and beautiful omega. Because he didn't bear my mark, but he smelled ripe and ready, fecund, an omega ready to mate, to be claimed and marked.

"Avery—"

"Can you do me a favor and get the club outta my ass?" he asked playfully.

I slid gently free, horrified that I'd caused him any pain. "I didn't mean to hurt—"

"Baby, you so did not hurt me," he purred, rolling over as

Muscle and Bone

I sat back on my haunches and stared down at him. "It was great. I hope we can do it again."

"You hope we—pardon me?"

He sat up, leaned sideways and opened the door of the dryer. His snicker was evil as he pulled out a white T-shirt and clicked the door shut before using the article of clothing to clean the gush of fluid seeping from his ass.

When he was done, he rolled to his feet in a seamless motion, moved his tailcoat aside and lifted the lid of the washing machine, threw the shirt in and was about to say something to me when his phone chirped. He checked the display, then put it down on the dryer, yanked up his pants, tucked in his shirt, zipped, adjusted his belt, and tossed the tailcoat over his shoulder. When the phone rang, he quickly picked it up again and put it to his ear.

"Hey," he said warmly to whoever was on the other end, and I found my jaw clenching as I stood and pulled up my underwear and trousers, unable to see anything but the golden skin of his throat where my mark needed to be. "Yeah, I got the text from him. Why are we—what?"

He was listening, which gave me a moment to admire the long, sleek lines of the man.

My mate was breathtaking.

His short hair was a riot of wheat and rich burnished gold, ash brown with streaks of silver. His eyes were the color of a cloudy day, an opaque gray that flashed like polished moonstone. There were heavy laugh lines etched into his fine angular features, and heart-stopping dimples that made my knees weak. His lips were full and lush and bewitching, as well as swollen from my kisses. I wanted to kiss him again, at my leisure, and it hit me then, as I braced myself on the washing machine for the second time, that he was not at all as affected by me as I was by him.

"I am," he growled. "I'm on my way right fuckin' now," he finished irritably, hanging up and turning to go.

"Avery."

He stopped with his hand on the knob. "I'm sorry to bail on you, but duty calls. If you go see my mother, she'll give you my number. I'd love to hear from you," he said, the annoyance that had been there before now absent. Then he gave me a wicked grin before he opened the door, slipped out, and closed it behind him.

He was gone.

I stared at the spot where he'd been seconds before, all the while thinking that at any moment he was going to pop right back in and tell me he was kidding. An omega didn't leave an alpha without permission, and certainly no omega had ever left their mate. It was simply not done. What was happening right now?

But it became glaringly apparent with each passing second that Avery Rhine was not aware of the rules omegas lived by, because he did not, in fact, come back. He'd left me, his alpha, of his own free will. It was without precedent, and I was utterly gobsmacked. Honest to God, I had no idea what to do. Not only had I never been faced with this situation before, but the whole thing was nonsensical and completely out of my wheelhouse. I dealt in logic, in things that made sense, and him leaving me—and even more alarming, him being *able* to leave me—was beyond my comprehension. How in heaven's name did he have the audacity to abandon his alpha? Didn't he understand it wasn't allowed, wasn't permitted? And now that he'd gone, what in the world was I supposed to do?

Did I run after him and drag him back to my house?

Did I go to his mother and get his number like some common suitor who found him appealing?

Did I report him to the council?

He said he knew I was a *cyne*, but did he know what that truly meant? That I had even more power to discipline him?

Did I report him to the *dryhten*? And if I did, what would they do to him?

And what the hell was I supposed to do about the rug?

He'd left me in the most ridiculous position with regards to the protocol of hospitality. Because while it was true that it wasn't my spend on the rug, I was the cause, and he had rolled over on his back before he wiped himself off, so technically my semen was on the rug as well, and if I kept thinking about it, my brain would explode.

And why couldn't I leave the room? It took me a moment to figure out, and then it hit me.

It smelled like him.

The room was practically pulsing with the scent of his sweat and musk, of sex, and I wanted to breathe it into my lungs. More than that, I wanted *him*. The longer I stood there thinking about him moaning under me, begging me, coming apart, the rasp of his voice, the catch of his breath, the madder I got. How dare he leave me? He had no right to leave me. He belonged to me. I owned him. He was...he was—I...

The second revelation nearly gutted me as I was struck by the irrefutable truth that he had made all the decisions. Not me. Him. I had corralled him and herded him into the laundry room, yes, I had kissed him, but that was all. He had gone to his knees; he had swallowed my cock; he had taken me inside his body. And he was the one who left when he was done. He'd called me his alpha, and I'd succumbed to my animal, I'd *wanted* to, and I allowed myself to believe the power was mine. But it was all him. I was merely a fun romp at a party.

This was a life-altering moment for me, and he left!

I felt the anger and possessiveness surge through me, boiling my blood, and it took all my self-control not to put my fist through the nearest wall or shift to my wolf. The animal in me yearned to run down his mate, to take hold of his throat and pin him down and claim him. Remind him to whom he belonged. I was ready to have Avery Rhine again. I wanted my scent and my tongue on every square inch of his skin before I marked him as mine. It was primal. It was life and death, more than a need or a want; it was necessary that his neck be scarred with the brand of my fangs this very instant. The fact that I could not make that happen, because he was gone, rocked me to my core.

I shivered, thinking about him, about his beautiful round ass, how my cock had looked sliding inside of him, stretching him open, and the mewling cries that had come out of him as I yanked on his hair and bowed his back as he took me in deeper.

My desire would undo me if I didn't make him mine. There could never be anyone but him again; my wolf would accept only him, and he didn't know it, because clearly he didn't understand the protocol of mating.

And for him, being an omega, his position was even more precarious. Newly claimed omegas were not at all like betas or gammas. Both could be claimed, but not marked, and go about their lives; they were so much stronger than omegas. They were made to be partners, separate but united. The same was not true of an omega. Omegas who were newly claimed needed to be bitten and to carry the mark of their alphas. Being unmarked was dangerous for them. Avery was, at the moment, oozing pheromones designed to keep his alpha close. His smell, the way he carried himself, the blown pupils and feeling like he was drugged, all of it was a siren call to his alpha, to make me take him over and over, to put my scent on him and mark him. It was like a dance of submission, of glances and touches, an open, carnal invitation. Crudely put, I'd kickstarted his heat, and every wolf who crossed his path would want him.

And any other but me he would run from.

When he left, he said he'd love to see me again, but the fact was, biologically, he had no choice. He would have to come to me. It was hardwired in him now to seek me out. Whether he acknowledged my place or not, I was still his alpha and his mate. He would need me for more than sex; he required closeness and comfort from me. Proximity to me would give him relief and balance. Without me, he would slowly fray, unable to eat or sleep, and eventually he would shut down completely. The problem was it could take days for him to figure that out, and in that time he'd be driving others mad and putting himself in real jeopardy. Just because he ran didn't mean that no one could catch him, and he'd *fight* not to be taken, and others would *fight* to have him. It was a recipe for disaster.

I hadn't thought it through when I steered him into the laundry room. I'd only meant to taste him and talk to him. Having him there on the floor never crossed my mind, but neither did him touching me. No one put their hands or mouth on an alpha without express permission, and no one took liberties with me, especially. I was far too frightening.

But Avery wasn't scared of me in the least. He'd looked at me as a conquest, and once his lips were stretched around my cock, my logic was drowned in a sea of frantic, desperate longing. I couldn't recall ever wanting anyone more, which made perfect sense. The man was my mate, my other half. He belonged to me. Not taking him, not acting, was counterintuitive. Why would I hesitate to claim what was mine?

I needed to find him and bring him home. And while it would not be critical for hours, even days, he would feel the eyes of others on him, see their covetous glances and feel their thirst, and he'd wonder why he was so prickly and short-tempered with that attention when it had never bothered him in the past.

If he had been properly educated, he would know better. But, by the same token, most omegas were not true mates, they were bond mates. They were taken as a second choice. Certainly, I never imagined I would have an omega for my other half. An alpha was best served with a beta or a gamma for a mate, someone who could stand up to them, argue, fight if needed, be strong but still subservient. An omega simply gave in, broke down, as my mother had with my father, a beautiful, elegant doormat, devoted to an alpha's care, to providing pleasure, unconditional support, and even, in some cases, love. I knew most alphas didn't love their omegas. They cared for them, protected and sheltered them, and lavished them in a lifestyle few others could boast of, but love was generally not part of the arrangement. True feelings, those from the heart, were not the norm. And while I had no idea if I could ever come to love Avery Rhine, I knew already, even in that short time, I wanted to know absolutely everything about him.

"You want more than that," I husked in the stillness of the empty room, leaning on the wall, feeling the truth wash over me.

The strain of his leaving was already wearing on me. I wanted the man in *thrall* to me. I wanted him beside me in bed, wrapped around me at night, and his hand in mine when I welcomed people to our home. I wanted to hear his laugh, talk to him at dinner, and to be the first thing those gorgeous storm-washed eyes of his saw when he opened them every morning. I wasn't sure if I could love him, but I certainly wanted him to love me. He was mine, and he would need to quickly wrap his brain around that fact. He was an omega. I needed to inform him of his place and what was expected of him—to live in my house and sleep in my bed.

Settled back into my skin, I straightened up, made certain I was put together, and texted Kat to meet me near the library. I needed to speak to Avery's parents, but first I needed my assistant to make sure I didn't have their son's scent all over me. It would be hard to take my claim seriously if they knew I'd had their son on his hands and knees next to their washing machine.

KATHERINE OLYMPIA HOLT was staring at me like I'd grown another head before she leaned in close and inhaled.

"Well?" I snapped at her.

She cleared her throat. "Yes," she stated flatly, "you smell like cum."

I threw up my hands.

"Should I lie?"

"No, but you could take more care with your words. You're always so crass."

Her squint made her look like she was in pain. I was annoying the hell out of her, that was certain.

I growled at her under my breath. "Go find his parents and ask them to meet me on the patio. At least if we're outside, it won't be as noticeable."

"Yes, sir."

"But first, call Izzy and have her find out Avery Rhine's

phone number and address, because my plan is to go there from here." Avery had told me to talk to his mother. Ridiculous. As though I was some poor suitor without my own ample resources.

"Absolutely," she agreed quickly. "I—oh." She gasped, and when I turned to look at her, I saw Mrs. Huntington, our hostess, standing there, arms crossed, staring up at me.

"Mrs. Huntington," I croaked out, floundering as I stared at the stunning woman, realizing, in that moment, where her son had come by the beautiful shade of his eyes, though his were lighter, nearly silver, and their effect on me was quite different from those of his mother. "I would like to speak to you and your--"

"Sir," she said, lifting one of her eyebrows. "I saw you duck into the laundry room earlier with my son. Do you perhaps want to speak to me about his contract?"

Oh dear God. "I--yes," I managed to get out, mortified by my behavior and illogically angry at Avery for being the cause.

She nodded sagely and stepped closer to me, and even though I was terrified she'd smell him on me, I had to stand my ground. "He's a police officer, my son. Did he tell you?"

"I don't know why what he does now would pertain to after our--"

"It's in his contract," she informed me. "He will remain on the police force for as long as he sees fit. It's a stipulation that is nonnegotiable."

I turned to Kat, unsure if I'd heard correctly.

She nodded, grimacing. "He told me about that, and I was going to inform you before you spoke to him, but you—" She coughed. "—went near him before I could mention it."

I'd done far more than simply go near him.

"He's not a 'make a home for an alpha' kind of omega," Mrs. Huntington explained solemnly. "He's built like a beta, to be an equal partner. He'll be an exceptional father, because he's been raised by one, and he has the nurturing of an omega built in, so children won't be a problem, but if you're looking for someone to welcome you home every night with a drink for you in their hand and food on the table, I think you should look elsewhere. Nine times out of ten, it will be you making dinner."

"I have a cook and a housekeeper and a butler," I defended automatically, the words out there before I could form a coherent thought.

"Perfect," she commended me, brightening, "that'll help."

I'd stepped into some kind of weird alternate universe where nothing made sense. How in the world was she telling me what her son, an omega, would and would not do in the home of his alpha? What the hell was going on?

"Are you well, sir?"

I turned to Kat and could not miss her grimace.

"You're kind of an odd shade of gray."

I looked back at Mrs. Huntington, trying to put thought into word.

She was waiting expectantly, brows lifted, head tilted forward.

I was...having trouble wrapping my mind around the fact they had written Avery's job into his contract. I'd never heard of such a thing. It was beyond all imagining.

"Ma'am, you understand that your son is an omega, do you not?"

"I do," she assured me with a knowing, gentle smile. "But I didn't raise an omega."

Before I could get a word out, she lifted a hand to stop me.

"Actually, let me amend that statement. His father and I didn't raise an omega. We raised alphas. Our first and second born are alphas, and we treated all our children the same. I have a fulltime job, so does he, and neither of us had the time nor the inclination to try and teach our omega to be anything but self-sufficient, self-reliant, and strong."

She was kidding. She had to be kidding. "Surely you jest."

Slow head shake from her.

"But that's madness."

"To you."

"To everyone," I retorted, trying to curb the anger in my voice. "I admire you and your husband's commitment to Avery's career, but to raise him an alpha when he so clearly is not, is, if you'll pardon my candor, the height of irresponsibility." Both of his parents had done Avery a grave disservice. It was like training a lamb to be a lion. It was absurd. "I appreciate you wanting him to be himself"—I clipped my words, my voice strained—"but in your efforts not to raise a subservient omega, you've missed something vital."

"And what is that?"

"The possibility that he would turn out to be not just a bonded omega, but an omega destined to be the *mate* of an alpha."

The statement hung in the air between us for several minutes before she jolted, my words sinking in, hitting the mark.

"No," she told me, shaking her head. "It's not possible."

"It's exceedingly rare, yes," I agreed, sighing deeply, "but not at all impossible."

Her eyes narrowed as she stared at me.

"I assure you that your son is, in fact, my mate."

Her gasp was loud, and I felt sorry for her when she clutched her heart, because in that moment she had to grasp the depth of her failing.

"You're certain?" Kat whispered roughly beside me.

"I am," I told her, keeping my gaze locked on Mrs. Huntington, addressing her as I continued. "And now your son is out there, alone, newly mated, without my mark, and without a clue of what will soon be happening to him because you didn't prepare him to be an omega, let alone a mated one."

She took a deep breath and, wonder of wonders, seemed to gather herself and calm.

"Ma'am, let me say that––"

"It's all right," she stated with absolute certainty, and I was stunned. It sounded as though she was trying to comfort me. "He'll be all right."

"Mrs. Huntington, he's going to be in heat."

She squinted. "No."

"No?" I was dumbfounded at both her denial and ignorance.

"I don't think so."

"You don't *think so*?" I rasped, repeating her words, my patience all but gone. "Madam"—I bit the inside of my cheek, the formality not helping my tone at all––"your son is an omega. He can't control what will––"

"No," she contradicted me again, adamantly. "You don't know him. He won't succumb to anything as base as being in heat."

How in the world was she so deluded? She was an educated woman; she couldn't simply brush off biological facts. "I beg your pardon, but––"

"I understand what you believe, sir, but my son isn't

some vapid, weak-willed, frightened little omega. He's made his own way. He doesn't even live here at home."

"What do you mean?" She couldn't be in earnest; it wasn't possible. "An omega must reside at home with their parents until they are claimed by an––"

"I just told you I raised an alpha," she replied, her voice dripping with sympathy for me. It was beyond all reason, but she was sincerely, incomprehensibly sorry that I was so mistaken.

"But he's not an alpha," I husked, my voice breaking with the strain it took not to rail at her. "He's an omega. His needs are different. First, above all, an omega needs safety. How could you not provide the first––"

"He has his own accounts, his own money, he's entirely self-sufficient. Sometimes we go weeks without seeing him."

I was stunned. She'd raised him in a certain way and then allowed him free rein. In what realm of possibility could any omega be allowed out in the world, unprotected, unsupervised, and unescorted, without consequence? It was madness. They were lucky Avery hadn't been taken from them long before I showed up. Any suitor could have followed him home, or wolves who had caught his scent on the air, known an omega when they smelled one, and taken the chance that he was alone. I had no idea how he'd been so fortunate.

"Are you certain he's your mate?" she asked gently. "I don't mean to doubt you, and I mean no disrespect, but we're very close, he and I, as I am with all my children, so it makes no sense he wouldn't have shared with me that he found his mate."

She was choosing her words carefully, and when I glanced at Kat, looking for an ally, I was startled by the way she was gazing at Mrs. Huntington—brows furrowed, face drawn tight, eyes narrowed so no stray tear dared well up or, heaven forbid, fell. She was the picture of concern and sympathy. But why? Why would my ultra-capable assistant be concerned with—and then it came to me.

I was standing there trying to make this woman see that everything she'd taught her son had been wrong, when it was him and his easy charm and swagger, nothing forced, nothing fake, no pretense, that had utterly bewitched me. He was who he was *because* the woman standing before me had raised him without the restrictions on mind and body that every other omega I'd ever met had been taught from birth. They cleaved to their limitations and looked for freedom and fulfillment through their mates. It was precisely Avery's independence that had me so enthralled. None of this, however, resolved my concerns over the heat that he would soon find himself in no matter what his mother's thoughts were on the subject.

"Mrs. Huntington—" I sighed, taking a breath before I continued. "—forgive me. I was thrown by your revelations about how he conducts himself and where he lives. I meant no disrespect."

Her face lit up in relief, and she stepped closer and took my hand. It wasn't at all proper, her touching me without my permission or that of her mate, her husband, but already I was coming to understand that Avery was unusual, and so was his family.

"I would further postulate that the reason he didn't go to you immediately upon learning I was his mate is owed to you raising him to believe his human side is more important than his wolf. He called me his mate, his alpha, but they were just words; he doesn't truly believe them. Not yet."

She pressed her lips together and nodded, almost

grimacing. "I suspect that's correct. Avery and his wolf do not get along."

"How so?"

Her deep exhale told me it was a long-running point of conflict and debate. "I've told him since he was young that his wolf is not something to be fought, but instead embraced and cherished."

"But he doesn't listen to you," I surmised as she withdrew her hand.

"No. He argues the point with all of us: me, his father, his brother and sister, their mates, aunts, uncles, anyone who brings it up."

I held her gaze. "And therein lies my contention," I apprised her gently. "Your son, who you have raised to be self-sufficient and strong, was educated about what to expect when he encountered alphas who might consider him for a bonding, but he was never told what it would be like to find his mate."

"Because omegas don't have true mates," she replied shrewdly. "They're made to create a home, raise and nurture children, conform to whatever environment they find themselves in, but not to join with a single alpha. It's actually tragic when they do."

"I know all about omegas. My mother was one." I needed the lesson on what an omega was and wasn't to be concluded. I didn't need to be reminded why Fiona Davenport had fallen into ruin after the death of my father; the fact she had was enough.

"Your mother was an omega?"

"She was, yes."

"And she's gone now," she surmised with a sigh. "I'm so sorry. But as your own mother was an omega, then you understand an omega bonding with an alpha is––"

"Pardon me for interrupting. I'm not talking about bonding but about mating," I stated, needing her to hear me. "I know how omegas who are bonded by contract behave, but I am not at all familiar with what occurs in those who are mated. I suspect not many are, yourself included."

Moments of silence ticked by as she stared up into my face before she finally nodded. "You're absolutely right. Forgive me."

"There's nothing to forgive; I simply need you to grasp what I'm telling you. Your son left here thinking that his mate is secondary to everything else in his life, and I am not."

"No. No, you're not."

"And I believe that him going into heat is not only likely but guaranteed."

She glanced at Kat and then back at me. "Because the two of you mating is a once in a lifetime thing," she concluded. "Yes?"

"Yes," I rushed out, thrilled that she finally heard me.

She reached for me, and I took her hands in mine, holding them gently. "Then we'll have to make sure we get the two of you back here first thing tomorrow."

Had I heard her correctly? "Mrs. Huntington," I blurted out, "we need to sign the contract now so that I may leave here and go to him."

"I'm sorry," she said, eyes narrowed, brows furrowed, taking a step back from me. "Without his informed consent? This is what you're suggesting?"

"Ma'am, he's an omega. He has no say, only the alpha who claims him does, and the head of this household, your husband."

She nodded slowly. "Certainly. Please come with me."

I glanced at Kat, who looked just as confused as I was, and then fell into step beside the matriarch of the Huntington family, very much off balance with her sudden deference. It didn't matter, though, how uncomfortable I was. Only having Avery's contract in my hands did.

When we stepped into the main room, as expected, everyone stopped and turned. I was a *cyne*, after all. We were few and far between, and I was an earl to boot. Money, property, and a huge dowry was in store for the Huntingtons, and every person in the room was aware of that fact.

I saw the faces of the omegas I'd brushed off, walked away from. As the crowd parted and we reached Mr. Huntington, his son and daughter joining us, I gave a slight bow, and as was custom, he gave a much deeper one, which was necessary given my rank and title, and then we were facing one another in silence.

"Sir," I began, my voice far steadier than I felt, "I would like to speak to you about your son Avery's contract."

The room erupted into a din of people all speaking at once. I would soon be fielding a circus of social invitations; of that I had no doubt.

"Of course," he replied over the cacophony, giving me a trace of a smile, extending his arm and pointing the way toward an archway that led from the great room, ballroom, whatever they called the enormous room in their home.

Once we were in the hall, along with Mrs. Huntington, his son and daughter, as well as Kat, Mr. Huntington addressed me.

"Mr. Davenport," he began, "I have a copy of the contract to give you to go over, and then when we set the date to discuss terms we can--"

"No, dear," Mrs. Huntington, declared softly, demurely, a tone that she had, as of yet, not used in my presence. "Mr.

Davenport means to sign the contract immediately and take ownership of your son this very evening."

He stopped and rounded on me so unexpectedly that both Kat and I took a defensive step back, with her moving in closer than usual, as unnerved as I was.

"What reason would you have for wanting your suit to move forward so quickly?" he asked, glowering at me.

Instead of saying, "I had sex with your son in your laundry room," I replied with, "He's my mate, sir. Not a bond mate, but a true one."

He was taken aback, as was everyone but Mrs. Huntington. I could see it in their stunned expressions, all of them appearing as though I'd told them I was a unicorn.

"There's no question about it," I pressed on. "If you ask him, he'll agree. He's mine."

Mr. Huntington nodded and then took a breath. "To be clear, sir, he's *mine*. And until I hear from my son that he is indeed your mate, and, moreover, he wants to be, all I can provide you with is the copy of his contract, as I stated earlier."

I glanced at Mrs. Huntington, who had her arms crossed and her brows lifted. The *I told you so* was clear as day. "Perhaps you don't understand his present peril," I apprised my mate's father. "But I firmly believe that I've put him in heat. And, as he is truly mated rather than a chosen bond mate, I suspect that what he will experience will be far more extreme than what occurs with a normal bonding."

Mr. Huntington's glower turned into an outright glare of disapproval. "Being an alpha myself, I know the only way you could put him in heat would be if you placed my son, my youngest, my unbonded omega, into a, shall we say, compromising position."

Four people staring daggers at me.

"Tell me, sir," he demanded, grinding out the words, "have you violated all rules of propriety, hospitality, respectability, and decorum this evening, and compromised my youngest?"

It was a horrific breach of conduct, and ridiculous at the same time. No one in their right mind thought omegas were virginal ingenues. Were some of them? Of course. The younger they were, the more likely the omega would be a virgin, but this was the twenty-first century, not some Regency nightmare. The issue wasn't with the omega being pure and untouched; the issue was with an alpha claiming an omega before the contracts were signed. Avery could have screwed whoever he wanted to as long as that person wasn't an alpha; for an alpha to sleep with an omega without signing on the bottom line was akin to stealing. It was not something any upstanding alpha, or *cyne*, would ever do, much less admit to...but for one very good reason.

"I did," I confessed, meeting his gaze, staring him down. "Your son is ruined for anyone else; no other alpha but me will ever want him."

"I will have you censured!" Mr. Huntington railed. "And--"

"You don't have to do anything," I assured him, my tone soothing, kind, "because, as I said, I want him. All I need, sir"--it was my turn to draw out the words--"is your signature next to mine on his contract."

"Absolutely not," Ambrose Huntington, Avery's brother, rasped. "Until we talk to Avery, we can't do--"

"No," his father murmured, his cold, hard gaze on me. "There's nothing to be done."

"Unless Avery was forced or--"

It was instinctive. My wolf processed his words before my human brain caught up. I had Ambrose Huntington off his feet, on the wall, my clawed hand wrapped around his throat. Second time that evening I'd lost control, but for two night-and-day reasons.

"That's my mate you speak of so lightly," I growled at him, making sure he heard my rage in every clipped syllable. "He's more precious to me than my own eyes, and I would sooner cut out my heart than cause him a moment of pain."

Time ticked by, wild, rapid beats of his heart and the loud, steady drum of mine.

"Yes," he choked out.

"I more than merely *want* him; he's my very breath, my home."

Letting him go, he dropped to his feet and would have crumpled to the floor, sliding down the wall, but I pinned him there with two fingers to his shoulder. "You insult me and my family name far more gravely than I have yours with the mere *suggestion* of something so loathsome and vile as rape."

"Please," he rasped when I stepped back, placing his hand over his heart, "forgive me, Graeme Davenport. I was concerned for my brother and misspoke."

Turning to face Mr. and Mrs. Huntington, I was surprised at the looks on both of their faces, especially Avery's mother, whose head was tipped, a fond smile curling her bow-shaped lips. The dimples, which she'd given to her son, were also evident.

I squinted at her. "Ma'am?"

She rushed forward and took hold of my hand. "You're a mess, just like him."

"Pardon me?"

Kat snorted, but I didn't look at her.

"You're all grouchy and cold and aloof and growly on the

outside, but I heard what you said, and that came from the heart."

"I have no——"

"Come"——Mr. Huntington's tone was now warm, pacifying——"let's set the terms and get that contract signed."

I turned to look at Kat then.

She shrugged. "Your mate is precious to you, Graeme; we all heard you."

It felt like all the air left my body at once.

Mr. and Mrs. Huntington scrambled to hold me upright, both of them chuckling. Evidently, the fact I'd put their son in a compromising position paled beside my confession that I needed him more than air.

"He's your treasure." Mrs. Huntington sighed deeply. "You don't expect him to *make* a home for you, because he *is* your home."

I couldn't get my voice to work.

She patted my arm. "Alphas, so ridiculous. If you'd just spoken up, I would have never doubted you. All I've ever wanted for my son was someone to see him for who he truly is. Someone to love him desperately and treasure him above all else."

When had I said I was going to do any of that?

The look on her face was sheer adoration. "You're going to be so good for him, so grounding, and you can make a home together, as equals."

As what?

Kat snickered, and I turned to look at her.

"Sign the contract, boss." She mouthed the words. "We need to find your mate."

We did, yes. I had to set Avery straight about a great many things. And even though whatever I'd said in the heat of the moment was crazy, and I had no idea where it came from, still, it was worth it because I would get what I wanted —Avery. The more I thought about it, I had to wonder, how did an omega, raised like an alpha, go about dealing with being in heat? Could he possibly turn to others to sate his carnal appetite?

I wasn't going to give him enough time to find out.

5

AVERY

Thank God I had clothes in the car. The idea of having to drive home to Hyde Park to change and then turn around and drive to the 800 block of West Sixty-eighth Street was not what my partner meant when he told me to get my ass over there after I received a text from my chief, Seamus Bannerman, letting me know that my night off was over.

As a shifter I metabolized everything quickly, so fortunately I was sobered up from the post-sex haze by the time I got to my Jeep Wrangler. I started the car to get the heater going and began stripping out of my formal clothes, moderately certain the dry cleaner could put everything back to rights, and into jeans, a T-shirt, a heavy wool sweater, and the canvas Nikes I had in the back seat. I chugged a couple bottles of water I always kept in my car, then maneuvered out of my parking spot and headed to Englewood.

As I drove, I caught a whiff of leather and spicy musk and bent my head, lifting the collar of my sweater and T-shirt, and inhaled. It wasn't my clothes or me, it was *his* scent on my skin, *his* scent that lingered like no one else's had before.

Beyond the sex being good or bad, I never thought about it once I was done. Sometimes I thought I'd like to see whoever again, but it wasn't a compulsion, not necessary, and my heart didn't rabbit in my chest with…anticipation. In the moment, lost in what I wanted, needed, and had to have, the afterwards didn't cross my mind. But driving away from him now seemed, inexplicably, like the wrong choice. I'd had the feeling, after I walked out, that it was a mistake, and had stood for a moment, on the other side of the laundry room door, and fought the urge to go right back in.

Then I muttered "the fuck" under my breath before I bolted for the hall closet, grabbed my coat, and was out the back door, fast.

Walking to my car, I'd stopped, turned, taken a couple steps to go back, and then whipped around, continuing on with what I was supposed to be doing, which was reaching my partner. But I couldn't shake the weird feeling that I forgot something, like I'd left my phone in the room with him or something. I had everything, though, so that wasn't it. If I could just figure out what was grinding away at the back of my brain, I was confident I could shake whatever it was.

Or I was going to call my mother and ask her if he'd gotten my number from her, because apparently I meant it when I said I'd like to see him again. If he hadn't, and didn't care about seeing me again, I realized, strangely, that would twinge more than a bit.

"Call Mom," I directed my phone, but another call came in, so I answered it instead. "Yeah?"

"Hey"—my partner, Wade Massey's, voice came over the

line, sounding even more irritable than usual—"where are you?"

"Where do you think I am?" I snapped, because it was a stupid question. "I'm on my way to meet you."

"No, Bannerman wants us in Highland Park, so turn around."

"Wait. What?"

"Yeah, I know," he began snidely, "you're wondering why we're going to Highland Park, since it's clearly *way* the hell out of our jurisdiction."

"Yeah."

"Highland Park still has not one lupine detective or any lupine officers, so anything at all to do with wolves rolls over to Chicago PD."

"That's bullshit."

"It is," he agreed, "but they just elected a new mayor, so hopefully that'll change. In the meantime, their deficit puts you and I on a dead guy in a mansion by the lake, while Pecker and Ness get to go to Englewood and scrape a dead prostitute off the pavement."

"His name's just Peck," I reminded him nicely. "He doesn't like it when you fuck up his name, as you well know."

"Is he on the phone right now? No."

"Why are you like this?"

"This is how my mother raised me."

"Lies. Your mother's lovely."

He grunted. "I blame you."

"Me?"

"You're rich, so whenever we get these murders in rich neighborhoods, you and I hafta show up."

"My parents are rich," I reminded him for the billionth time. "I am not. Are you rich?"

"Fuck no."

"Then how can I be since we do the same fuckin' job?"

"Because your family is all wealth and privilege and the 'one percent'."

"Which has what to do with me, other than lavish Christmas gifts?"

"Whatever," he groused at me. "I'm having Marcie––"

"Meggie," I corrected him.

"––Meggie," he amended, "drop me off at the train station in Highland Park, so swing by there and get me. You have thirty minutes; I'm starting the timer now. Hurry the fuck up."

I was quiet, intentionally not hanging up. We sat there silently, listening to nothing but each other breathing until I finally broke. "Really? Marcie?"

"Leave it alone."

"If you can't even remember their names, it might be time to slow down."

"Can we just focus, please?"

Since it wasn't an argument I was going to win, I let it go. "Be there shortly."

He hung up without another word.

When I made detective three years ago, the push was to have a human and lupine together. The balance was supposed to be favorable. A human tempered the animal instincts of a lupine, and the extrasensory facets of a lupine —smell, changes in body temperature, the ability to distinguish the highs and lows of speech, awareness of those imperceptible nuances—were an asset to the human, especially during questioning. This was the rationale, which was why I'd been paired with another new detective, Dion Abernathy.

He couldn't keep up with me, though, and wanted to skate by doing the bare minimum—no overtime, no brainstorming, just punch the clock. It lasted a month before he asked for a new partner. And while I appreciated my chief, Seamus Bannerman, keeping me when he transferred Abernathy back down to patrol, the other guys had looked at me like I was a leper.

There were two more partners in the next six months, one who didn't understand why I checked in on people, even if we had no new information on their cases, and the other, who felt that I was too intimidating and too physical with suspects, especially those cases involving women and children. I was a lupine, and that meant I was "unpredictable and passionate." Bannerman looked pained when we both stood in front of his desk as he'd told the second guy his transfer to vice was approved. I was left without a partner again.

The following day we got a transfer from the organized crime division, and being the only detective without a partner, I found him sitting at the desk butted up to mine when I got to work that morning. As I sat down, he looked up.

Stunning man, dark umber skin with bronze undertones, scalp-trimmed hair, copper-colored eyes, like new pennies, long lashes, high cheekbones, and a sharp-angled square jaw.

He rose and offered me his hand. "Wade Massey," he said, introducing himself, his voice whiskey-smooth. "I'm your new partner." I shook his hand, and he smiled. "Can I call ya wolf boy?"

I squinted. His answering smile was wide and evil, as was his chuckle and the eyebrow waggle. I liked him immediately, and it didn't take long to realize he was the other half of me. I felt, at times, there had to be some wolf somewhere in his ancestry, and asked him about it.

"Listen," he told me the first time we went drinking, "there's Cherokee in my family, and African and Scottish, Quechuan and German. There's no wolves, you got it?"

But sometimes I could swear I caught a whiff of wolf on him. We could speak without talking, and I could look at him and convey what I was thinking. We were so attuned to each other that when we went undercover, we rarely, if ever, used our earpieces.

What solidified us as more than friends, and more like brothers, was when a guy had turned a gun on us, and I had stepped squarely in front of my partner. There had been no thought, just pure instinct on my part. Afterwards, on the way to our car, once SWAT had secured the scene, Wade grabbed me and pinned me to a wall.

"The fuck?" I groused at him.

"What the hell was that?" he rasped, staring at me, shaking.

Seeing how wrecked he was, I tried to defuse the situation. "I'm a wolf; I can take a bullet and heal more damage than––"

"That's bullshit," he croaked out, swallowing hard, breathing through his nose. "You may heal faster, but you're just as dead from a point-blank shot as I am."

I was. No question.

"But you––"

"You're my best friend, my partner. What do you want me to say?"

When he stepped back, I lunged at him, wrapping him in my arms, and he finally allowed the closeness that had been missing, the last piece in our relationship. Wolves were tactile; we needed, craved touch for true connection. Lots of human and lupine partners didn't have that, which kept everything professional but also not locked in, not a true pairing. The ones who had that functioned far better than two humans or two lupines, no matter how close they were. Wade had always been strong and independent. His father, a Marine, was killed in action when he was young, and he became the man of the house for his mother and little brother. Leaning on anyone else was not something he did. I was, in fact, the only one he let down his guard with. His mother told me often, when I was alone with her in her kitchen, that she was so thankful for me because, finally, there was someone in his life he could lean on.

"Well, it goes both ways," I told her.

And then, inevitably, her scowl would appear at dinner as we scarfed down her food. His brother, Ethan, would watch us with wide eyes, and Ethan's wife, Delilah, would keep her hands in her lap, staring at us as well.

"What?" Wade would ask her.

"I just don't want to risk getting my fingers between you two and the food."

His mother would shake her head at us. "You need a wife," she would tell Wade. "You need a husband," she would tell me. "The pair of you need lookin' after and to be fed something decent more than once a week."

"We both date," he lied to her the last time we were there.

Her eyes narrowed, and I kicked him under the table because, holy shit, didn't he know that lying to his mother was a sin?

"What you two do," she told us, her tone disapproving, like ice water through my veins, "is *not* dating. You need to stop fornicating and settle down."

He groaned. I whimpered.

"You both need Jesus."

And Ethan, that asshole, sat there all smug because he was a lawyer who'd married a doctor, and was basically every mother's dream child.

"I hate you," I told him after dinner.

"Me too," Wade assured him.

"Mom," he called over to her, "Wade and Avery are going to a strip club after this."

Only a call for a homicide saved us.

Where I was concerned, she wanted me to find a nice man and settle down. Since I hadn't told her son about me being an omega, I certainly couldn't tell her, so I simply did a lot of smiling and nodding whenever the subject came up.

Where her son was concerned...she wasn't wrong. He was running through women, looking for something, a connection that was just not there. It always started well, hopeful, and then there would be what I called *the moment*. I'd see it in his eyes when he looked at them or talked about them, and I knew it was done. The last eight or so women, he hadn't even introduced to me, and if I wasn't meeting them, that was the kiss of death. I was the step right before meeting his mother. I'd met Meggie, but only by accident. I was coming out of a club, he was going in, and he'd grabbed my bicep and spun me around to face him.

"Where were you?" he snapped at me.

"Here," I told him, tilting my head at my date, who was waiting with a cab for me at the curb.

"We were supposed to get burgers."

"Yes, and you know how much I love to watch you wolf down a side of beef...no pun intended," I teased.

His snort let me know how funny he thought I was,

which was not at all. "Huh," he scoffed. "It's my fault how that you're a vegetarian werewolf?"

He was trying to banter with me when he should have been paying attention to his date. That was never a good sign. I grinned at the woman behind him, reminding him that she was there. "You said you had a date, so I made other plans."

He looked pained; it was clear he would have rather been eating greasy fast food at our favorite diner than be at a club. He introduced me to Margaret "Please, call me Meggie" Edmonds, a high-end real estate broker, and when I told them to have a good night, he kept his hand on my arm, clutching tight.

I covered quickly. "We're about to have a late dinner; would you two like to join us?"

"Oh, I would love that," Meggie almost squealed. "I haven't met a single one of Wade's friends, and I was beginning to worry he didn't have any."

I fake laughed, then led them over to meet Ross Ingersoll, a corporate relations manager who had bought me coffee two days prior on my way in to work. As pickups went, it had been a smooth one. I gave him my number, and he called—many times. I finally relented, since Wade had a date, and agreed to go out to a club and maybe get food after that. He, like Margaret—sorry, *Meggie*—was thrilled to meet a friend of mine. Somehow people thought meeting other people in your life solidified things. I also felt it made them think, *If they have friends, clearly that means they can maintain relationships*. If they only knew.

By Monday afternoon, I'd missed eight calls from Ross. Wade missed five from Meggie. The difference was, he didn't call her back, but I called and explained to Ross that it wasn't him, it was me. And even though he was mad and called me a few unflattering names, at least it was a clean break. As far as Meggie knew, she and Wade were still together. And now him asking her to drive him to the train station sent the wrong signal.

When I arrived at the train station, it was deserted except for a Mercedes sedan. I pulled in next to it and was going to roll down my window when the passenger door of the sedan opened and Wade got out, looking nice in a sweater and dress pants, wingtips, a cashmere-and-wool trench coat, scarf, and gloves. A woman got out of the back seat, braced her hands on his chest, lifted to kiss his cheek, and then took his place in the front. Wade jogged around my Jeep and got in as the front and rear passenger windows of the Mercedes both rolled down at once, and I was faced with the woman who'd just kissed Wade and a blond man who was sitting behind her.

I rolled down my window, and Meggie leaned across the woman to wave at me.

"Hi, Avery, how are you?"

"Good," I assured her, fiddling with the controls to put the heat on high. "And you?"

"Well, we were on our way to dinner when Wade got the call to come up here."

"I'm sorry your night was ruined," I told her.

"I'm just bummed that you had a thing tonight, because we wanted you to come with us so you could meet my friend Steven."

"Yeah, it happens. When mothers call, you gotta show up."

"That's so sweet," the man in the back seat chimed in, smiling wide at me. "I'm the same way with mine."

He was handsome, but at the moment only one man held a drop of interest for me. Unless power was rolling off of them in waves of dominance and strength, they were not even the smallest temptation. I wanted…

The rush of arousal that surged through me was unexpected, and I jolted without meaning to, catching my breath.

"Ohmygod, are you all right?" he, Meggie, and the woman who'd kissed Wade goodbye all asked at the same time.

"What the hell?" Wade muttered beside me, hand on my shoulder, as if to steady me.

"Sorry," I husked, momentarily overwhelmed, my body having never reacted that way before, shivering with the cold as I tried to calm my racing heart. "I didn't eat," was all I could think of to say.

"His blood sugar just dipped," Wade leaned forward to explain to the others. "I'll have to feed him, but we gotta go now. Thank you for driving me, Meggie. And Skye and Steven, thanks for keeping her company. You guys have a good dinner."

I took several deep breaths.

"We'll miss you," Meggie said, blowing him kisses.

Skye did as well, her gaze on him speaking volumes.

"I'd love to double date," Steven called over to me. "Or just date."

"Sounds great," I barely got out, gripping the wheel tight.

"Drive away," Wade muttered under his breath. "Now. Drive away…now."

But doing that was a bad idea until I didn't feel like the world was spinning.

"I'll be waiting," Steven apprised me. "Just gimme a call. Anytime."

"For God's sake, drive away," Wade growled, poking me in the ribs.

His touch startled me, the uncomfortable jab stilling my fugue state, making everything slip back into focus.

"I'll be looking forward to hearing from you," Steven concluded, hitting me with a similar look to the one Wade had gotten from Skye.

I waved, rolled up the window, and pulled away from them, exiting the parking lot by the same route I'd entered.

"What the hell was that?" he barked at me.

"I—sorry."

"Look at me."

I turned slowly.

"Shit, pull over."

I complied immediately, stopping on the street beside a mailbox.

"We need to change places; you shouldn't be driving."

"No, I—"

"Now."

Following directions, I got out of the car. We passed each other in front, and then he was behind the wheel and I was in the passenger seat, both of us pulling on our seatbelts.

"I thought wolves couldn't get stoned," he griped at me, pulling away from the curb.

"We can't," I answered, realizing that I needed more water. "I must—I'm dehydrated, I think. We need to stop and get me some water."

"You have water in the back."

"I drank it all."

"Okay, I'll stop, but what's with your eyes?"

Pulling down the visor, I flipped open the mirror, and when the light came on, I was faced with blown pupils that made my irises appear jet black. I looked lobotomized.

"Did you take something?"

"No...I—no."

"Then what the hell?"

I had known what Graeme Davenport had wanted to hear. When we were in the laundry room and he said I knew who he was, I knew what to say to get what I wanted. He wanted to be called alpha, the wolf equivalent of "Daddy" for many members of the *jarl*, and for me to go all weak and willing on him. I knew how to play it, how to get an alpha believing they had all the power and that I was just a docile little lamb of an omega. They got off on that, and it was the quickest way to get laid. Because yes, I'd slept with many. It was a secret, a huge one, no one could ever know, but it had never meant anything. I had wanted Graeme just as badly as I had the others, so I said and did what I knew he would respond to. It was my regular act. Only after did I show them that they'd fucked a tiger, not a kitten, because I was even more unaffected than they were. As their dicks were in the process of shriveling up, that was when I made my exit.

But was that what happened? Because now that I was thinking about it, Graeme had been looking at me oddly, like he was confused, like I was not what he expected. But he hadn't turned away from me, had maintained direct eye contact, and was just as strong and powerful standing there as he'd been initially. His look conveyed irritation, perhaps a bit of confusion, but that was it. What did it mean? And what was with me feeling unbalanced when my mind had drifted to him earlier? I had thought about being in bed with Steven, and the revulsion—

My chest tightened, and it felt as though my heart seized, like every muscle in my body clutched at once. The choked cry tore from my throat as Wade stomped on the brakes. I heard him yell my name, but it was like he was far away instead of right next to me.

I grabbed for the door handle as my body spasmed, and I lifted up off the seat, my back arching up tight in a rictus of pain.

Frozen there, I felt a blast of cold air when the door opened, and there were hands on me, between my shoulder blades, on my abdomen, trying to force me down into the seat, to make my body fold in half so I could sit once more. But his hands, Wade's, were not what I needed.

I had pleaded with Graeme to take me. Had called him not just alpha, but *my* alpha, and now, suddenly, I could hear the words vibrating down deep inside.

My alpha.

But that wasn't possible. I wasn't a beta or a gamma. I couldn't be his true mate. And if I wasn't, then this couldn't be what I thought it was. I couldn't be calling for him. Omegas didn't mate. Omegas *bonded*, that was all. All we were capable of.

I concentrated on my breathing, on the beating of my heart, and then latched on to Wade's smell, the scent I knew as well as my own, crisp and clean, always, even after a night in a smoky club when he drank too much; underneath that was him, fresh, like the sun on your skin, and soap, and man.

Counting, I felt the need peak inside, almost like an orgasm, like climax, and then the grip loosened, and I collapsed down into the seat. Sound came back at the same time.

"...hospital?" he rasped.

I turned to Wade. "What?"

"I think I need to take you to the hospital." His voice shook and rose, his fear a palpable thing. I reached for him, and he slapped my hand away. "The fuck was that?" he yelled at me.

What could I...? "I need water," I threw out lamely.

His eyes were huge. "That's you needing water? Fuck," he gasped, slamming my door, running around the front of the Jeep, and scrambling back into the driver's seat. "I'll get it, we're going, just, fuck...hold on, all right?"

He gunned the motor, flying down the street, nearly rolling the Jeep as he took a left, seeing a gas station and crossing four lanes to get us there. We came to a jerking stop, and he was out of the car fast, bolting inside to find me some water.

I felt like crap for scaring him, but needing fluids was the only thing I could think of. Whatever else this was, I definitely needed to speak to Graeme Davenport. Hopefully he wouldn't blow me off when I called him later...after I went to the station and ran his name. I didn't need him to leave his number with my mother—I was a detective, after all—but reminding an alpha I had more access to them than any other omega probably wasn't wise.

6

GRAEME

It was agreed.

Mr. and Mrs. Huntington would come to my home tomorrow, with their son and daughter and their mates, to meet my brother and his wife, and we would all dine together and set a date for the wedding. Our nuptials, of course, would be a spectacle, where people would come and formally acknowledge my mating to Avery. An over-the-top extravagant event was expected from any member of the *jarl*. As my family was, in essence, the pinnacle of the social hierarchy, the affair would be obscenely lavish. To say I was dreading it would be the understatement of the year, but truly I could endure anything, because starting tomorrow, Avery was mine. He would live with me, dine with me, sleep in my bed, and most importantly, stand at my side.

I wanted that more than I ever thought possible. I had no idea I would care as much as I already did. And yes, I'd have to be crazy not to want to be back inside of him almost desperately, but even more, I wanted him wrapped around me in the night. To see him had become, in a little over an hour, as necessary as breathing. His presence was greater than a need or a want but, instead, an absolute that I would not, could not, live without. He was mine, and I would have him.

"Why aren't you happy?" Kat asked, seated beside me in the back of the Bentley Bentayga Mulliner we had driven over in. Isabella Straeger, Izzy, my other shield, personal bodyguard, and in her case, driver, was, as usual, navigating us expertly through traffic. "You have your mate."

"May I offer my congratulations?" Izzy asked from the driver's seat.

"Yes," I whispered, meeting her warm henna eyes for only a moment when she turned her head, glancing at me over her right shoulder.

Izzy, like Kat, was a beautiful woman, and men hit on her a lot, even after noting the rock and accompanying band on her left ring finger. It was her smooth russet complexion with the warm undertones and bewitching smile that drew admirers like flies to honey. The high bun she wore at work, her long box braids swept up, showed off the delicate line of her throat, and men, especially alphas, noted the lack of a mating mark. That didn't matter, though, because if they were too forward, Izzy would put them on their ass. She was, first and foremost, deadly. No one tried to touch her twice.

"Congratulations, Graeme," she imparted kindly, and then, because it was how she was made, added, "it's about time you chose."

"Really?" I snapped at her.

"She's not wrong," Kat threw in, making a face, nodding. "I can't wait to send word to your grandfather. Maybe he'll visit and it won't be a horror show."

"At least he won't bring unannounced visitors anymore," Izzy stated, shuddering for good measure. "When he brought those two betas with him the last time, and that omega with all the...what were those?"

"Yorkipoos," Kat informed her. "Five of them."

"And they peed whenever Graeme looked at them," Izzy groaned. "Remember that?"

"How could I forget? The rugs were being cleaned on a continual basis, and we had a revolving color scheme every day. It felt like we were living in the middle of a going-out-of-business sale."

Izzy snorted. "Well, at least we're done with all that now Graeme is bonded. Again, sir, I'm thrilled you finally settled on an omega who pleases you."

"No, no," Kat corrected her. "He's mated, not bonded."

Izzy caught her breath. "Graeme," she whispered, her voice failing her, "that's amazing. I wouldn't have teased you if—I'm over the moon for you."

I nodded.

"This is the best news. Now I really can't wait to meet this amazing man who—Graeme? Whyever are you making that face?"

"What face," I demanded, hearing the annoyance in my voice.

"The one you get when you have heartburn."

"I do not get heartburn," I growled at her.

"He left," Kat explained to Izzy.

"What do you mean? Who left?"

"Graeme's omega."

Several seconds ticked by.

"I'm sorry, what?"

"Could you two not discuss me as though I weren't sitting right--"

"Graeme seems to think," Kat continued on, ignoring me

completely, "from the conversation he overheard, that Avery had to go to work."

"Ah, well, that's under—"

"No. You're not getting it. Avery didn't get Graeme's permission first; he just left. And he's keeping his job even after the mating."

"I don't understand."

"He's an omega raised like an alpha."

"I'm *sorry*?"

"His mother raised him and his siblings the same."

"I don't understand," she repeated.

"You *do* understand. She raised her omega as one would an alpha."

"But that's not a thing," she told Kat. "It's not. It can't be. And how would that even work? My God, the freedoms allowed an alpha could be the death of an omega."

"Wherein lies Graeme's concern."

"You're telling me that Avery's family allows him to do as he pleases?"

"No, it's *way* better than that. He's a police detective, and he's going to remain a police detective even after the mating. It's in his contract."

Izzy sucked in a breath.

"Yeah."

"You're screwing with me," she accused Kat. "Why the hell are you screwing with me?"

"I'm not, I swear. Hand to God."

"Well then, that section or clause, or whatever the hell it is, needs to be stricken. Draft an addendum or whatever needs to—for fuck's sake! That's the stupidest thing I ever heard. An omega, even a mated and marked one, is still far too vulnerable to be out alone in the—"

"Let me tell you about his crazy-ass family," Kat stated, leaning forward in her seat.

I tuned out the conversation, because it wasn't helping in the least. Izzy had the same concerns that any lupine with a modicum of good sense would. Omegas needed to be protected, and even those who were mated and marked, as she'd said, were in constant danger. And Avery was neither of those things. He wasn't carrying my mark, and the mating ceremony, our wedding, had yet to be performed. My omega, my mate, was out cavorting in the world, free to be accosted by any alpha, beta, gamma, or human, for that matter, who he came across. It was like a ticking timebomb in my chest, and even his contract beside me on the seat did little to reassure me. I needed to see him and convince him to come and stay with me. There were ten free bedrooms; he could take his pick if he didn't want to...

Who was I kidding? If I got him in my house, I would make damn sure he'd be sleeping with me, because it was all I wanted. The reality was, waiting a whole day to see him would be the death of me. By tomorrow at this time I'd be a raving lunatic.

"Graeme!" Kat nearly screamed my name, and I understood I had been lost deeper in my own thoughts than I realized.

"I'm sorry, what?"

Her face was stricken, and when I glanced over at Izzy, I saw that her hand was pressed across her mouth. She'd pulled the car over, and we were idling beside the curb.

"What's wrong?" I demanded.

"It's Remy," Kat answered, her voice catching. "The police are at his home. There's been an attack."

"What kind of attack?"

"That's why he wasn't at the party tonight," she apprised me.

"Kat," I said hoarsely, fighting not to yell at her. "What kind of attack?"

"Oh, Graeme," she replied shakily, "the police are saying we need to go there now. Your cousin's been killed."

And as I sat there and absorbed the news, Izzy turned away from the mansion I shared with my brother and his wife on Dearborn Street in Lincoln Park and directed us instead toward Remy's home in Highland Park.

THE MANSION on Sheridan Road was newer and built right on the lake, with a private beach, a heated indoor pool, an enormous kitchen, a vast library, and a media room with leather seats. Those were the things Remy had listed when he explained to me why he wanted an advance on the monthly payments from his trust fund. He sought to purchase the property. I had made the arrangements promptly, because it was a good investment—for once—and I didn't want to get in the way of him finally growing up. In exchange, he was taking the job I'd been pushing him to take in marketing, where I felt his ideas and enthusiasm would be most beneficial to the company.

A month later, when I was informed by the director of marketing that my cousin had not shown up for work in three weeks, I'd visited his home for the first time. I found the mansion filled with people in various stages of undress, with drugs and alcohol for the humans and all manner of blood play for the wolves. It was the last time I'd been there, and we didn't speak. I'd seen him, poolside, sharing a man with another, turned and left. It was, as it turned out, the last time I saw him alive. Now, in hindsight, I wondered if I would have done anything differently, and if I was being honest with myself, the answer was no. I had thought, after I defended him in mortal combat, we might become close, my only uncle's only son and I, but it was not to be. So while I wanted to know how he died, and why, I found grief was not tied into those questions. Stone reacted much the same when I called to give him the news. He was shocked, but he had no feelings beyond that.

"If it's a crime perpetrated by a human—" He sighed. "—then that's one thing. The police can be allowed to do their job. But if it's a lupine attack, which you'll know when you see him, then that's another matter entirely, and you have to be included in every part of their investigation as the *holt* leader."

"Yes," I agreed woodenly.

"If someone is coming after our family, we need to know who and why. Shall I call Burman now, or do you prefer me to wait?"

"Wait. I may have answers here shortly, and I'd hate for you to call Shivani and have her come all this way for nothing."

His snort was unexpected.

"What?" I asked, my tone sharper than I meant it to be.

"Only you get to call her Shivani. She'd gut any of the rest of us who tried."

"I'm the only *cyne* in the *holt*, or have you forgotten?"

"No. It was always like that. Even when we were younger, at boarding school, only you. The rest of us had to use her last name. She has only one soft spot, and it's for you."

"I don't know. She's awfully fond of that husband of hers, and her twin sons."

"You know what I mean."

"Perhaps now is not the time to--"

"I think you should call her. If you don't, and it becomes a situation where you or I or Gigi are in danger, she's going to show up breathing fire and brimstone, and we'll all be sorry."

"I'm certain that between Kat and Izzy, we're in good hands." I glanced over at Kat, who mouthed the words *thank you* since I had him on speaker phone.

Kat leaned forward and clasped Izzy's shoulder in solidarity to get her to stop growling. Just the insinuation that the two women couldn't take care of me, my brother, and his wife had both of them irritated.

"Then call me the minute you know something," he told me.

"I will. And when I get home, I have other news."

"Oh?"

I sighed deeply. "I found my mate. He's an omega, and I signed his contract."

Long silence.

"The hell are you talking about?" he roared over the line. "You mated with someone I haven't even met, and I'm sorry, but did you say an *omega*?"

"Just do me a favor and tell Gigi. We'll talk as soon as I get home."

"I—no, you can't just drop a bomb like—I forbid you from hanging up and not explaining this all to me right this second!"

"Maybe if you hadn't insulted Kat and Izzy, I would have had one of *them* explain it to you while I go in and talk to the police, but we're here now, so I have to go," I muttered before I hung up. Before I could even get out of the car, the phone rang again.

I hesitated, kept myself from picking up, and instead, glanced at Kat.

"I'll talk to him," she affirmed curtly. "Because it's what *you* want."

"Tell him the part about Avery being a police officer first. That might stun him long enough for you to get the whole story out without being interrupted."

She nodded, and I got out, met immediately by a uniformed police officer who instructed me to turn the car around because I wasn't allowed into the crime scene.

"I was called here," I informed the man. "My assistant spoke to a detective Massey."

After that things moved quickly.

I was given booties for my shoes before entering the house, and told not to touch anything. As if I would. I wasn't allowed into the master bedroom, where Remy's body was, instead being directed to remain in the living room and await further instructions. Standing in front of the doors leading out onto the enormous back deck, I suddenly caught Avery's scent and pivoted to face him, stunned by the turn of events that would lead us to cross paths twice in one night.

"Mr. Davenport?"

But it wasn't Avery there. A strange man—tall and muscular, handsome, his eyes an unusual color—stepped into the room. The shield hanging from a chain around his neck proclaimed him a detective. I would have been interested in what information he had to impart if he wasn't absolutely steeped in the scent of my mate. I could barely think. Coherent thought came second to a craving that lived, dark and brutal, inside me. I wanted to eviscerate him.

It wasn't that Avery's smell clung to his clothes. This went deeper. This detective carried my mate's spoor on his skin and in his hair, as though they'd spent considerable time in close, intimate contact. When the detective exhaled,

Avery's scent flowed from in his lungs, and strands of his golden hair were caught on the man's dark trench coat. To witness these signs of intertwined lives, outside of familial connection, was yet another reason omegas were to remain cut off from others. The rage I felt, rage any alpha who'd found their true mate would feel, was immediate and incendiary. I was nearly drowned in the desire to tear the man limb from limb. It took everything in me not to act upon that.

"Sir, I'm Detective Massey," he began, oblivious to the danger I posed. "I regret to inform you there's been a terrible mistake. We apologize for causing you any undue emotional distress, and...we're just so sorry."

My hands were clenched into fists, and I was shaking.

"We fu—we messed up, badly."

"What?" He'd lost me. Mostly because I was trembling with my need to disembowel him. "Speak plainly," I reproached him.

He cleared his throat, and I felt the surge of anger he stamped down, allowing me to see only his professional façade. "Sir, your cousin is alive. We were worried about him hurting himself, or someone else, so we had him sedated. We're ready to transport him, but we wanted to wait until you arrived."

Wait. Remy was alive? "My cousin isn't dead?"

"No, sir. A man fitting his description was found here when officers responded to a 911 call, and they jumped to the conclusion that it was him."

"Well, I..." The news jolted me from my anger. I had to be the *holt* leader, the *cyne*, not some besotted alpha out of his mind with jealousy. "That seems a reasonable deduction to have made."

He brightened like a weight had been lifted. "Thank you for your understanding."

"But you said something about transporting him?"

"Yessir. He's going to Geary Hospital, downtown. We have only two facilities in the city rated for lupines, with locked wards. The closest one, in Parkridge, is full."

Any lupine could go to any hospital—there was no issue there—but locked wards, those made specifically to withstand the added power of an alpha or beta who was in police custody, those were few and far between. As a rule, lupines were dealt with by their alphas. If the crime was committed by an alpha, then that alpha was dealt with by their *cyne*. If they didn't belong to a *holt*, then the *dryhten* stepped in and either took justice into his own hands or tapped the nearest *cyne*. Even those lupines charged with murder, who were sanctioned to be put to death by the state, were executed by alphas. Lethal injection might or might not work on wolves, as they each had different tolerances, different shifting speeds, and just plain strength. But when your alpha tore out your jugular, that was certain death, without question.

"So now he's a suspect? Is that why you're holding him?"

"He attacked my partner, and——"

"Is your partner all right?" I rasped, heart in my throat.

He squinted at me, the look conveying his annoyance. "What? Yeah, of course. He's a wolf himself, so he put him down easy."

But Remy was an alpha and Avery was an omega, so the "easy" part was in question. "You're certain your partner sustained no injuries?"

"Yeah, I'm sure. Thanks for your concern, but we're trained for this, Mr. Davenport, and like I said, my partner's a wolf too."

I needed to see Avery to confirm Detective Massey's claim.

"As I was saying, we're not sure why your cousin came at my partner, and yes, Mr. Talmadge is a suspect. To be frank, at the moment he's our only suspect. It's his house, after all, and the dead man was killed by another wolf; that's obvious to our ME, as well as to those of us who have worked homicide for more than a minute."

"So you're saying this dead man, his throat was punctured?"

"I'm saying he was torn to pieces."

Which meant the crime scene was a thoroughly gruesome sight.

"We're going to question your cousin tomorrow, so you and your family can arrange to have a lawyer present at the hospital. As *cyne* of his *holt*, you are, of course, welcome, by law, as well."

I nodded.

"Also, we would like your permission to perform a search of the premises. As you know, even at a murder scene, we're required to have a warrant, as even a murderer —though we're not saying Mr. Talmadge is one—is still entitled to a reasonable expectation of privacy."

"I understand, Detective. A homicide occurring on the premises doesn't magically make it constitutionally permissible for you to search the house."

"Exactly."

"I, on the other hand, as Remy's *cyne*, may grant you permission per lupine law that supersedes human law in this area."

"Yes," he agreed. "So will you?"

"I will."

He drew his phone from the breast pocket of his coat to

pull up a document for me to sign, which was immediately dated and time stamped.

"Do you know the identity of the dead man?" I asked him.

"We do, but I'm not at liberty to divulge that information at this time. We need to contact his family first, and we're having a bit of trouble finding them."

"As you've noted, Detective, I'm not only an alpha but a *cyne*, so I have contacts who won't be in your database." I pulled a small gold case from the breast pocket of my tailcoat, flipping it open and extracting a business card I handed to him. "If you need any assistance, please don't hesitate to call on me."

He took the card, and his eyes flicked to mine. "Thank you, that's very generous."

"Now," I began, clearing my throat, "if I may be permitted, I'd like to see my cousin before you move him. And, more importantly, have a quick word with your partner."

"Seeing my partner is more important than seeing your cousin?"

"It is, yes," I answered, trying to keep the leeching coldness out of my tone, but not altogether successfully. "So, if you would point me in his direction."

He scowled, unsure of me, but he asked me to follow him. We walked down a long hallway, where a cluster of men stood at the doors of Remy's bedroom, and I heard the charge and discharge of a camera flash, over and over. As we passed the open doorway, I didn't turn and look. The metallic scent of blood was nearly overwhelming.

Remy was being held in the second to the last bedroom, the door guarded by two uniformed police officers. He was disheveled, possibly feverish, passed out on a bed that looked as if it could comfortably accommodate five adults.

And there was my mate, sitting beside the bed in a Chesterfield wingback chair.

He stood up as soon as I walked into the room, and moved behind the chair so it was between us as I came around the end of the bed. His beautiful silver gaze held mine for mere moments before he turned to look at Detective Massey.

"I need to go talk to the forensic guys, Avery, so I'll leave you to explain things to Mr. Davenport. He was concerned that maybe you got hurt when his cousin jumped you. I'll be right back."

Avery nodded, and then his partner was gone, slipping back out the door and closing it behind him.

I moved fast, beside the chair, the only thing separating us. "What happened?"

"When—wait, what's wrong with your eyes?" he asked, and the genuine concern I heard in his voice touched me deeply. "They're all red and watery."

"It's nothing," I assured him, knowing, of course, that there must have been a number of omegas in and out of Remy's home quite recently. There were so many scents, piled one on top of the other, suffocating, cloying, it was causing something like an allergic reaction in me. It happened sometimes at gatherings, but if I moved around enough, didn't get stuck in one spot for too long, I wouldn't smother under the weight of roses and peonies, strawberries and vanilla, and what I could discern now was the rich scent of caramel. "The residual omega pheromones are a bit overwhelming."

"From the party, you mean?"

"No, the scent is—"

"So it's me?" He jumped to the conclusion, moving as though to take a step back.

"No, not yours." I rushed out the words, needing to make myself clear. "Your scent cuts through the others, allows me to breathe. Like tonight, when I met your friends, those who carried traces of your scent on them...I didn't want to breathe in theirs for fear I would lose yours."

"Is that right?"

"Yes," I murmured, staring into his beautiful eyes. "I suspect they didn't mention that I asked about you."

"No," he replied, giving me a slight grin. "But I'm not surprised. They were both so pissed off, that was all they could focus on."

It was typical omega behavior, and the polar opposite of everything I already knew Avery to be.

"Tell me what happened here," I ordered, wanting to get this part over with so I could speak to my mate.

He took a breath. "When we arrived on the scene, I asked who made the call to 911. Since no one had an answer for me, I figured it had to be an alarm."

"I don't understand what this—"

He lifted his hand to stop me. "With me"—the grin made his eyes glint—"you always get the whole story."

"Police officer," I murmured, smiling in return. "Please, continue."

"According to the incident report, a security alarm was triggered, and the monitoring company followed up and alerted the police. Someone had locked themselves in a panic room."

"And that someone was Remy? He locked himself in, and that's why the police showed up."

He nodded. "The uniforms were first on the scene, and missed the panic room on this floor when they initially swept the house. Knowing there had to be one up here, I was walking around looking for it, and when I passed it by, he must have caught my scent and couldn't help himself; he came charging out at me...I think, because I smell like you."

I nodded, putting my hand on the back of the chair, taking a step closer. "And so he came at you?"

"He came *to* me, not *at* me. In spite of whatever he witnessed tonight, or did, I was able to subdue him fairly easily because he recognized your scent."

"But he's an alpha." I looked my mate over, seeing marks that would become bruises and scratches that had not been there a few short hours prior. The scrape on the side of his neck, in the exact place where my mark would go, was especially startling. "He could have killed you."

He scoffed. "Not today, and I've tangled with many alphas and come out just fine."

I scowled at him. "You've fought other alphas?"

"Among other things," he confessed, holding my gaze, making the connotation crystal clear just in case I missed it. "You should know that in case it changes anything you might be thinking about me."

The only thing it changed was that I felt even luckier to have found him. Other alphas had not only seen him but had him in bed, and then made the deliberate decision to let him go. I was dumbfounded. They had missed his value completely. I wondered at their blindness, and was grateful even as I was bone-deep jealous.

"Graeme?" He croaked out my name. "Does it...change anything?"

"No," I declared, letting him hear the truth in my voice. "I'm sorry, I'm merely surprised. Normally, an omega would inform their family immediately to secure a bonding. In your case, you could have forced any of the alphas you slept with to offer for you, given the liberties they took."

"Nobody *took* anything," he assured me. "I gave what I

wanted to, nothing more, and I had no interest in seeing any of them again."

I was quiet, didn't push. I wanted him to say more. Hoped he would say more.

"I would—" He took a gulp of air. "—like to see you, though, if that's okay."

"It would be my privilege," I promised him, driven to distraction by his abraded skin. "Where did you––how was your neck scraped?"

His gaze met mine and held. "In the scuffle with your cousin."

Remy…had tried to mark my mate.

A cold jolt of fear slammed into me, and anger coursed alongside it through my veins. I closed my eyes and breathed amid the tremor of raw hatred that thundered close behind.

"It's not what you think," he murmured, and I heard him, but his voice was muted, as though he spoke to me from across the room. "When he saw I wasn't you, he went for my throat. He was scared, so yeah…he was trying to kill me, not mark me."

I should have been more horrified over Remy attacking my mate, but I was embarrassed to admit to myself the greater fear was that another had tried to mark him.

"He came at me, but his attack was clumsy. One of his claws caught me, not a fang. His mouth was nowhere near my throat."

Simple words, illuminating words, and they cleared my head and meant my cousin would live. It was my right to take his life for any trespass I saw fit to punish. Certainly, I would have gutted him for trying to put his mark on my mate, whether he knew who Avery was to me or not. One did not mark omegas without their permission, and since Remy was raised better, I had to wonder what happened.

"Was he drugged?" I asked Avery.

"I don't think so, but they'll do a tox screen at the hospital."

"Your best guess?"

"My guess would be no. I got a good look at him when I put him on the ground. His pupils weren't blown, and he seemed lucid. I mean"--he gestured at Remy on the bed--"he hasn't moved since we put him there. We can both hear that he's breathing, and his heart is pumping. This reads like shock to me."

I nodded. "So the chances are good that whatever he saw in his bedroom scared him to death, and your scent--or mine, as it were--jolted him, but only momentarily."

"Yeah, that's what I think."

"And who is dead in the other room?"

His brows furrowed.

"This shouldn't have to be said, you should know it, feel it, but you can trust me."

He took a breath. "It's just not—this is a police matter."

"But perhaps I know the man and can be of assistance."

His gaze held mine, weighing his decision. "We know who he is; we ran his prints. His name is Trent Highmore," he revealed. "Do you know him?"

"I know *of* him," I answered, scowling. "We belonged to the same country club, but his membership was revoked after the charges."

He nodded. "Yeah, I bet. Suspicion of felony criminal sexual assault and criminal sexual abuse by force will get you bounced out of lots of nice places."

"And they were human women."

"What I got from the case notes was that he preyed on

them because he was banned from any interaction with omegas, even as an alpha, for his treatment of several of them at the gatherings."

"That was my understanding, yes."

As a *cyne* I was given access to information that others were not, and that included sensitive information about crimes that had been committed. I couldn't recall them all, but certainly Trent Highmore's offenses had made an impression.

"If the omegas who accused him are mated now, their bond mates should certainly be questioned," I prodded Avery.

"I'll have to track them all down, but another alpha would have challenged him to a duel, wouldn't they?"

"It depends on how highly the alpha values their omega," I replied honestly. "Certainly, I would challenge and defend you, but you're more than my bonded omega."

He said nothing, just continued to stare at me.

I took a step closer. "You're certain my cousin didn't hurt you?"

"Yeah," he answered, and my breath caught when he took a step toward me, around the chair, still holding my gaze. "Like I said, I'm stronger than you think, and even though there's something wrong with me, I held my own."

"Wrong with you?" I questioned, noting again the scrape on the side of his throat where my mark should have been. It was gnawing at me, looking at it, seeing the abraded skin, but instead of grabbing him and holding him down and claiming him right then and there, overpowering him as I knew I could, I turned from my raw animal instinct to my thoughtful humanity and reached a hand toward him.

Taking the last step into my personal space, he pressed

his cheek into my palm, and when my thumb slid across his skin, his eyes fluttered closed.

"I can't...focus," he murmured, pushing forward, bumping his head on my chest, hands hanging limp at his sides. "And I lost it in the car on the way over here."

"What do you want me to say?" I put both hands on the sides of his neck, holding him gently, savoring the feel of his skin, the brush of his hair, and his intoxicating scent, smoke and newly turned soil. "Shall I tell you I'm sorry, when I'm not?"

He gave a clipped whine, breathing slowly, working, I knew, to remain calm.

"Every alpha dreams of finding their mate, their true mate, and I'm certainly no exception," I confessed, stroking both his cheeks, even that small amount of contact comforting me. Touching him, feeling the rightness of the action, was grounding and illuminating. Because yes, I wanted him, there was no question, but I knew, even in this short time, seeing and hearing and touching him, that he wanted me too. Amazing how much tension and anxiety drained from me in a flood of relief, like a great knot had been untied deep in my heart. I wasn't alone; he felt the pull every bit as keenly as I did. "You're a gift," I whispered. "I wouldn't have it any other way."

"But I have things to do here, and...I was thinking about you in the car, and I don't—what's going on? Do you know?"

"You're not listening," I crooned, feeling a terribly uncharacteristic flutter in my gut over the news that he'd been thinking about me. I would be laid low, reduced to a quivering simpleton who lived and died by how much or little their mate esteemed them, and somehow, I couldn't be made to care. "Try to pay attention."

His head lifted and his eyes snapped open, and I was hit

with his silvery gaze, the indignation clear as day. "What'd you just say to--"

It was impossible not to smile. "You're my mate," I reminded him, and noted that even as affronted as his expression suggested he was, he didn't move an inch away from me. He would argue, yes, but not break contact. "Or had you forgotten?"

"Yeah, but"--he shook his head as though whatever he was thinking couldn't have possibly been real or right or true--"I'm an omega, and we don't mate like everybody else."

"You're wrong," I assured him, sliding my thumb across his cheek again before slipping it under his chin and lifting until those glorious eyes were gazing up at me in absolute wonder. "Some omegas, just like some betas and gammas, find the alpha that's meant to belong only to them."

He shook his head. "Alphas don't mate with omegas; it can only be a--"

"Listen to me," I urged, releasing my pheromones, soothing him, giving him comfort so he could shore up the cracks in the wall between the two parts of himself, man and wolf. I never wanted to weaken him or cause him to doubt himself. That wasn't my place. Ever. I was there to lean on, to offer my strength when he came undone and lacked his own. "You're my mate, and I know that beyond all reason. I know it down deep, in muscle and bone where my wolf lives."

His eyes filled then, and his jaw was clenched, his hands fisted, and he trembled violently.

"Please," I murmured, bending close, speaking into his ear, "trust me, Avery Rhine. I belong to you. I'm yours. You called me your alpha, but what you didn't realize at the time is that I truly am."

He began panting softly as he stared up at me, and I watched his gaze transform from pain and uncertainty, widening and then slowly narrowing down to silvery slits of moonlight. It was ravenous, that look, and I wanted, more than anything, for him to feast on me, and only me, for the rest of my life.

When he parted his lips, gazing at me like he was drunk, the longing there for anyone to see, I couldn't resist. I bent and took his mouth, and was immediately rewarded with his whimpering moan of pleasure as he tangled his tongue with mine, staking his claim, kissing me boldly, hungrily, with blatant possessiveness. He held nothing back, allowing me to feel his desire for all I had to offer, secrets he admitted to no one, even himself, that he craved a mate and a home. And I knew, because I could taste the need in him, and the fear at the same time. He'd been led to believe that having a mate equaled limits, and while it did, and the desire to cage him and keep him safe was overwhelming, I would never take his freedom from him, because it would change who he was now––the strong, virile man that drew me like a moth to a flame.

My hands were all over him, and the mauling kisses grew harder and deeper, verging on savage. When I tasted blood on my tongue, I broke the kiss, panting hard. "That's enough," I husked, seconds away from putting my mark on him, wrenching him away from me and holding him out at arm's length.

His lips were swollen, as they'd been earlier in the night, his eyes glassy and heavy-lidded, and his hair was tousled, falling into them. "I thought you were mine," he whispered.

"Make no mistake, I am, but I refuse to have you any place but my bed when I give you my mark."

He stepped back, out of my hands, and walked to the

glass doors that led out onto a small balcony, turning his back on me. I watched him stand there, shivering, and wanted to comfort him even though I knew better. This time, he had to find the strength within himself rather than drawing it from me.

In that moment, I understood that his mother was right. He was not the kind of omega who lost all sense of self and would, while in heat, rut with anyone who came along. He would not lie down in the middle of the floor, naked, head down, ass raised, presenting himself as a vessel for anyone to fill, as I'd seen others do, both men and women, at private invitation-only affairs I'd attended. My mate, *my omega*, was having difficulty focusing his thoughts, and his control was shaky because he was unmarked. That was all. That was the extent of the "heat" that I'd seen others completely abandon themselves to. He wanted me, and only me, desperately, but could and would wait for the claiming, because his needs took a back seat at the moment to a murder investigation.

I was in awe of his control.

When he turned, his rough, erratic breathing was level, his eyes were clear, he was steady on his feet, and there was even a ghost of a smile for me.

My heart swelled with pride just looking at him.

"Tell me, do you know how your cousin and Mr. Highmore knew each other?"

I shook my head. "I don't, no."

"Had Remy made any offers for omegas?" he asked, pulling a notebook from the back pocket of his jeans.

"Not that I know of, and he would have had to notify me."

"Okay—" He took a breath. "—so you're going to go with him to the hospital. I'm going to be here for a bit longer, and then—"

"After I get him settled at the hospital, would you meet me at my home?"

He shook his head. "It's not a good idea. While we're in the middle of this investigation, we should probably keep our distance."

"You don't understand; that's not possible."

"Graeme, I––"

"Your signed contract is in my car."

His brows furrowed as he stared at me. "I'm sorry?"

"Your contract has been signed, and it's in my car."

"But why...why would you do that?"

"What do you mean *why*?"

"I *mean*, why would you without talking to me?"

"Avery––"

"And why in the world would my––" His eyes widened as he caught his breath. "What did you say to my father? Did you tell him we––"

"They didn't want to listen, and your brother––"

"Did you hurt my brother?" he yelled, fear and anger mixing in his voice.

"No, I didn't hurt your brother," I rasped, furious that what I wanted and needed was veering further and further off course with every passing second. "I might have grabbed him, but I didn't hurt––"

"You signed my *contract*?" he shouted at me, unable, it seemed, to come to terms with that part. I couldn't decide whether he was horrified or indignant or gobsmacked. He wasn't making himself clear, and the yell was open to interpretation. "How could you do that without discussing it with me first?"

"You left me!" I roared back. "How dare you leave me!"

"And that gives you the right to take my choices away and question my freedom and––"

"I didn't take any of your *precious* freedoms away," I retorted vehemently, the anger searing through my voice. "I signed that contract as-is, without a single modification."

He jerked back in surprise, staring at me with wide eyes, utterly stunned.

"Didn't expect that, did you?" I reproached him, nearly snarling.

The smile I got almost put me on my knees. I thought the argument, the back-and-forth, would escalate, grow until we were at each other's throats, putting a chasm between us that, at least for the moment, would place him beyond my reach, but he surprised the hell out of me. Instead of reacting to me like everyone else in my life, he listened. He stopped, weighed everything, put himself—I could only imagine—in my shoes, and then...smiled. And what a smile it was. I could see the gratitude in his hooded quicksilver gaze.

"No, my alpha," he replied hoarsely, "I didn't expect you not to try and change me. But I should have known better. You're *my* mate after all, so of course you knew, didn't you?"

I had needed to leave with the document. I didn't want to take the contract to study, to prepare arguments, and to come to terms. I couldn't have left his parents' home without having that signed agreement in my possession. It was frankly impossible.

"Thank you," he husked, his gaze brimming with gratitude.

I was going to command him to come to me, but he rushed across the room and wrapped his arms around me, his sigh of contentment so sweet that my mind went blank. I might have recovered enough to speak to him, to say something, anything, but Detective Massey opened the door, and Avery stepped back as his partner led the EMTs into the room. There was no time to say anything more, as I was left answering questions while my mate cast me a longing look before he was gone. I didn't see him again before I climbed into the back of the ambulance.

It was strange, leaving him, as I'd been frantic to find him, terrified over the heat that I was certain he was dealing with. Now, after spending even a short time with him, I realized my fears had been alleviated, having seen his innate strength for myself. I wanted him home with me, yes, but I wasn't afraid of him losing control or having another incident like the one he told me about. He knew he belonged to me and, more importantly, knew now that he was my true mate, and I was his. I was shored up mentally, emotionally, and him physically, with a single quick meeting. I could only imagine how much good we could do one another when we lived together.

7

AVERY

With all the squad cars and the lights and the ambulance, everyone was awake and out on the street even though it was late. Wade and I took the opportunity to question Remy's neighbors on both sides, as well as the Gregsons, who lived across the street from him.

Jodi Gregson and her wife were worried about Remy and were going to call the police earlier in the night, because they'd seen a man who was so much bigger than him at the house.

"Hold on, go back," I instructed, because they'd lost me. From Wade's expression, he was just as confused, and it didn't help that they were talking over one another.

"There was a man, and he was really scary," Jodi explained.

"Like, really, really scary," Tiffany backed up her wife. "That guy had muscles on top of muscles, and he picked Remy right up off the ground. And Remy's an alpha, so I got super freaked out; we both did."

"But the guy left," Jodi chimed in, "and Remy waved at

us and yelled over that it was just a misunderstanding before he went back inside."

Wade nodded. "So you got the feeling that Remy knew him?"

"I did," Jodi granted, nodding.

"But you can't describe him to us?"

She winced. "He was wearing a hoodie, so I can tell you the size of his arms and his back, but that's about it."

"I took a shot of his car," Tiffany told me, showing us the blurry picture, "but it was parked at a bad angle, and then he tore out of here."

"No idea of the plate number, even a partial?" Wade queried hopefully.

She shook her head. "No, I'm so sorry. That's why I take pictures of everything; my memory is total crap."

"Don't worry about it," I soothed her. "Remy has several exterior security cameras, so hopefully one of them caught something."

"I wouldn't bet on it," she apprised me. "As far as I know, they're all for show—at least that's what he told me—except the one at the front door."

At least maybe we'd see someone on that.

Wade and I questioned the Morenos, the neighbors on the right, next, and while they had a lot to say about Remy's parties—the dozens and dozens of people who came and went at all hours, and that it was not right he should have orgies in his house—they couldn't help with much more. They'd been downstairs in their theater room, and Mr. Moreno liked watching his movies loud.

"He's not having orgies." Mrs. Hurley, Remy's neighbor to the left, contradicted the Morenos. "That's not it."

"What is it?" I asked her.

Both of them, Mr. and Mrs. Hurley, looked at me, then at Wade, and back to me.

I turned to my partner. "Could you give us a moment?"

He shot me a scowl but walked away, and I turned back to them.

"Omegas," Mrs. Hurley announced, stepping in close to slip her hand around my wrist as she laid out the story for me. It was a lupine's instinct to touch, we needed to make physical contact, and I knew at first scent, of course, they were wolves, an alpha and a beta. "I know them when I see them," she assured me. "And smell them."

Except, it appeared, where I was concerned. I guessed she believed I was a beta like herself. In my experience, when you expected something, it was what you saw. "You're a hundred percent sure?"

"Absolutely," she said, glancing at her husband.

"I stopped one of them," he admitted, shaking his head. "Tiny little thing I thought had to be barely legal, but he showed me his ID, and he was twenty. I told him it wasn't right that he was there, in Mr. Talmadge's home, unescorted, and I threatened to inform Remy's *cyne*, but he begged me not to. He said that Mr. Talmadge was a blessing because, for a minimal fee, he was helping to put omegas into *les fausses chaleurs* before the gatherings to make them more likely to draw a mate."

In short, Remy Talmadge was paid to arouse them.

It was a horrible practice. I'd heard of it being done, *les fausses chaleurs*, or fake heat, mock heat, but I'd never met an omega who felt they had to use it. I was friends with omegas like Linden and Bridget, who were genetically blessed, and others from rich, powerful families who could afford the latest couture, who had every advantage by way of stylists and entire teams of hair and makeup artists. But for those less fortunate, those families who had three or four omegas and couldn't possibly afford to provide for them long-term, it wasn't enough to *hope* to find a suitable alpha to buy their contracts. They had to do everything possible, exhaust every advantage, to snag one. Being put into a fake heat would greatly improve their chances of making a match.

Omegas would allow a willing alpha to arouse them so they were no longer in control of their own pheromones, drowning potential suitors in the lush scent of sex. From what I understood, it didn't last long, three hours tops, but that could be just enough time to get the job done. An unsuspecting, younger, more vulnerable alpha would offer for their contract before they were even aware they'd been duped. It wouldn't work on stronger, older alphas, but those weren't who the omegas were after. Most alphas, like my brother, wanted to find their mate when they were young. They were expected to settle down, have children quickly so they could turn their attention to running businesses and heading their families. Alphas who went into their thirties unmated were normally *cynes* from families of exorbitant, old money wealth, and could breed at their leisure. Those alphas were rare, powerful, and did not succumb to doe-eyed ingenues reeking of pheromones. Men like my alpha, like Graeme, they were drawn in by something deeper, truer. He would never look at—he...

"Detective?" Mrs. Hurley sounded concerned.

I met her worried gaze. Shit. "Sorry, I—"

"Are you quite well, dear? You look a bit flushed."

"No, no, I'm fine." I cleared my throat, looking from her to her husband. "Please continue, Mr. Hurley."

The older man coughed softly. "Well, after speaking to him, I didn't think it was fair of me to limit the chances of all the omegas who were coming to Mr. Talmadge for help, so...

I turned a blind eye," he confessed sheepishly. "I knew it was wrong, but Detective, if you'd seen all those poor boys and girls, you might have too."

"Our son Kevin's an alpha," Mrs. Hurley chimed in, "and he's been a bit down on his luck lately, between jobs, and I mentioned to him that perhaps he might think about helping the omegas as well."

Being a detective, I heard the strangest confessions.

"But you see, our Kevin would probably end up impregnating the girls, because he'd be tempted into rutting."

And people overshared. A lot.

"But you see, now, Remy is gay," Mr. Hurley explained, wanting to contribute, talking over his wife. "So the female omegas don't have to worry about him going too far, because he's not attracted to them, and the males, he couldn't get them pregnant even if things accidentally got out of hand."

There were so many things wrong with Mr. Hurley's statement. For starters, anything getting *out of hand* with an omega in fake heat was rape. Secondly, I suspected that Remy Talmadge was bi. If he had no interest in having sex with female omegas, his pheromones would have never aroused them enough to trigger any kind of response. It all started the same way, with that urgent, excited roll of awakening that flared quickly into desire. Talmadge was jump-starting that cycle and then sending them out the door. The *Maion* council frowned on the practice of placing omegas in mock heat, as did everyone I'd ever spoken to about it, but I was fairly certain it was punished at the discretion of the individual *holt* leaders, which was why, as Mr. Hurley had said, he looked the other way. As far as human law was concerned, the omegas were all consenting adults, were all there in Mr. Talmadge's home of their own free will; they weren't forced or drugged, and they were free to leave at their leisure. I had nothing to charge the man with.

"Tell me, did you ever see any other alphas here with Mr. Talmadge?"

"That cousin of his, who was here after you all showed up tonight, the *cyne*, he came once, right after Remy first moved in. There was another one a week ago, huge, all muscle, and I think he and Remy had words, and they might have even fought, but I'm not sure."

Muscular guy, like the Gregsons saw tonight. I needed to find him.

"Remy's a nice man. Good neighbor. I hope he won't get in any trouble."

Had they missed the body rolled out on the gurney?

"And we both know he didn't hurt anybody."

"Did you, perhaps, see the man's face? The one with the muscles?"

"No, he was wearing a hoodie," Mrs. Hurley explained. "He had it pulled way down."

I nodded, gave them my card, and told them to call me if they thought of anything else. Once I was nearly to Wade, I noted his crossed arms and scowl as he perched on the hood of one of the police cars.

"Why didn't they want to talk to me?" he barked when I got close. "Too Black?"

I shook my head. "Too human."

"Oh." He grunted, uncrossed his arms and stood up. "I don't know why that's better; it's still something I can do nothing about."

I grimaced, knowing he was right.

"Anyway, what'd they say?"

"I'll tell you on our way back into the house."

"Why?"

"I'm wondering, did the CSIs check the panic room for cameras? The neighbors said nothing worked outside, but I don't know. It's an expensive home; I'm thinking maybe he let them believe that because he didn't want anyone freaked out that he had eyes on the whole block."

We put new booties on before we went back inside and up to the panic room, talking through this as we moved down the hallway.

"The Hurleys told me Remy Talmadge was putting omegas into *les fausses chaleurs*, so I'm thinking that to protect himself, he had to have had those cameras hooked up throughout the house. Plus," I added, grimacing, "I'm wondering if he had footage of what he was doing with the omegas."

"I have no idea what you just said. Lay-what?"

"*Les*—mock heat," I corrected myself. "Sorry."

"I'm afraid to even ask, but what does putting them into mock heat entail?" Wade's face scrunched up, bracing himself for the answer.

"You really want to know?"

"Hell no, but I think I have to."

"The alpha gets them all hot and bothered, aroused and ready, and then shoves 'em out the door. It's all the edging, none of the screwing," I explained bluntly.

"And why would omegas want to be in that state?"

"Because then they're oozing pheromones."

"Which I'm guessing gets an alpha all horny."

"Bingo."

"And then?"

"And then the omega says, 'You want me, sign my contract.'"

"But what if an alpha just bangs the omega in their car?"

"An alpha can't *bang* an omega without a contract."

Which was, for all intents and purposes, correct. Only an omega who didn't need to find a mate, who was completely self-sufficient, could afford to screw an alpha without a signed contract. As far as I knew, into that group fell only one, and that was me. Because others, like Linden and Bridget, could afford to be picky. They came from rich families, so they could wait on the best match possible, but I was the only one who had a job and a way to take care of myself if my family ever tossed me out on the street. And that would never happen, they loved me too much, but it would not have been the end of me if it did. No other omega I'd ever met could make that same claim.

"Can't?" Wade questioned my word choice, drawing me from my thoughts.

"Fine. They can, it's just against lupine law, and the alpha is screwed if anyone finds out."

"So all omegas are virgins until they get married?"

"Hardly. Lots of them have sex with humans and betas and gammas. They just don't fuck alphas."

"Why?"

"Because of the contracts. A beta or gamma can bang an omega and leave once they're done, and it doesn't matter who knows. But an alpha has to put a ring on it."

He nodded. "You know, it occurs to me that even though alphas are supposedly at the top of the food chain, they get the short end of the stick in a lot of scenarios."

"Yeah, but they can have sex with betas and gammas, even other alphas. No one's telling them they *have* to fuck an omega."

"That's true, I guess; though aren't omegas supposed to be really hot?"

When we first became partners, Wade made the assumption that I was a beta, and I never set him straight. At this point, it was unnecessary to reveal my true nature to him; for all I knew, he'd be hurt that I hadn't told him the truth. It was, I was certain, best to let sleeping dogs lie.

"I think, much like many things in life, the reality has been greatly exaggerated."

"As in, not all female omegas are Victoria's Secret models, and the guys aren't all right out of the pages of *Esquire*."

"Exactly."

"Okay."

"Regardless of what you've heard about omegas," I added, "they are far worse off than alphas. They don't always get to choose where they go."

"Yeah, I agree. Being stuck in some fucked-up Regency nightmare sounds like a horrible way to live."

He didn't know the half of it.

WE HIT the motherload in the panic room, in a cabinet built flush into the wall.

"Why wouldn't Talmadge just use a flash drive or two instead of all these DVDs?" Wade asked me, holding one up between his gloved fingers.

There were shelves full of them, named and dated, and while we concluded that Remy didn't want what amounted to his pheromone-fluffer collection on the cloud where it could be hacked, the DVDs made little sense.

"I bet he's got them all stored on an external hard drive as well, but I think this way, he has a DVD ready to go for his viewing pleasure or, more importantly, for blackmail."

"I guess," Wade concluded. "Whatever his reasoning, this is a racket."

He started unloading boxes of DVDs from the cabinet

and stacked them on the floor. "We know the omegas pay Remy to put them in mock heat. Once they've snared an alpha, he then most likely threatens to tell the new spouses how they got honey trapped unless the omegas pay him again."

"Our suspect list could be endless," I groaned, watching him pull more boxes from the cabinet. "Jesus, how many more are there?"

He stepped back, and I saw three more shelves behind him, with boxes stacked two high.

Christ.

"I *really* hope Remy can identify the murderer," Wade said, turning to me. "Or you and I are gonna be watching werewolf porn for days."

Neither of us was looking forward to that.

I CALLED Highmore's family once we got back to the station. It was early in the morning there in Paris, just after eight, and I got his mother on the line before his father joined us. They were devastated over the news, his mother openly sobbing.

His sister was in Manhattan, his father apprised me, on a buying trip for her jewelry business, so she would be the one making arrangements for the body, as well as dealing with his finances and the house in River North. Once the scandal had hit the year prior, the rest of Highmore's family had relocated overseas to the city of love. They couldn't face people they knew, even as they assured anyone who asked of his innocence. In the end, they were right, nothing could be proven, but most people were of the opinion that was because the women were paid off not to come forward.

Sitting at my desk, I was contemplating whether to go

get food or have it delivered when Bannerman came out of his office, into the bullpen, and crossed to Wade and me.

"You guys need to go home or you'll be useless in the morning," he ordered in that raspy tone of his.

"We're gonna nap in the waiting area upstairs," I informed him. "We wanna go by the hospital first thing, and that's only a few hours away at this point."

He nodded. "Well, after that, give me a status update, and then both of you go home. I don't need you sleepwalking through your days, missing shit, or being assholes."

I snickered.

"Bigger assholes than usual," he amended irritably.

"Yessir," we both agreed.

"Where are you with this at the moment?" he wanted to know.

We brought him up to speed, and he told us to hold off looking at the videos until we talked to Mr. Talmadge.

"No use having that shit fused into your cerebral cortex if it doesn't have to be."

It was good advice. We had slept maybe an hour and a half when Ness and Peck came tromping up the stairs, which were creaky and old on a good day, and woke us up.

Peck nearly sat on Wade before my partner moved his legs, and Ness grabbed a chair and flipped it around close to the couch where I was lying, near my shoulder.

"The hell're you doin', Peckinpah?" Wade groused at him.

"Give it a rest, Massey," he growled back. "It's Peck, and you know it."

Wade may have just woken up, but he still had a savage grin for him. "Do I?"

"Hey," Ness barked, and when I turned to him, he passed me a tablet.

Sitting up, I swung my legs around and put my feet on the floor. Wade flopped down beside me as I made the picture on the screen bigger so I could see what was left of the face of a dead girl. "Why am I looking at your victim?" I asked him.

"We confirmed her identity," Ness told me. "Not a hooker at all. You're lookin' at Imogen Lowell with her throat torn out."

I lifted my head to meet his gaze. "And who is she?"

"She's an omega who had her debut earlier this year," he informed me.

I couldn't place her, didn't remember the name, but that didn't mean anything. I was in and out of the gatherings, saw Linden and Bridget and a couple others, but for the most part I didn't socialize with the male and female debutantes.

"I checked the society pages, found her pictures," Ness explained.

I went back to examining the photos with Wade. The attack had been particularly vicious. "So why show us?"

"Guess where the GPS on her phone shows her as being earlier tonight?"

I looked up at him. "At the home of Remy Talmadge?"

"Yep. Right before Highmore's time of death. That's what the ME is saying. She may be off by a little but never a lot. She's a wolf, yanno; she can smell it."

One of the things that had happened, from the Feds on down to police departments all over the country, was that there were two MEs in each department, one human and one lupine. And if there was only one position available, it would be held by a lupine. Because, like all wolves, they had a heightened sense of smell, but in lupines, they were specifically trained to scent certain biological markers as they broke down. I could tell if someone was dead from their scent, but our ME could scent, during the autopsy, each postmortem interval like algor, rigor, and livor mortis. Each carried its own smell specific to lupines, and our ME could gauge, with a fair amount of accuracy, the decomposition rate, to then trace it back to a narrower time window.

Wade sighed deeply and turned to look at Peck. "What're you thinking?"

He shrugged. "Maybe things got rough between her and Trent Highmore. He ends up losing it, wolfing out––"

"That hardly ever happens," I said defensively.

"I know," Ness snapped at me. "I got a brother-in-law who's a wolf, Rhine, so don't bust my balls."

Betas, gammas, and even omegas could marry humans, and some of them did. Alphas could not. Many alphas were far too powerful to have sex with humans. Some of them with absolutely rigid discipline could, but having sex when you had to be careful wasn't something alphas were known for.

"But it does happen," Peck jumped in. "Alphas especially can get overstimulated and freak the fuck out."

"Young alphas," I corrected him. "But still, you're reaching."

"Maybe," he agreed. "But maybe since she's brand new to bein' an omega, she doesn't get how she's drawin' in these guys fast and hard, and you know what they say about omegas: that other wolves lose their shit around them."

I grunted my agreement.

"Turns out Remy Talmadge was putting omegas into a kind of fake heat," Wade told our fellow detectives. "And then blackmailing them over it down the road."

"No shit. You see?" Peck almost shouted. "That's the answer right fuckin' there."

"It follows," Ness affirmed with a shrug. "Think about it. Talmadge gets her all going, kissing on her, fingering her——"

"Could you not," Wade groused at him.

He scoffed. "Whatever, Massey, sack up."

"Anyway," I pressed him.

"Yeah, okay," Ness groused, turning from Wade in disgust to meet my gaze. "So Talmadge has got the girl all wet and ready, her pheromones are off the fuckin' charts, and Highmore's there for who knows what, and he loses it, he attacks her, knocks her out, and now he's shittin' bricks, 'cause just like that, suddenly there's someone who will for sure say what he did, 'cause she's rich, and he can't do nothin' to her."

"That plays," Wade agreed.

"Oh good, thank you" came the sarcastic reply.

"Don't be a dick," Wade ordered, slipping his arm around the back of the couch, pressing into my side. "Fuck, she's lying in a pool of blood. That can't all be hers."

"It is." Seeing Imogen bathed in blood shook me more than it probably should have by now. The aftermath of violence, both human and lupine, was an unavoidable part of the job, but she was so young and vulnerable, and I was sad thinking about how fragile life was and how relentlessly cruel fate had been to her. "Lupines have double a human's supply to allow for the shift. It's all hers."

"Poor kid," Ness commented.

"Your story makes pretty good sense," I assented, glancing at Ness, "but what've you got as her time of death?"

He gave me the estimation that the ME gave him, between nine and nine thirty.

"Yeah, see, that's the same window we're getting on Highmore's death. So maybe he knocked her out, I can buy that, but he couldn't be dead *and* in a car driving from Highland Park to Englewood."

"Okay then, next suspect," Peck offered. "Where was Talmadge?"

"Locked in a panic room."

"You're sure?"

"Yeah, it's a coded lock system. We have the log from the monitoring company showing when he went in, and the door didn't open again until he came out to get to me."

"And Talmadge's car was there, at his house," Wade told them. "CSI took it to the garage, so we'll know if her DNA can be linked to it pretty quickly, but do we think Talmadge drove from his house to Englewood, ripped out her throat in an alley there, and then drove home and locked himself in the panic room? Does that work?"

"Not with the time lock on the panic room," Ness replied. "Unless Talmadge found a way to hack the system and close the door to make it look like he was locked in when he wasn't."

"But if he's out driving his car, that means he has to park it in his garage without any of the first responders spotting him, and then slip back into the panic room to then come out later and attack me."

"That window of time is really tight in Chicago traffic," Wade threw out.

"Yeah, not likely," Ness agreed with a sigh.

"You guys should have the hospital take a swab of his mouth anyway," Peck told us. "Get an imprint of his teeth in human form, then have him shift and take one in wolf form as well. You should do the same with his fingernails and claws."

"Already ordered those kits done." Wade sighed heavily and lifted his head, done looking at an eviscerated young woman. "Because traffic or not, panic room door or not, I like Talmadge for this. He wasn't hurt, and the blood on him wasn't his."

"So it could be Imogen's, then."

Wade squinted. "My money is on it being Highmore's. I think he was there when Highmore was torn up, and that's what sent him into the panic room."

"Makes sense," Ness concurred, "if the scene was as bad as everyone says."

Wade took the tablet, pulled up pictures of Highmore in Remy Talmage's bedroom, and passed it back to Ness.

"Jesus Christ," Ness groaned as he flipped through the shots. When he handed the tablet back, Wade and I were looking at Imogen Lowell again.

She was young, just turned eighteen. Despite all the blood, she looked like a doll.

"It certainly wasn't a robbery," I commented, zooming in on her wrist so everyone could see. "That's easily five grand worth of diamonds."

"No shit." Peck whistled, and I wasn't sure if he was stunned, impressed, or maybe a little of both. "I thought it was costume."

"I have a question," Ness began, whatever was on his mind clearly eating at him. "I'm just thinkin' out loud here. Why the fuck does Talmadge bring the omegas to his house?"

"Yeah, I don't get that either," Wade agreed. "That's the part I can't work out. It seems stupid, and this guy ain't stupid."

"Maybe because he's a world-class fuckin' douchebag?" Peck offered.

"Absolutely no question the guy's an asshole," Wade easily conceded, "but he came up with this whole scheme where he gets paid twice. Once for the heat, once for the blackmail. That's fuckin' brilliant."

"It is," Peck commented, suddenly sounding weary. "Repugnant as it is."

"And he's been doin' it awhile, right?" Ness asked us.

"By all accounts, yeah," I replied sourly. "He's been a pariah for years."

"Okay," Ness clipped the word, "then what the fuck, why his house? That part makes no sense at all. Why let his neighbors see? Why open himself up to that kind of scrutiny? Why not get a fuck pad downtown or find a——"

"His scent," I answered flatly.

The other three men went silent.

"Would you care to elaborate on that?" Wade snapped at me.

I hated explaining anything lupine. I felt like it reminded my partner and my peers that we weren't the same. Ponting out differences was something I worked hard to avoid.

"Now," Ness ordered me. "It's time to share."

"Okay, so an alpha's home smells like them. Anywhere else, an unmated omega wouldn't feel safe, wouldn't be able to stay there, wouldn't be able to get aroused, because they'd be so fearful for their safety."

"But an alpha can carry their scent with them wherever they go, so why can't they do the pheromone dump thing at an apartment just as easily as their own home? It has to be something more than smell to justify this."

Leave it to Wade to delve.

"It's like grounding," I told him. "Think of it like a wolf's den, that everything in there is steeped in not only smell but use."

"Keep going," he prodded me, "I'm not there yet."

"A lupine can own multiple houses, but only one of those can be its true den, a true home. Lupines form a bond with their 'hearth home' that can't be replicated anywhere else, whether they own the place or it's a hotel room, whatever."

"Like, no matter how much I loved the suite at the Wynn when I was in Vegas, I still had that relieved feeling when I walked into the front door of my place in Brookfield," Ness suggested. "That's what you're saying."

"Yes," I told him. "Exactly."

"And other wolves, like the omegas that were in Talmadge's place, they can sense that?"

"Yeah. Remy Talmadge could only perform the service in his own home. The omegas would have walked into some apartment, and even if, say, he was there often, they would have known instinctively that it wasn't his home. And once they sensed it, they would have run. For them, for omegas, the flight reflex is all there is."

It made the omegas sound weak, and they were, and I hated that they were. But the truth was, most unbonded omegas would have needed that small piece of grounding to trust Remy with their bodies. The women and men who had allowed Highmore to touch them had done so only because they were in Remy's home. His smell in the air, in his bed, on every surface, had reassured them, helped them relax enough to become aroused. It was a horrible abuse of his power, and did I think it should have been outlawed? Without question. The problem was, until omegas were raised differently and their rights were changed—until there was an entire cultural shift where we were concerned—mock heat to trap a mate would still occur. If the practice was criminalized, maybe some alphas would rethink their decision to *help*.

"That's fucked up," Wade concluded, shaking his head. "And I tell you what, if I were an alpha, I would hope my mate would have enough faith in our bond to tell me what they did so I could go kick the shit outta Remy Talmadge."

I shook my head. "No omega would tell their alpha, someone who has the right, by lupine law, to banish them or worse, what they did to secure their mating."

"Are you serious?"

"Yeah, he's serious." Peck took over the conversation. "My brother-in-law told me that back before the laws changed, before there were contracts drawn up that are legal in our courts and can go before the *Maion* council, an alpha could have their omega killed or tossed out on their asses with nothing. It was brutal, but completely legal."

Wade nodded. "This all makes more sense now. I knew that omegas were totally controlled, but I had no idea how many rights they don't have."

"Shit," Peck muttered, looking at me. "Thank God you were born a beta, huh, Avery?"

I was saved from having to agree, thus lie again, by my phone buzzing. I answered and listened while Remy's doctor gave me an update on his condition.

"Thanks, Doc." I hung up and then stood. "Remy's awake; let's all go. Breakfast is on me after."

"Good plan," Peck agreed, and even though we usually didn't drive together, it seemed like the thing to do.

8

GRAEME

Trent Highmore had been torn limb from limb in my cousin's bedroom. My cousin, however, had escaped, at least physically, unscathed. Mentally, emotionally, he was in a weakened, battered state, and therefore had not appreciated being poked and prodded, having his nails scraped, his hair combed, his penis swabbed, or the hundreds of pictures taken of his naked body. Then he was told to shift, and it was all repeated. When he was given permission to return to his human form, only then was he allowed to rest. Small abrasions were bandaged—likely from his fight earlier in the evening—drugs were administered, and he was allowed to hydrate, which was, I was certain, the most helpful. Shifting required fluids, so replenishing those were the first step in recovery.

Standing near the head of the bed as my mate outlined what he knew, and didn't, about the evening, I was by turns enraged and horrified. Those feelings were in sharp contrast to the warm ones I felt for my mate. He was, again, impressive. The others deferred to him. Some of it, perhaps, because he was the only wolf on the case, so they were taking their cues from him. But as they regarded him, as their gazes flicked to him and then away, I saw only respect in their eyes.

Our family lawyer, Agatha Chun, had given Remy permission to speak to the police, but only in reference to the omegas. Anything else, anything pertaining to the murder or other charges that might come up, fell to me to make a decision on. She counseled that if the police wanted any footage or pictures Remy might, or might not, be in possession of, they should supply me with warrants and subpoenas, and stipulations would need to be secured before anything could be shared. When I told Avery and the others that we would hand over everything Remy might have, Agatha left, annoyed with me as usual. I understood; she was there to protect me, to protect my cousin, and as I was certain Remy was guilty of exploiting and betraying omegas, but not murder, I wasn't going to impede the investigation by dragging out the judicial process.

"Mr. Talmadge," Avery began gently, putting his phone down on the rolling tray table beside the bed. "Now that your lawyer has left you in the hands of your *cyne*, and he has agreed that you should cooperate with us, I'm going to record this conversation while we all take notes."

Except for a faint whimper, my cousin remained silent.

"Now, Mr. Talmadge, will you please walk us through the events of the evening as you recall them."

He took a breath and slowly turned his head, his eyes lifting to me. "I need to know what my *cyne* is going to do to me first."

"No," I replied flatly. "Tell them everything now, and then we'll talk."

Trembling hard, reacting, I was certain, to the utter revulsion in my voice, he rolled his head on the pillow, returning his gaze to Avery. "I don't—it was just a regular night, like all the other gathering nights."

Which was why Remy was never at the parties, he was at his house putting omegas into mock heat for money on those nights.

"And the omegas," Avery prompted him, "can you tell us who was there?"

"Not by name off the top of my head. Most of them were nineteen or twenty and had already attended their first gatherings, but weren't successful at securing a bonding. The brand-new omegas, the debutants, young and fresh, they rarely come to me. I get a few here and there, those who want to assure themselves a quick bonding, but it's typically the older ones who are starting to panic."

"Thank you," Avery replied. "Please continue."

"I was in the living room, giving them the rundown of how things work, how I take each one into my bedroom, but the doorbell kept ringing, so I had to start the explanation over and over, and soon there were more omegas than I was expecting." He went to rub his forehead, but the bandage stopped him, and his hand dropped back down beside him on the bed. "I didn't know what was going on at first, but then I remembered that my cousin, him," he whispered, "Graeme, he was supposed to attend the gathering. He'd missed others, but for whatever reason, everyone was pretty sure he was going to show up to this one."

"Did you attend, Mr. Davenport?" Detective Ness took that moment to confirm.

"I did," I replied.

He nodded and then looked to Remy. "So the possibility of Mr. Davenport attending this gathering in particular, that's why more than the usual number of omegas were at your place?"

"Yes. They come to the house, I put them into heat, and they go from my place to the gathering. Some of them have cars waiting, some drive themselves—that part's not important to me, but I do tell them if they're not having someone circle the block, they need to park a street over to avoid suspicion."

"So you're telling us there were extra omegas at your place tonight." Detective Massey was clarifying.

"Yes," Remy answered. "Like I said, because of Graeme. He's a *cyne*. He leads a *holt*. There's not a lot of them to begin with, and even fewer who aren't mated. When he attends a gathering, a party where omegas are presented, all of them show up. No one wants to miss out on——"

"Move on, Remy," I demanded icily.

"Please, Mr. Davenport," Detective Massey urged me, "let him speak."

I was quiet as Remy shivered.

"I was—it was hard to hear all the omegas chirping about my cousin being there and how excited they were, but I know better, right? I know what my cousin wants, and it's not some throw-away omega. He was only there because he had to be, but he'd never settle for a waifish little doll. It's so stupid that they don't just say what an alpha is to save everyone from wasting their time. Like with Graeme, he wants a beta or a gamma, someone strong. And I wanted to tell the girls they were especially out of luck, because he's not bi like me; he's gay, and he's looking for a——"

"Never mind," Detective Massey cut him off. "I thought this was gonna be important, but you can stop with all the bullshit and whatever the fuck you're tryin' to do here. We don't care who your cousin wants to fuck, Mr. Talmadge. Unlike you, he's not a suspect."

"What?" Remy gasped. "No. You can't think I did anything to--"

"We do," Avery assured him sharply, but then quieted his tone, softened it purposely, "until you give us reason to believe differently."

Remy stared at him a long moment. "Okay. Once I saw how many omegas were there, I knew there was no way I could put them all into heat, so I made a call to my friend Trent."

No one said a word, all of them waiting on him, all with notebooks in hand, poised to take down every new word he uttered.

"Trent was the only one I told about my business, because I knew I could trust him to keep it quiet."

Of course Highmore wouldn't tell; he was a predator himself.

Remy had taken a couple of the omegas back to his bedroom where the camera was set up, and was readying them when Highmore came in with two more.

Finding out that Remy had been putting omegas into fake heat, was getting paid, and then was blackmailing them if they secured a mate, was nauseating. Having to listen to the play-by-play, I was thankful I hadn't eaten.

"I had to explain to Trent that most of the omegas were virgins. He didn't need to give them oral, he just needed to use his fingers, gently, and that would be enough."

My stomach lurched, and I rolled my neck to try and displace the tension that had settled at the top of my spine.

Avery cleared his throat. "So you gave him those instructions, and was he good with it?"

"He was. Once he started, the omegas calmed down, and soon they were all whimpering and whining, like they do, and he was great. He told them good luck and good hunting and got them out. He was even faster than I was, and we got them done and sent on their way, but then there were stragglers."

Silence in the room. I could hear the ticking of the Breguet Classique 5177 my grandfather had given me when I graduated from Oxford. I was glad, in that moment, he wasn't Remy's grandfather, only mine and Stone's. I couldn't wait for Avery to meet him.

"First there was a girl at the door, so young, I didn't think she was eighteen. I was fairly certain I hadn't seen her picture in the paper; I comb through the society pages so I can match the announcements with a face, for reference. But she was young, like I said, so I was going to ask her how old she was, but before I could even get the words out, there was a man, the same one who'd been there earlier that night, and the week before, and he yelled, grabbed me by the jacket and yanked me outside."

"You didn't know him?" Avery questioned.

"No, I…I mean, I recognized him by his size and build, but I don't know who he was. I don't know his name. And I'd never seen him before he came to my house the first time."

"Did you get any pictures of him?"

"Yes, but it didn't matter." He shook his head. "It doesn't matter. He was wearing a hoodie and a gaiter or balaclava or—I don't know, but I just couldn't see his face at all."

"Okay," Avery prodded gently, "please continue."

"The first time he knocked on my door, he threw me up against the wall when I answered, said he knew what was going on, knew what I was doing with the omegas and didn't give a shit, but what he did care about was a girl with platinum hair."

Avery and the other three detectives were all listening

intently, no one saying a word, not wanting to interrupt my cousin.

Remy swallowed hard. "He said as long as I turned away any girls with platinum hair, he wouldn't tell my *cyne* what was going on."

Avery looked up then, and our eyes met briefly. Something, a thought, perhaps an emotion—I couldn't discern which—flickered in his, there and gone before he returned his focus to Remy and continued the interview.

"Which scared you, because he knew who you belonged to. He'd done his homework."

"Yes," he whispered shakily.

"Okay," Avery stated, clearing his throat. "So this man warned you about a specific girl, and he came to your house just that once before tonight?"

"Yes, just the once, and then, as I said, twice tonight," Remy declared.

"Twice tonight," Avery repeated. "And then what happened?"

"She screamed when the man came up behind her."

"So she screamed because she was scared?"

He shook his head. "No. She was screaming *at* him. Definitely at him. She was telling him something about how it wasn't fair, that it was her turn. I don't—he scared the crap out of me, so that was all I was focused on. Well, that and I do know her hair was black, not platinum blond."

"Could you tell which direction the girl was headed when she left? Was she on foot, or did she have a car?"

"I think she ran, but that's just a guess. He started hitting me, and I couldn't do anything but try not to be killed."

To the humans looking at Remy, it had to sound absurd, because whatever damage the man had inflicted was already healed.

"It looks like your X-rays corroborate your story, Mr. Talmadge," my mate told him.

"I wouldn't lie, not about this. It was so scary. I'm an alpha, but this guy was big and strong; he had to be an alpha too, and I'm guessing trained in some kind of martial arts or —I would have died if Trent hadn't started yelling and threatening to call the police."

"Which he would have never done since there were still omegas in your home," Avery commented. "Correct?"

"A few, but yes," Remy agreed. "Which perhaps my assailant realized."

It seemed reasonable.

"Let's continue, then," Avery prodded him after a couple moments of silence.

In the story Remy continued to tell, the alpha, or the man Remy assumed was an alpha, chased him out to the street, where Remy had fled. His assailant punched him for the final time and then took off. By then, there was an audience, his neighbors. After assuring them that he was fine, he walked back inside. Trent had been waiting, and helped him to the hall bathroom because Remy was going to be sick and couldn't make it to the one in the master. Remy heard the doorbell ring while he was vomiting. When he finished, he splashed water on his face and rinsed his mouth, then headed to his room to change out of his sweat-soaked, filthy clothes.

"I noticed my bedroom door was closed, but was sure I heard a woman's voice and assumed it was another omega. I was going to go back to the living room, figuring Trent was taking care of her, but then I heard a scream. I was worried that maybe he forgot my instructions, so I opened the door and saw a girl bent over the end of my bed, passed out." His voice was monotone, as though he was back there, in the moment, narrating what he was seeing. "She probably screamed before she fainted, and because I was so worried about her and what Trent must have done, it took me a second to register he was in the middle of the floor, choking to death."

I watched Remy filter through his memories, saw him wince and jerk before tears welled in his eyes.

"There was so much blood and that awful, wet gurgling."

"Could you tell why he was choking?" Avery asked.

Remy lifted his hand to his neck as though in a trance. "Because a wolf had its jaws clamped around his throat, suffocating him and ripping at the same time. When it yanked free, it kept its jaws locked, didn't let go, so most of Trent's neck was gone," he rushed out, his voice catching on a sob.

"What'd you do then?"

"Trent was convulsing and trying to shift, but he'd lost too much blood, and then the wolf just—the wolf..."

"The wolf," Avery prodded him. "Go on, please."

"It started pulling him apart, ripped into his stomach with its claws and bit through his wrist, and then it stopped and turned its head to me, like it was in slow motion, and stared at me for a long time. I mean, it felt like a long time, and I watched the blood drip off its muzzle, and then it opened its mouth and went back to Trent."

"And then?"

His eyes had flicked away, but he returned his gaze to Avery. "It was going to kill me. I knew it was seconds away from being done with Trent and would be coming for me next, so I ran."

I could imagine how terrified Remy had to have been, faced with his own mortality.

"I rushed out of the room, and I was going to go out the

front door, but the girl suddenly flew by me, into the hall, headed that way, so I went in the opposite direction, to my panic room, and locked myself in."

"Did you hear anything after that?" Avery was in full interrogation mode now, pressing Remy for the final details.

"No, the...the room is sealed and soundproofed, so no."

"Okay—" Avery took a breath. "—thank you, Mr. Tal--"

"If the room is sealed and soundproofed, why did you come out and attack my partner?" Detective Massey phrased it as an accusation more than a question.

Remy's eyes widened fearfully as he turned to Avery. "Are you the one who was outside the room?"

"I was, but it's—"

"I'm so sorry," he apologized, his voice bottoming out. "I just—I was so scared, and I could have sworn I smelled Graeme, and I knew if I could reach him I'd be safe so—oh God, I didn't hurt you, did I?"

"No," Avery assured him. "You were out of it, so it wasn't much of an attack."

"But I... I seem to remember there were marks on your face and...your neck, and...thank God you're not mated. I don't think I could fight a wolf for--"

"It's fine," Avery affirmed, shooting Detective Massey a pointed look before returning his focus to Remy. I suspected that Avery wanted to get on with the investigation and not delve into the reason he was carrying my scent on him. "You didn't hurt me; I just don't heal as quickly as an alpha. I'm fine now. The important thing is that we found you; you needed medical attention."

He inhaled deeply. "Thank you. I—" He inhaled again, parting his lips, tasting the scent in the air. "It's so odd, but all I'm getting from you is Graeme."

"That's because he's standing right beside you," Detective Massey groused at him. "Of course he's all you can smell."

"We found your DVDs, Mr. Talmadge," Avery redirected, "but not the location of the camera in your bedroom, and we need to look at the footage from tonight."

"The camera is behind the mirror above the headboard of my bed."

"I was just in your room," Detective Massey told him. "There's no mirror above the headboard. There's a mirror on the opposite wall, beside the armoire in the corner."

"No," Remy assured him. "It's a two-way mirror, with shelves behind for positioning the camera."

"There's a painting above the headboard...and two shelves behind it. But nothing else."

Remy caught his breath. "Detective, I assure you that's where the camera was. The mirror was there, the painting was next to the armoire. If they're switched now, whoever did that has the camera and the footage of Trent's murder."

"Okay," Detective Massey said after a moment. "We need to go back to that house."

"Are all the copies of your interactions with the omegas on DVD, or do you keep them backed up in cloud storage as well?"

"I don't trust a cloud not to be hacked, so I have the DVDs and an external hard drive."

"Which is where?"

"In my safety deposit box."

"We already have access to your phone records, but I'd like to look at the phone as well, if that's not a problem."

I moved then, from where I'd been standing near the head of Remy's bed, to the foot, pulled Remy's phone from my outside suitcoat pocket, and passed it to Avery.

His eyes met mine. "Thank you," he murmured.

I tipped my head at him. "And now, gentlemen, if there's nothing more, I need to speak to my cousin, and then to his doctor."

Avery promised to return the phone as soon as possible.

"I look forward to hearing from you, Detective, but perhaps in the meantime you can give me your number in case I need to contact you."

"Absolutely," he acceded, his voice husky, gravelly, as his gaze met mine for only a heartbeat, but it was enough.

He and the others were gone moments later.

In truth, I had nothing to say to Remy, so I ordered him to be silent and rest, and then pulled out my phone to call Kat.

"Make arrangements to send a *vordr* to Remy's home."

"No," Remy gasped behind me. "Graeme, you can't do that. It's not——"

"It is," I snarled at him before speaking into my phone. "Kat."

"Yes," she replied hoarsely. "Yes, Graeme, I'm here."

"Did you hear what I said?"

"I did," she replied softly, steadily, not asking the question that my brother would have—if I was certain of my decision. "Anything else?"

"Not at the moment." I clipped the words before I hung up.

Walking to the door of Remy's room, I stepped outside, nodded at the two police officers there standing guard, and then walked down the hall to a deserted seating alcove I'd seen earlier. Only then did I call Stone.

"Tell me everything," he said when he picked up, even though it was a ridiculous hour of the morning. "Gigi's here too."

I cleared my throat. "I'm sorry to have kept you both up with this."

"That doesn't matter, Graeme," my sister-in-law assured me. "We're family, this is a family matter. Now tell us."

I explained all about what Remy had done, not bothering to sugarcoat the details about him preying on the omegas, or my plan to make reparations.

"We're going to have to agree to disagree on this." Gigi's sigh was long.

"You don't think a *vordr* should be called?"

"No, not that," she rushed out. "I agree there's no recourse but for him to have a watcher, starting now. The blackmail is despicable, and he deserves to be stripped of his freedom for that trespass alone. Alphas must be held to a higher standard or the entire system will fall into chaos. If we cannot look to our leaders, then we're lost as a species."

"Agreed."

"Apart from the blackmail, however," she began, exhaling slowly. "Graeme, those omegas are all of age."

"Yes," I conceded, because she wasn't wrong.

"They all sought Remy out. They made the choice; they paid him; no one forced them. And, as far as you know, none of them were violated."

"Of course they were vio––"

"Their trust, their faith, absolutely. That's not up for debate. But Graeme, to dismantle whatever's left of Remy's trust fund, selling his home, liquidating his possessions in order to return money to omegas who got exactly what they wanted from him, is that fair?"

"I can't believe you're defending him," I chided her.

"I'm not *defending* him," she retorted, bristling. "I'm spreading the blame, as it should be. There's plenty enough to go around."

"They're young," I stated. "They didn't know any better."

"Okay, into the deep end we go," she declared before sucking in a breath. "I think the fact that your mate is an omega is clouding your judgment."

My fury was instantaneous. I was never to be questioned. I was going to attack, absolutely annihilate her, put her in her place, but I hung up instead, because in that instant my mate, my beautiful golden-haired, silver-eyed mate crossed my mind.

Acting on instinct, I called him.

"Hi" was all he said, but his tone, low and husky, instantly soothed me.

"I wanted to ask you what you thought about something," I apprised him. "Concerning the omegas Remy mistreated."

"Hit me," he replied gamely.

"First, though, I must tell you that I'm going to have a *vordr* assigned to my cousin."

He was quiet for a moment. "I think that's great. Remy deserves a *vordr* who will, in essence, strip him of his alpha status and the ability to make a decision about anything beyond what he wants for lunch."

Succinctly put.

"What are your thoughts on the omegas?" he asked me.

"My first thought is to pay them all back."

He was quiet a moment. "May I speak frankly?"

If anyone had ever told me, even a day before, that I would be waiting to hear the thoughts of an omega—ever—I would have told them they were insane. But the truth was, to me, Avery had no rank; he was neither lowest nor highest. He was my mate, and I wanted to hear all his thoughts on everything.

"While I think it's quite chivalrous of you to want to

make things right with them, first you have to speak to their alphas and explain what you're paying them back for."

He was right, to a certain degree. No one was allowed to speak to a bonded omega without first speaking to their alpha. It was, regardless of the circumstances, not permitted. By virtue of my position as a *cyne*, however, I was entitled to more leeway and wasn't bound to those protocols. But given the circumstances surrounding this case, Avery raised a valid point.

"That would be problematic," Avery apprised me, "wouldn't it?"

"It would."

"And if you spoke to an alpha who had been tricked into a bonding with their omega, and told them the truth, you could potentially be putting those matches in jeopardy that have been working great for years now, even though they started out shady."

Quite true.

"So maybe," he began, "since you have a lot of money and resources, you could put a team together to track down each and every omega. Then the team could look at each case individually and determine which omegas are in successful relationships. Not happy, because not all wolves are, and deciding who is or isn't wouldn't be within the team's purview. All they would be judging is which bondings are successful as it relates to the financial and familial benefit of each party. You can also look at those omegas who weren't able to secure a match, even after Remy put them in mock heat."

With every word he spoke, I warmed more to the idea.

"If you do that, you could provide for those omegas who are currently a financial drain on their families by helping to offset whatever costs are being incurred, without divulging why, of course, and give omegas who would prefer not to be mated the necessary funds to stay single."

He made good sense, but I had a terrible thought.

"And for the unsuccessfully mated ones, you could provide a parachute, a way out of the situation they're in."

I was quiet.

"What do you think?"

Quick clearing of my throat. "I think that's a well-thought-out plan."

"Really? Because you sound like you're not sure."

"No I...I just—you didn't want to remain unattached, did you?"

It was his turn to be silent, and with every passing second I died just a bit.

"Avery, you——"

"I thought I did," he murmured. "And I'm sure I would have...if there was no you."

Amazing how such simple words from him could settle me so quickly in my own skin.

"When I saw you at Remy's tonight, you helped, you know? Like, I felt calmer just seeing you, more grounded, almost——"

"Settled in your skin?"

"Yeah." He exhaled, as though relieved to have his feelings put into words. "Exactly."

The man was made for me, and all I wanted was to have him close, right there, so I could touch him.

"Graeme?" He sounded tentative.

I had no idea I could enjoy hearing my own name so much. Other people using it had certainly never resulted in this swell of pride and possessiveness rolling through me. "Yes?"

"Remy was adamant when he was talking about you and

what you wanted from a mating, and that you would never want an omega."

The truth was always the best. "Remy knows very little about me, but that is true. My mother was an omega, and she was, perhaps, the textbook definition of one, delicate and easily broken. At the gatherings, one is treated to the worst kind of alpha and omega interaction, and never, no matter how beautiful, did I ever look at any of them twice."

He was quiet, listening.

"But Avery, your scent had me bewitched," I confessed. "I had to find you, and when I did, imagine my delight at discovering you to be a beautiful, strong, virile man who is exactly the mate I've always needed and wanted."

"But still an omega."

"It doesn't matter what you are, only *who* you are. I need to put my mark on you so you'll know how I feel and won't second-guess my words."

"I won't do that. I believe you...or, I want to believe you."

"Good. Wanting will suffice for now until I claim what's mine."

His breath caught.

"Avery?" The low, seductive, husky chuckle from him was a surprise and sent a roll of heat right to my cock. "Something funny?" I barely got out.

"No I—it's just, you're very sure of everything, and I should mind that you think of me as belonging to you, but for whatever reason, I couldn't breathe there for a second."

"I'm thrilled to hear it."

"Okay so, about the omegas, is it a plan?"

"It is," I agreed. "I'll task my brother with it. He's quite discreet, and it should go without saying, but I will have him wait to contact anyone until the police—you—conclude your investigation. We certainly don't want to risk tipping off a murderer in our zeal to make amends. That would be exceedingly counterproductive."

"Yes, it would," he agreed, and I could hear the mirth in his voice.

"Something you find humorous?"

"*Exceedingly counterproductive*. I would've said it'd be a shitshow. You're so proper and smart and gorgeous and..."

"Gorgeous?" I stopped him, hating myself because of how pathetic I probably sounded, as though fishing for a compliment. But this was my mate. "I'm horribly disfigured, you know. Perhaps gorgeous isn't the adjective you were looking for."

"It's the right one," he replied, his voice thick, smooth like honey. "And I...I see the scar, but to me it only adds; it doesn't take away."

The man rendered me mute so easily.

"I see you, okay?"

"Yes," I managed to croak out.

"There are life and death parts of being a wolf that most people never think about because they're not *cynes* who have to put their lives on the line for members of their *holt*, like I'm sure you had to do, right?"

"I did," I confirmed for him.

"You being a champion, taking care of everyone—I don't want to change you, but I also wouldn't want to lose you," he murmured, his voice like a caress. "And there's so much for us to talk about. I would like one of them to be us discussing who you'll put your life on the line for in the future, since you'll be mine first."

Mine first...the words echoed in my mind. I knew I had wanted things, important things, but for the life of me, at that moment, I couldn't think of anything I'd ever wanted more than to belong to Avery Rhine.

"I would like to see you before dinner this evening," I told him, realizing that it was very early in the morning at this point, and neither of us had been to bed.

"Dinner?"

"Your family and mine are convening for cocktails at seven and dinner at eight, to make arrangements for our mating ceremony—our wedding—but also to meet."

"Oh no, we can't do that until the investigation is—"

"I must insist," I broke in quickly, wanting to make certain the next time I slept in my bed he was with me. "While I appreciate the fact the police must investigate all crime, we both know when you find the murderer, that person will be punished by their alpha. This won't be a matter for the human courts. The attack was perpetrated by one lupine on another."

"Yeah, I know, but—"

"Then there's no reason for us not to move forward."

"We should wait."

"For what?" I asked gently. "Truly? For what?"

He had no answer.

"Avery," I said hoarsely, "I want my mark on you."

"Yes," he rasped, and I knew I had him.

"Now tell me, if Remy has a master list of the omegas he mistreated, would you want that? Would that be of help to you?"

"That would be amazing," he breathed out.

"Hold on," I said, and walked quickly back to Remy's room, my phone pressed to my chest. One of the officers held the door open for me, and I was at his bedside in moments. "Do you have all the names of the omegas? Is there a master list?"

"Yes," Remy whispered, his face ashen. "It's in my safety deposit box with the hard drive."

"Which bank?"

He told me.

"There is a list," I reported to Avery, crossing the room to the window. "I'll send my brother for it when the bank opens and have the list and hard drive delivered to you."

"But it's Remy's box, how will——"

"I'm a *cyne*," I reminded him. "I have access to the possessions of everyone in my *holt*."

He chuckled. "Privacy laws will catch up with the wolves, mark my words."

"Perhaps," I agreed. "But not today."

"No," he conceded, and I heard the smile in his voice. "Not today."

I got his email address, stressed how much I was looking forward to seeing him later, and then, even though I didn't want to, I let him go. I then called my brother back.

"You scared us," he told me. "You never hang up. You always make us aware of your anger, and it takes weeks to——"

"I'm sorry," I muttered. "I'll work on changing that."

Long silence.

"Stone?"

"I'm here, and I need you to tell me, what were you doing the nine or ten times I tried to call you back?"

"I called Avery, and he had an excellent idea."

"You...you called your mate and—Gigi," he yelled, thankfully not into the phone, "he called his new mate."

"Stone," I barked.

"You should see her," he mused, and there was a trace of pain in his voice. "She's been scrunched up on the couch, waiting, certain that when you did call back you would hit her with both barrels."

"I..." What did I want to say?

"Yes?"

"I don't want to attack her."

"No?"

"No."

"Well, I'm terribly glad to hear it," he announced dryly.

"I hate you," I assured him.

"Yes, I'm aware." He sounded thoroughly smug, but somehow, from him, it wasn't annoying. "So let me see if I understand. This new mate of yours, this omega, has a terribly calming effect on you that resulted in you and Gigi not clashing, me not being thrown in the middle of it, and he had an idea you seem partial to. Are those the facts in evidence?"

He was a lawyer, so he got a bit high-handed on occasion, but he was right. I was the leader of my family, what I said became law, and Gigi, who belonged to my *holt* through her mating, did not always agree with me. Our rows were epic, we were both alphas after all, and Stone almost always ended up stuck in the middle of a ruthless game of tug-of-war. It had to be exceedingly difficult on him, and while I loved him, it was in my nature to win. That same need was instilled in Gigi, and I had never given a lot of thought to what it must be like for Stone. Not until now. Many siblings I'd come across were not close, but I loved my brother and was thankful that was not the case with us. I needed to make certain the warmth remained.

"Yes," I admitted, "those are indeed the facts in evidence."

"Well, Graeme," he said, sounding quite pleased, "I can hardly wait to meet this man, and I know I can speak for Gigi when I say she feels the same."

"I do," Gigi revealed, and I knew I was on speaker. "Now

tell us about this plan your omega came up with. I want to help in any way I can."

"Excellent," I stated, and then outlined everything for them as Remy lay there in the bed, listening to every word of the plan to try and make amends for some of the horrors he'd committed.

9

AVERY

No one was hungry after listening to Remy Talmadge recount his evening, and even my talk with Graeme didn't help my mood for long. It had been hard to let him go; I wanted to keep him talking, his voice warming the cold pit in my stomach. Amazing that not even twenty-four hours after meeting the man, I could yearn for something as simple as sitting with him. I could almost feel my wolf pacing inside, wanting his mate, whimpering, whining, becoming more and more agitated with each passing hour. I'd be crazed by the time the evening rolled around if I couldn't figure out how to placate the animal inside.

It turned out grief was the answer.

At eight in the morning, Wade and I went to the Lowells to deliver the death notification for Imogen. It was horrible. Her mother screamed, turned into her husband's arms and sobbed. Mr. Lowell appeared shattered.

He clung to his wife, his eyes telegraphing a deep well of pain and horror. "Where is she? When can we see her?" he asked me. "We need to make arrangements for..."

I glanced at his wife, saw her face was still buried in her husband's chest, and shook my head. Mr. Lowell took a breath.

All we could do now was promise to find her killer.

"Please, when they call to let you know her body is being released, have her sent directly to the funeral home." His gaze met mine. "Perhaps have your wife go lay down before she collapses." I suggested gently.

He called for his housekeeper, who rushed in, and when his wife was halfway across the room, I stepped in close to him, my mouth near his ear. "Make certain it's a closed casket," I whispered. "Please. Neither you nor your wife need that to be the last image you have of your child."

He nodded quickly.

Back in my Jeep, Wade and I both sat there for a while outside the Lowell mansion, neither of us speaking, before I drove us back to the station. Hours later we were in the briefing room with Ness and Peck, staring at whiteboards, facts and details and timelines laid out on them, three of us sitting in a row while Wade paced, the only one of us still capable of being upright.

The camera had, in fact, been taken. Our forensics team determined the house was a perfect storm of smudged prints, trace evidence pointing to everything and nothing, and, surprisingly, not a drop of fluid found anywhere that would suggest sex. Even Remy Talmadge's bed was pristine. All of it, every square foot of the house, was a wash. The word of the day was *inconclusive*.

"Who do we think took the camera?"

"Maybe the person who killed Highmore," Ness offered, his head resting on his arms folded on the table. "Maybe not. Who the fuck knows?"

This was the day we were having. No answers, just more

questions. Sitting there listening to him, I recalled a time before I valued his words and opinions.

The first time I'd met Craig Ness, I'd thought, with his blond hair and blue eyes, square-cut jaw, ruddy, wind-chapped complexion, and the "aw-shucks" grin, that he just got off a train from Iowa or Idaho or someplace where they ate a lot of potatoes and corn. I thought he was a hick and couldn't be all that bright, especially since he was built like a linebacker. Big and dumb was my initial conclusion. It was stupid and judgmental, and when he solved a cold case his second week on the job, I found out that while *big* was applicable, nothing else I thought about the man was. His brain worked lightning-fast, and God help you if you thought you could outrun him. He was like a tank charging down the sidewalk, and folks tended to scatter. What always impressed me was how quickly he could calculate angles and trajectories in his head, and how strangers opened up to him right away. It was a gift I didn't possess, putting others at ease. I tended to get on people's nerves.

Wade turned, arms crossed, to look at all of us. "Okay, this person, this killer, decides on the fly to kill Highmore; we heard from Talmadge himself he didn't plan on calling his buddy, but because so many omegas showed up that night, he needed the help."

"Yes," I agreed and then nudged Ness who echoed my affirmative.

"So our killer strips out of their clothes, shifts into wolf form, kills Highmore, shifts back because they need thumbs now, puts their clothes back on, grabs the camera, moves things around on the walls to throw us off, and kidnaps Imogen Lowell."

"Without leaving a single print or strand of hair, or anything else, anywhere in that bedroom," Peck chimed in.

I often said if anybody was smoother than Eddie Peck, I didn't know who that would be. I was never sure if it was the walk—all swagger and attitude—his crooked grin, his devotion to fashion, the deep, rich sepia skin that had both women and men reaching for him, or the infectious laugh that made you want to join him in whatever he was doing. He'd been a transfer from narcotics, and Wade never missed an opportunity to remind him that homicide was a step up. Peck, not to be outdone, explained that narcotics worked ten cases to our one. At some point they would put the rivalry to bed, but it wouldn't be any time soon, as evidenced by Wade still calling him everything but his actual name. It didn't help that they had a similar taste in women.

"Rhine," Ness snapped at me, "pay attention."

"Sorry, sorry," I apologized quickly, hating that I'd been caught with my mind drifting. "What'd you say?"

"I asked, why would Imogen leave with Highmore's killer?"

"Talmadge said she was passed out. Maybe she didn't see anything, didn't know that the person she left with killed Highmore."

"Yeah, but Talmadge said she ran down the hall. Why do that other than to get away from the murder scene?"

"Right," Wade agreed. "Then maybe whoever Imogen ran into when she left the house, that's the person she left with, thinking she was safe."

"Then there have to be two people," I concluded. "Two killers. Whoever killed Highmore didn't kill Imogen."

"I agree," Peck declared. "She ran away, left with whoever, and the killer messed around in the house."

"Does the person who killed Imogen even know that someone was murdered there?"

"Maybe not," Wade admitted. "Maybe someone,

whoever, was just picking her up. Talmadge told us that all the omegas left in different ways; it could be the person who drove Imogen was prearranged to be there."

"So no savior, just someone she trusts and knows," Ness proposed.

"Right," Peck agreed. "But then why kill her?"

"Something must've happened in the car," I advised him.

"And this all makes sense unless Talmadge is lying and Imogen never ran by him, in which case we could be back to one killer."

"I tend to think that part's true, though," Wade apprised me, "because it makes Talmadge look bad that he didn't do anything to help her. I mean, he could have yelled at her to get in the goddamn panic room with him, but he didn't, he was too scared and put his own safety before that of a frightened young woman. Who admits to something like that unless it's the truth?"

"I agree." Peck's voice gave out on him, hoarse because he—all of us—had been up for so long. He cleared his throat and continued. "He's terrified, he sees Imogen run by, and all he's worried about is savin' his own ass. I think she's runnin' out the front door, away from the bloodbath, just like Talmadge is, except he's running to his panic room."

"She's scared to death," I began, imagining the layout of the house, "and gets all the way to the street. She snuck out of her own house earlier in the night, and we know from her phone records she took an Uber to Talmadge's, so she has no car. Now she's there, alone, on the street, lookin' around, and...someone appears."

"Yeah," Wade agreed, nodding, "Either prearranged or not, she's freaked out, and she goes with whoever it was, thinking that person is saving her life."

"That's the only thing that makes any sense," I told him.

"Okay, so two people," Wade affirmed and wrote down the number. "One person butchers Highmore and steals the camera, the other one kills Imogen Lowell."

It made sense.

"Why, though? Why kill Imogen?" Peck asked us.

"Maybe that was never the plan," Wade surmised. "Maybe it started off good, like whoever this person is really was going to help Imogen, but at some point during the trip from Talmadge's house to wherever, something changed. Instead of dropping Imogen off safely at her house, this person took her from Talmadge's, then ends up killing her and making her wounds look similar enough to Highmore's that we think there's only one killer."

"Except there is a difference," Ness pointed out. "Highmore was aware he was choking to death on his own blood, and had to have been in excruciating pain before he died. Miss Lowell, on the other hand, had her neck broken. Yes, she was torn to pieces as well, but she was dead long before that happened. All that damage was done postmortem."

"Okay," Wade said, lacing his fingers behind his head. "Both people were murdered, Highmore because he was in the wrong place at the wrong time. And Imogen, technically for the same reason?"

Then something occurred to me. "Maybe whoever killed Highmore thought they were killing Talmadge. I mean, uniforms on-site even made a false identification and called Mr. Davenport to tell him that his cousin was dead."

"Yeah, that was fuckin' great," Wade groaned. "Way to make us look like assholes."

"We're so lucky he's a good guy," Peck declared with a yawn, "and not calling the mayor. That would be all over the news, and whoever called Mr. Davenport would be so out of a job."

"Focus," I ordered them. "If Highmore was killed by mistake, then whoever did it might make another attempt on Talmadge's life."

"He's got police protection now, but lemme make a call and double it," Wade said, walking out of the room.

Getting up, I walked to the back of the room and called Graeme.

"Avery," he murmured, sounding tired.

"I'm sorry to bother you, but––"

"You could never bother me," he professed.

"Just wait, I will."

"We'll see," he rumbled, and his voice was like a caress that I wanted to lean into. "What may I do for my mate?"

Would I ever get used to that? "Uhm, we think your cousin might be in danger."

"Yes," he stated. "Our family *vraekae*, her name is Shivani Burman, and––"

"Holy crap." I was in awe. "Your family has a *vraekae*? Really?"

He chuckled. "You sound very excited. I'll introduce you to her at our wedding."

The *vraekae*, or wolf-warriors, were the oldest continual security force in the world. They were palace guards for pharaohs and emperors and kings. They had been Vikings, samurai, knights, and a part of every elite fighting force throughout history. Now they were private security for a small number of lupine families that had made ancient blood oaths with them, as well as for human clients who could afford to employ them. The price tag for their service was astronomical, but if the hype was true, they'd never lost anyone on their watch, from the Bronze Age to the present.

"I would love to meet her," I gushed, "and sorry, I interrupted you. Go on."

More soft laughter, and God, I loved the sound of him. "When my assistant called for a *vordr* for Remy, that immediately prompted a call to Shivani, and when I explained the circumstances to her, she sent two men to watch over Remy until the police have the guilty party in custody."

"She must care about him."

He scoffed. "No. The oath is with my father's line, the Davenport line, not my mother's, which is the Talmadge line. She's doing this because she doesn't want someone to try and get to me through Remy."

"But then, why isn't someone guarding you?"

"I have two bodyguards, Kat, who you've met, and Isabella, who you will meet. Shivani believes them both to be quite capable of taking care of me. When I travel abroad, she sends extra people along with me, and them, as is protocol, and I suspect, once we're mated, she'll assign you your own *skyld*."

"A what?"

"A shield. If you were kidnapped or placed in danger, you could be used as leverage against me, so she'll want to take that temptation off the board early."

"Yeah, but Graeme, I'm a cop. I can't have someone with me or––"

"Oh no, you never see a shield," he snorted. "I had one for years when I went to school abroad, and I wouldn't be able to give you a name or tell you what they looked like."

"Really?"

"Yes, it's all very cloak-and-dagger. But I've known Shivani for years, even before she became a member of the *vraekae*, so we have a different relationship, which is why she'll be at the wedding."

"I can't wait to tell my father that your family has a *vraekae*, but okay, thank you for letting me know. I'll get the CPD detail off your cousin and save the city some money."

"Good."

I hung up then, even though I didn't want to, and was going to find Wade, but he found me first.

"Hey, I just got a report that Talmadge has private security now, so I'm gonna pull the guys we have there with him. Once Talmadge is released from the hospital, we can have a patrol car roll by his place, but it sounds like his *cyne* has it covered."

"Yeah, I was just gonna come tell you. I talked to Mr. Davenport, and he explained that his family has a *vraekae*, so--"

"No shit?"

"I know, right?" I wasn't sure I'd ever get over being in awe of that.

"Jesus, who is this guy? I've never heard of a *cyne* who had a *vraekae*. A *dryhten*, sure, but how big is his *holt*?"

"I have no idea." But I was damn sure going to find out.

AN HOUR LATER, Peck was pacing in front of the rest of us; Wade was sitting next to me, slouched in his chair, arms crossed; I was leaning so hard on my fist that if it slipped, I'd hit my head on the table; and Ness was doing that thing where you squint to try to keep things in focus.

"I wanna know how Muscle Guy fits in, and who the girl was that Talmadge got beat up over," Peck informed us. "I mean, I don't know that this has anything to do with the rest of the case, I feel like a lot of things were happening at once, but we still gotta find that guy and the girl he was trying to protect."

"Okay, so how do we find Muscle Guy?" I asked Peck.

"We know he was warning Talmadge about a girl with platinum hair, so maybe we do like Talmadge and check the society pages and see who's got platinum hair."

There were so many dead-ends, but that one actually sounded promising. Bannerman came in and told us that new leads would have to wait until the following day. He was sick of looking at us—and smelling us—and it was time to sleep on it and see what, if anything, we came up with. I was going to argue, but the man's glare was sharp enough to cut glass, and I was too exhausted to be logical.

Driving home, after dropping Wade off, was dicey. I was exhausted and afraid I'd fall asleep at the wheel, so I called Graeme. I could have chosen anyone to talk to during the ride home, but I picked him because, more than needing just any voice on the other end of the line, I wanted to hear his. If I could have driven to his house instead, I would have, but that was—

"Avery," he greeted me, sounding genuinely pleased to hear from me.

The fact that his voice was gruff and deep, like he just woke up, pinballed through my chest, lighting everything up. The whimper escaped before I could even think about stifling the needy sound.

"Where are you?" he wanted to know.

"In the car driving home so I can—were you sleeping?"

The yawn and the sound of stretching was ridiculously sexy. "I was," he rumbled. "I wanted to make sure I was fresh and alert for this evening, since I didn't get much sleep last night, as you well know."

"Yeah" was my brilliant reply.

"Wait, driving home?" He growled at me. "Do you mean

to say you haven't slept? It's almost two in the afternoon, and you haven't slept yet?"

"I'll be fine for tonight. I just—"

"You should pull over and I'll come get you," he apprised me. "I wouldn't want you to fall asleep at the wheel or—"

"Why do you think I called?" I teased him. "And I'm really not that far from home."

"Avery I must insist," he was adamant.

I snorted. "And yet, I'm still driving."

He was silent a moment and I was about to tell him that him not talking wasn't helping anything when he spoke again.

"Wouldn't it be better," he began, speaking softly but with a husky, ragged edge that had all of my attention, "if you drove here to me? Then you could have a bite to eat, shower, and go to bed knowing you could sleep in longer?"

The *driving to him* part sounded so good I had to pull over and give myself a minute to calm down. "Should you have an unbonded omega in your house, though? You're a *cyne*, and I wouldn't want to hurt your reputation or—"

"Avery," he murmured, and I got the feeling he might have known I was a bit susceptible to his voice, captivating as it was. "I have a copy of your signed contract here in the safe in my den, and the original is flying, with a courier of Shivani's choosing, to Bern as we speak, to be placed in my personal vault. My reputation, as well as yours, is above reproach."

My contract was so important to him that he was having it flown to Switzerland? He didn't trust it to the mail? It had to be hand-delivered by someone his *vraekae* had chosen?

"Now, please...come to me."

"But my clothes—"

"As soon as you get here, I'll send Kat to your home to

collect whatever you need. Just leave your keys in your car and—"

"It's not a home; it's just a crappy apartment with—"

"Even more of a reason to *come to me*," he stressed, sounding silky and growly, and the few brain cells that were still functioning shorted out as my dick thickened in response.

"Where do you live?" I barely got out.

My house, or my old house, my parents' house, was impressive. It had six huge bedrooms and thirteen bathrooms, not to mention the garden terrace and the central courtyard, an abundance of natural light, which my mother insisted on—she hated a dark house—and a carriage house in the back where my grandmother had lived before she passed.

Linden's home, which I'd been in a million times over the years, was also impressive. There was an open gallery that spanned the entire first floor so you could look left or right and see everything, like at a museum. It was a huge, wide-open space, and you got an immediate idea of the volume of the home.

Neither house had anything on the place I rolled up to.

Because Graeme's home was in the city, in Lincoln Park, there was no big circular drive out front. Instead, a wrought iron gate blocked unauthorized entrance to the cobblestone driveway. I was about to open my window and lean out to speak into the intercom but noticed the camera, so I waved, and the massive gates opened inward, allowing me to guide my Jeep down the drive to the back of the house.

I wasn't sure where to park, but Graeme was there, standing near the ten-car garage, and raised a hand—as if I'd miss him. I parked where he indicated and took a moment to look at the man before I got out, leaving my keys on the seat before I slammed the door. In his white T-shirt, black lounge pants, and heavy socks, he looked decidedly normal. With his arms crossed, biceps bulging and hair tousled in the wind, all I could see was home. He looked like home to me. It was hard to breathe for a second.

When he gestured instead of meeting me halfway, presumably not wanting to get his socks wet from the rain earlier, I jogged over to him, but stopped when I got close. He looked sort of sleep-rumpled and warm, and my instinct was to lunge, but I resisted. Somehow.

"Avery?" He lifted his arms, beckoning me.

"I haven't showered, and I probably stink, badly, and—"

"Come here," he demanded, and his tone, all alpha, told me not to fuck with him.

I lost it.

Rushing forward, I hit him hard. For other men I'd been with, had in my bed, it would have been too much. Too much exerted power, too much speed, too much raw, clawing desire.

Not Graeme. I didn't move him a fraction, and he absorbed my frantic movement as I writhed against him and tried to get closer, pressing my face to the hollow of his throat, inhaling his scent as my hands slipped up under his T-shirt to his warm, sleek skin.

"Avery," he murmured into my hair, and when I lifted my head, met his gaze, he bent and kissed me.

I wanted to drown in that kiss, and the hand that cupped the back of my head, and the other on the small of my back, were perfect. Coiling my arms around his neck, I hung on as his tongue rubbed over mine, tangled and tasted, sucking and gently biting my bottom lip. His hand fisted in my hair, yanking my head back gently so he could breathe me in, and he slid his other hand down to my ass, fingers sliding over my crease. I bucked forward, my cock hard and, I was embarrassed to admit, leaking in my underwear. When he grabbed hold of my ass with both hands and lifted with those powerful arms, I hopped at the same time, held against him, arms and legs wrapped around him as I mauled his mouth.

He held my thighs tight in his hands as he turned and climbed the steps, like my hundred and seventy-five pounds was nothing. It was impressive, but then, everything about the man was.

I didn't stop kissing him to look around, couldn't have even if I'd wanted to. I was peripherally aware of passing room after room, and while I would have been horrified, under normal circumstances, that I was grinding over the man's abdomen in full view of anyone who might see me, the friction was the only thing allowing me not to howl in desperate, ravenous hunger.

The open door he went through put us in a room that was warm with the lingering scent of cedar and musk. I heard the door slam behind us and thought he must have kicked it shut, but then my brain was entirely too occupied with him falling down onto his bed with me in his arms, pinning me under him before he took a quick gulp of air and kissed me again, to care.

I heard a sound that took me a moment to realize I was its source. It was a whimpering, panting cry, and when he lifted up off me, I growled.

"I know," he soothed me, sitting with his long, muscular legs folded under him, lifting one of my feet, then the other, taking off my sneakers and socks before reaching for my belt.

Pulling the sweater up over my head, I got caught in it

and the T-shirt underneath. His low chuckle should have been embarrassing, but it was so warm, like I was dear.

"I'm stuck," I whined.

"For the moment, yes. Stay there," he ordered, the sexy, seductive rumble in his voice making me arch up off the bed.

He worked open my belt and the button, pulled down my zipper, and I called his name as he yanked my briefs and pants halfway down my thighs.

The air hit my hot cock and made me shiver.

"You're so hard," he almost purred, and he licked the underside of my dick.

"Graeme," I rasped, my breath catching, "please."

He took me down the back of this throat then, sucking hard, and I screamed, rough and hoarse, and tore my arms free from the restraint of my sweater and T-shirt, wrestling them off. I meant to fist my hands in his thick, glossy brown hair and hold him still while I thrust into him, but I ran my fingers through it instead, gentle, savoring the feel of the silky strands on my skin.

My cock slipped free of his lips, and I felt hot tears in the corners of my eyes. He sat up, scrambled off the end of the bed, and reached for my left ankle, pulling off one pantleg, then the other. He took the time to kiss each ankle, reaching up and dragging my underwear down and off before rolling me to my stomach.

I lay there and watched as he went to his nightstand and pulled what looked like a small bottle with a ground-glass stopper from a drawer and came back. He lifted my ass, and I heard the clink of glass striking glass before two fingers were pressed inside of my tight entrance. It should have hurt, had hurt in the past when other lovers had done it without first loosening me or rimming me, but all I felt was good, the consuming ache, the want and need of his kiss, his sweat, his cum. Between my own raging desire and his possessive touch—the way he pushed in deep, twisted his fingers inside of me, and then slid them free only to repeat the motion, over and over until I shoved back against him, aching and begging—I was lost.

"Avery," he growled, and the wide head of his cock notched against my opening, "are you mine?"

"Yes," I cried out, lifting my ass as he pressed inside, filling me, stretching me around his club of a cock, going slow but never once stopping until he was buried to the hilt.

"My mate," he ground out like it hurt, hands on my hips, holding tight, bracing himself as he eased back and then bottomed out again, his moan decadent and filthy.

I hooked my feet around the backs of his thighs, holding on to him as he slid out and in, each time increasing the speed and the depth of the plunge until he was thrusting to my core as he closed his fingers like a vise around my cock.

I shivered hard. The only sound that crawled out of my throat was his name.

"Tell me," my alpha demanded, the sound savage and feral, as though he was on the cusp of his shift.

My alpha.

Mine.

It wasn't just a word anymore. It wasn't a rank that was important to others but not to me, or something that had no real relevance in my life. And it certainly was not a word to be taken for granted or spoken lightly to get what I wanted in the heated rush of passion.

I always tried to be a man first, to bury my wolf under layers of humanity, to fan the fires of logic and reason that kept the animal at bay. But now...my wolf smelled blood when Graeme bit my lip, tasted salt and sweat when I licked it from his skin, and felt the euphoric high when I was manhandled by my mate, my alpha, made to do solely as he desired. I was nothing more than his, and the animal I was reveled in the knowledge that I was safe, forever, in his den.

The man was the only alpha I would ever have, my one-in-a-million shot, and I knew, under my skin, in the blood rushing through my veins, down deep in muscle and bone, as Graham had said, that my wolf would run with his.

"Tell me," he snarled as he turned my head, and his fangs were there, catching on and grazing my skin.

"I'm yours...my alpha."

I expected pain, and it was there, blinding and choking, so overwhelming for a moment I thought I was drowning. Until, in a heartbeat, it rolled into pleasure as my climax roared up my spine when he bit down into the hollow between my shoulder and neck.

Fangs piercing flesh was agony.

The claiming bite of an alpha...*my alpha*...was ecstasy.

"Graeme!"

He was rutting hard, pistoning inside of me, pounding me through my orgasm, claws on my hips, teeth holding me still—his to do with as he pleased, taken and used.

Pumping into me even as cum ran down the inside of my thighs in warm rivulets, he released my throat and lapped at the wound, bathing it in saliva before he took my mouth.

The thrusting was endless and I reveled in the feel of him, of the claiming, of his dominance and my complete submission.

After long moments, he slowed then stopped, kissed me deeply, lifting me to my hands, and then broke the kiss to drape himself over my back.

"What're you doing?" I asked, and heard the gravel in my voice. I had perhaps done more screaming than I thought.

He was panting. "I need a minute."

"Lemme understand," I said gruffly, biting my bottom lip so I wouldn't smile. "You put me on my hands and knees so you could rest on top of me?"

"No," he grumbled. "It's because you're so beautiful, and I'm admiring your––"

"Liar," I accused him softly, chuckling as he rubbed his face in my hair and then slowly, carefully, with a tenderness I hadn't expected, slipped free of my still-clenching channel.

"Do you feel that?"

"I feel your huge dick sliding out of my ass."

"Your muscles are holding on; you want me to stay right there inside."

I grunted. "I know you're very pleased with yourself at the moment, but you need to get off me before I collapse."

Smug male chuckle before he toppled me sideways and scrambled up toward the headboard of his ridiculously huge four-poster bed. It could easily sleep four comfortably.

Sitting up, I stared at him. "Usually have lots of company, do you?"

"Sure, of course—" He snickered. "—orgies every night, are you kidding?"

I scowled, and he laughed at me. "You know, I had no idea you were such an idiot."

"That's because I'm so relieved I put my mark on you, and heard how sweet my name sounded when I was inside of you, that I'm entirely undone."

"You're an ass," I stated flatly.

"Yes," he agreed, far too pleased with himself. "Always have been. But I would point out that whatever I am, I'm yours."

The warmth as he stared at me, as though I was, without

question, the most beautiful thing he'd ever seen, was overwhelming.

"That's enough of that," I groused at him, glancing away, noticing the pitcher of water on the nightstand and getting off the bed to walk around to it. Between not eating or sleeping and the energy I'd just expended, I would have dropped to the floor if my mate hadn't moved so quickly to reach me. Staring up at him, I noted the swirls of amber in the dark mahogany-colored depths of his eyes. "Thank you."

"Ask me for the water next time," he directed, carrying me around the bed and putting me down gently at the head. "I'm dying to take care of you."

"I think that's supposed to be the other way around," I assured him, accepting the glass of ice water he poured me. "I'm supposed to take care of you."

He scoffed. "What you don't know about alphas is a lot. All we want to do is take care of everybody, but more than anyone else, our mates."

The look on his face, the earnestness, ran right through me.

"I know you haven't seen that from me yet, because so far, there's only been the pull of the mating between us."

He was right. What was raging between us up to this point was frantic and urgent, all hunger and heat. Intuitively he knew what I needed, and I was brought back instantly to how dominant he'd been when he had me under him, knowing every button to push, what I craved and longed for. My ass twinged as I gently touched the already healing wound on my neck, and there was an immediate and familiar throb of arousal. I wanted him again.

"But now you bear my mark, and everything inside me that was desperate and anxious feels settled, down deep, and all I want to do is care for you."

I felt the same. Because yes, in his bed, he'd made me his, but more importantly, he was mine. He belonged to me, and that meant how I wanted to be cared for was my choice as well.

Draining my second glass of water, I put it on the nightstand, turned my back on him, and slid under the sheet and heavy comforter, burying my face in his pillow and inhaling deeply.

He was under the covers behind me a moment later, spooning around me, face in my nape, left hand on my hip, his right arm sliding under the pillow. "I know you're tired, but maybe you should eat first and then––"

"I know what I need; I'm a grown-up and everything," I teased him, turning my head so he could not only see his mark but smell the coppery scent of blood drying on the wound.

"Yes, I know that," he rumbled, kissing my shoulder, breathing me in as I arched my back, pressing my ass into his groin before I took hold of his hand and guided him to my already semihard cock. "Avery, you have to rest. I don't want to hurt you."

"If you make me beg, I'll never forgive you," I warned him, my breath catching as he rolled me over to face him.

"No," he murmured, sliding his tongue over my bottom lip before he bit down gently and sucked it into his mouth.

I bucked forward, and he kissed me, his tongue slipping inside at the same time he reached down and took hold of my right thigh. He pulled it over his hip, opening me up so he could angle the head of his cock to my entrance. When he pushed forward he filled me, the lube now mixed with his cum easing the way.

I moaned his name.

Anchoring me to him, he rolled to his back, and I gasped

at being fully seated over him, my ass plastered to his groin. He gripped my thighs tight, and when I took hold of his chest, piercing each beautiful pectoral with claws where my fingernails should have been, he shivered with pleasure. Levering myself up, his dick sliding out of my ass to the tip, I let myself drop, taking all of him before repeating the process, slow lift followed by sinking down over him, again and again until I was riding him hard, my thighs squeezing his hips as I used my claws in his flesh to keep hold of him.

His fist on my cock was more than I could bear. "I'm gonna come all over you," I rasped, rocking into his hips, so close, right there, cresting, feeling the sizzling heat snaking up my spine.

"My mate," he rumbled, wrapping me in his arms as he rolled me to my back.

The feel of him, buried inside of me, bottoming out, my legs lifted, my knees draped over his forearms as he eased back only to shove in deep again, was the end of me.

I howled his name, my orgasm causing my muscles to clamp down around him, milking every inch of his impressive length and girth as he tried to move, to press deeper, harder, even as he bent and took my mouth, swallowing my cries as I came apart under him.

I felt it then, as though my chest burst open and everything I was, all of it, rushed out like a wave and flowed into him. When he broke the kiss, and I saw the amber eyes of his wolf, I felt a tightening, a wrapping, two separate things coiling together and becoming one. All my life I was certain that fated mates, true mates, was not something that would, or could, ever happen to me for the sole reason of being born an omega. But when he bent and bit down into his mark, ejaculating inside of me, his orgasm making him clutch me so tight that breathing became a secondary consideration, I knew I was wrong. My mate was right there, with me, just as I'd always dreamed deep in my secret heart.

A tumbler clicked into place, my heart settled in my chest, and I knew in that moment I would never be alone again. He was mine. I was his. He was my alpha, and I was his mate. The tears were of no consideration.

"I've got you," he soothed me, kissing my eyes. "My mate. I'm here and I've got you."

And for once, I let down my guard and trusted that if I fell, he'd be there to catch me. "Don't ever let me go."

"No, not ever." He crooned the vow before he kissed me.

10

GRAEME

I meant to get up. I needed to get up. But when I lifted off of Avery and slid as carefully as I could from his body, I found that getting out of bed was impossible. I didn't have it in me to leave my mate. I lay there, facing him as he succumbed to sleep, pushing his sweaty hair out of his eyes, utterly transfixed by the sight of his long gold lashes lying on his flushed cheeks.

I'd felt the joining, the cogs whirring into place, that moment my grandfather had told me about, the one Stone had raved about, the moment I'd never believed in. I'd felt the mating. Never in my wildest dreams, in my secret, dark dreams, had I imagined I would find my other half. I had the most ridiculous urge to carve his name on my chest. I also wanted to lick every inch of his skin. And kiss and bite and then lick again.

Reaching for the covers, I pulled the sheet and comforter over us, tucking them around him, feeling the slight chill on his skin and wanting to make sure he stayed warm.

I might have gathered the strength to leave, it was possible, but he scooched into me, nuzzling his face into the hollow of my throat, inhaling deeply and wedging himself into my chest. I had no choice then but to wrap him in my arms and hold him tight.

In the past, other lovers had complained that I crowded them, suffocated them. No one wanted to be clutched close as they slept; it was too much. I had always craved it, though, giving shelter, protection, but no bed partner had ever allowed it. Avery, my mate, my omega, craved the possession, the domination, even in sleep. I heard his contented sigh, and I smiled like an idiot.

"You're perfect," I husked into his hair, rubbing my face in the thick golden mop.

I wasn't sure when I succumbed to sleep.

THE POKING WAS ANNOYING, had been since we were children. He knew I hated it when he tapped incessantly on my temple, and yet he did it anyway. One of these days when I killed Stone and made Gigi a widow, he was going to be sorry that he––

"Why?" I grumbled, opening my right eye—not brave enough to open both—and rolling my head on the pillow so I could see him. The only light in the room came from the gas fireplace he must have turned on when he walked in, and the soft glow from the hurricane lamp on my nightstand.

"It's six in the evening," my brother informed me cheerfully, giving me a nod and a grin for good measure.

He looked good in his navy Prada suit, and I had to wonder where he was off to. "You and Gigi going out?" It was Saturday night, after all, and they had a million friends to field invitations from.

He shook his head, still with the annoying smile, indulgent, like he knew something that I...I—

I jolted hard, which upset Avery, who was sleeping in my arms. He blinked several times, trying, I was sure, to get his bearings, squinting up at my brother.

"Hi," he acknowledged Stone.

"Good evening, Avery," my brother greeted him kindly, smiling at my mate. "I'll wait until you're vertical and dressed to welcome you to the family. But"—he tapped the Omega De Ville Prestige watch I'd bought him for his birthday in August—"it's now five after six, and as your parents and siblings will be here in less than an hour, I thought perhaps you and my brother might want to rise. Greeting people when you reek of cum isn't polite, don't you agree?"

"What?" Avery gasped, turning to me, eyes wide. "I don't even have—oh dear God," he moaned, sitting up and covering his face with his hands.

I growled at my brother, who took a step back in self-preservation, still grinning like he was enjoying all of this immensely, which, of course, he was. "I told Kat to go to Avery's place and––"

"It's all here," Stone informed me, "on his side of the closet, but honestly, shopping is paramount and should be on the top of your to-do list. His wardrobe is a quarter the size of yours, and I can't even begin to calculate how it compares to mine."

Stone was a bit of a clotheshorse, as well as whatever the equivalent was for shoes.

"He also has a cat, did you know?"

"No, I—was it brought along?"

"Of course *it* was brought along," Stone snapped at me. "And it's not an *it*, he's a *he*, and he's here in the suite. Jane had the small sitting room across the hall renovated for his food and litter box, and well, if you ask me, she's going a bit overboard with what she's having done, but far be it from me to--"

"We've never had a pet besides fish." Was all I could think of to say.

"And they don't count, as they don't sleep on the end of the bed."

"I don't mean to be rude," Avery interrupted, "but my folks are on the way, so could you get out so Graeme can show me where my clothes are, and then the shower so I can actually be clean and shaved before my mother shows up?"

"Yes, of course." Stone smirked at me before he walked to the door leading to the outer suite, opened it, and kept walking, heedless of the fluffy white panther he let into my bedroom.

"That's your cat?" I asked Avery, watching as the creature lifted his head, sniffed the air, and then made the oddest trilling noises, almost a grumble, before he quickly crossed the room, leaped gracefully onto the bed, and walked over to Avery.

"Yep," Avery assured me, grinning. "Twenty-eight pounds of pure power."

I'd never seen a bigger housecat in my life.

"Hi, Maxie," he greeted his pet happily, and seeing him calm as the beast got close, then dip his chin as the cat lifted his so they could rub foreheads, made my stomach flutter.

It was ridiculous, but even if the cat hated me—as most animals, horses, dogs, birds did not like alphas—I would allow the creature to live under my roof. Avery and his pet clearly adored each other. "Is it some kind of illegal breed?"

He turned to me as the cat flopped into his lap and

purred loudly, like the engine of a motorboat. "He's a Maine Coon," Avery informed me, petting the cat and scratching behind his ears. "I saved him from a hoarding situation when he was a kitten, like my second or third day as a cop, and he's been with me ever since. He's not much for people, so don't be upset if...he—huh."

The cat rose from Avery's lap, walked the inches between us to me, and climbed into my lap. He was heavier than I thought he would be, but when he made himself comfortable and looked up at me, I was compelled to pet him. His fur was like silk, and when he purred, his eyes narrowing, I glanced over at my mate and saw the delight on his face.

Yes, the cat and I were good. The cat could stay, had to stay, because having his pet here would help Avery to think of my home as his. And who was I kidding before? What I would allow, as though the choices of what came into the house and what stayed were mine alone. Avery was as empowered as I was; he was my mate.

"He likes you," Avery stated happily, leaning sideways to kiss me.

As he slid his hand around the side of my neck, holding me there to prolong the kiss, parting his lips, his tongue slipping inside my mouth to mate with mine, I realized I never, for the rest of my life, wanted to wake up without this man.

Breaking the kiss, Avery leaned back, threw the covers off, and headed toward the door. "Okay," he announced, "come help me find my crap so we can get this show on the road!"

When Avery got off the bed, Max followed him, making the grumbling noise again, and I already missed his company—what that was about, I had no idea.

"No," I heard Avery tell the cat before I scrambled off the

bed to catch up with him, "we're setting new boundaries. You watching me shower has always been creepy as hell, and you know it!"

I couldn't stop smiling as I darted through the suite, naked, after him.

Avery must have said a hundred times how much he loved my shower. I, of course, was thrilled to hear it, and enjoyed watching my mate with his head thrown back, eyes closed, water sluicing over his wide shoulders, broad chest, flat stomach, round ass, and down his long, muscular legs. All the burnished gold skin made me ache to touch.

"Get in," he demanded, and though under different circumstances I would have bristled at being ordered about —no one but my grandfather got away with it—I heard the teasing in Avery's tone, saw the warmth in his eyes, and immediately did as I was told. The fact that he kissed my shoulder on his way out sent a roll of heat through my entire body.

I was already ridiculously attached.

HE WASN'T in the bedroom waiting for me, so I went to check the rest of the suite, the chairs in the reading nook, and I even went out on the balcony overlooking the garden —though why he'd be out there when it was cold was beyond me. He wasn't there.

Leaving my suite, I headed for the stairs at the end of the hall. My home wasn't small. The mansion measured 25,000 square feet, was built on eight city lots, and had luxuries like a media room, a game room, an Olympic-size indoor pool, and a gym and spa. The finery—the chandeliers, curving grand staircase, polished wooden floors with marble inlays, and cavernous vaulted ceilings were merely part of its aesthetic. Scattered about the grounds were ornate fountains, a reflecting pool, and manicured gardens. It was a lovely house, but the cottage I owned in Portree, on the Isle of Skye, in Scotland, was my favorite. It was small, cozy, and quiet. The sea air always soothed me, and I couldn't wait to show it to Avery...if I ever found him again. Where the hell was my mate?

Turning into the great room, a toy mouse flew by me, followed by Max, who looked even bigger in full running mode.

"Oh my God!" Gigi squealed, and I looked around the room until I found her. She was wearing a gorgeous, slinky black strapless Dior gown, and was currently on her knees, on the floor, clapping her hands in glee as Max proudly carried the toy back to her, the mouse's tail hanging out the side of his mouth as though he'd actually killed the neon-colored creature.

"You're going to get white cat hair all over you," I informed her.

She gave me a dismissive wave, tucking an errant auburn curl behind her right ear. Obviously my warning was inconsequential, as evidenced by the praise, and petting, she lavished on Max, who lifted his head so she could scratch under his chin and then tore off in another direction when she threw the toy again.

Shaking my head, I walked by her to the couch where Avery was sitting, sipping a beer from the bottle, of all things, and listening to my brother, who was perched on the coffee table—something I'd never seen him do before—telling some kind of story that involved him waving his arms around like a crazy person.

"...and Graeme is scandalized because not only are our grandparents having sex, but they're doing it in his bed!"

Avery swallowed hard and nearly choked, then burst out laughing, barely able to breathe. Stone was wheezing, laughing so hard he was crying from the memory.

"It wasn't that funny," I commented dryly, which must have been hysterical because they both stopped, looked at me, and lost it again.

Taking a seat beside my mate, I took the bottle from him, set it on a coaster on the coffee table, careful not to get it anywhere near Stone, and put my hand on Avery's denim-clad thigh.

"You know, you were meant to get dressed for dinner," I told him.

He was wearing a white T-shirt under a heavy beige cardigan, soft, faded jeans, and a pair of beaten-up jump boots that should have been thrown out years ago. The man was not at all ready to have a meal with our families.

"I'm so dressed," he assured me, and then gestured with his hand, wanting me closer.

He needed to understand the rules of propriety, that as the head of the household I would not candidly display my feelings for––

"C'mere," he husked, and leaned sideways.

I inhaled sharply, tipping my head so he could reach me, his lips brushing under my jaw, and the sound that crawled out of his throat, a soft, decadent, carnal whine, made me close my eyes and press closer.

"Mr. Davenport," Tomlinson, our family butler, said as he stepped into the room, "may I bring your scotch and water, sir?"

"Yes, please. Thank you, Tomlinson," I told him, and then he turned to my mate.

"Mr. Rhi—er...Avery, would you like another?"

"I shouldn't," he answered with a smile. "I haven't eaten anything. Can I have a giant glass of water instead?"

"Certainly, sir."

"Dude," he replied, shooting my butler a pointed look.

"Certainly," Tomlinson corrected himself and left the room.

I turned to look at my mate.

"What?"

"It should be Mr. Rhine until you officially become a Davenport as well."

Avery scoffed. "Yeah, no, not in this lifetime," he told me, bumping me with his shoulder before he got up to walk to the fireplace, yawning as he stood there.

"He's already made a few changes," Stone apprised me, standing up when I did. "No one is allowed to call him Mister Rhine or address him as sir. He told Francisca she should continue to cook whatever she wants, he won't be taking those decisions from her, though he would like a pizza night, and taco night, and I swear to God I had no idea she could squeal like that."

"Well, of course," I replied, glancing over at Avery, who looked a bit gray all of a sudden. "I mated with an omega, so she was certain her place in the hierarchy would change. She assumed that with the coming of an omega, he would run the household and oversee the staff, and now she knows nothing at all will change."

"Trust me, it's even more than that. She's excited to wake up with him in the mornings and have his coffee ready and make him breakfast, and when he mentioned that once a week he has to take in the morning pastries for all the other detectives and asked her what was good around here, she told him she would, of course, make all manner of delicacies for him to share with everyone he works with."

I grunted.

"Seriously, you would have thought he gave her a million dollars."

I smiled, thinking about our cook, Francisca Sandoval, and all the things the rest of us didn't like, didn't eat and wouldn't try, and how Avery had just given her free rein to create all manner of cuisine for him. I would have to remember to tell her I would become a foodie with him. Whatever he was doing, I wanted to share in.

"Did he speak to Mrs. Roe as well?"

He nodded. "Yes. Your head housekeeper was thrilled when he asked her if it would be all right to change out all your bedding from silk sheets and the goose down comforter to cotton sheets and quilts. He also wants heavy rugs, lots of them, in your bedroom, because the floor is freezing, and he asked her to 'please bring some color into the room.'"

I shook my head. "She's wanted color in my bedroom for years."

"Not that she came out and shared that with you."

"No, of course not," I agreed. "But the look on her face every time she walked in, shaking her head as she glanced at a rug or a chair, made her opinion fairly clear."

Stone snorted. "You know, you could put a stop to any and all of his changes. The only reason they're listening to him is because they think he has the authority to make these decisions, like a typical omega would," he pointed out. "But he should have also discussed anything he wanted altered with you first."

"Do you think I care?" I asked him. "Whatever it takes for him to be happy and comfortable in our room and in our bed, I want done."

"Really?"

"Weren't you the same with Gigi?"

"Gigi's my alpha, I would do anything to make her happy, it's hard-wired in me, and of course, I love--" He stopped himself mid-sentence, and after I realized he wasn't going to say anything more, was instead going to stand there and stare at me like I'd grown another head, I demanded he speak. It took my brother a moment to gather his thoughts. "Are you trying to tell me you love this man?"

I took a breath. "I don't know, but what I do know is that whatever he wants, if it's in my power to give, he'll have it."

Stone clapped me on the shoulder. "Brother, what do you think love is?"

I scowled at him. "What else did he do while I was in the shower?"

"Avery hates dead things. Did you know?"

"He's an omega; they're about life, never death." But even as I spoke the words, I wondered how that worked with Avery being a police officer. He investigated murders; dealing with death was an inevitability. That he might ever get caught in the crossfire and cause someone's death if it meant saving the lives of others was an unthinkable paradox. My mate was a puzzle I might never gather all the pieces of.

"Well, that means all the animal rugs throughout the house, the mounted trophies on the walls, and even the zebra-covered chair in the library, he wants all those gone," Stone continued, not noticing I'd gone quiet.

"Mrs. Roe must be in heaven," I imparted when I realized Stone was looking at me, waiting for some kind of response.

"She hated them when grandfather sent them here from the estate in Edinburgh," he reminded me. "Now your mate has given her a free hand to send them all back, immediately, and handpick items to take their place."

"Avery told her to choose those things without consulting with him first?"

"He asked specifically for antiques and paintings that would remind us of our father, bring him to mind, as it were, and to include whatever our mother had loved."

I sighed deeply. "That's terribly intuitive."

"Agreed," Stone replied, his voice shaky for a moment. "Already, in less than an hour, he's made quite the impression on your staff."

I turned to look at my brother. "What about you and Gigi?"

He gestured to his wife, in couture, sprawled on the floor, stroking the paws of a cat who was purring next to her, allowing her ministrations. "She adores him, she adores his cat. He walked right up and hugged her without permission. Just grabbed her and said he was so happy to have another sister."

I grunted.

"She cried, Graeme. My wife, the dragon lady, cried."

"And you?"

"He hugged me too, and well, he's terribly confident, and he's an omega, and…I can't imagine him not being here with us. I have a picture in my head of the four of us in the library, in front of the great hearth, sprawled out on those overstuffed couches, reading and napping an entire Sunday away." He seemed almost embarrassed by the confession. "It's strange, but I can see it so clearly."

It sounded heavenly, warm and familial. I couldn't speak, surprisingly choked up over my brother's admission, and wrapped my arm around Stone's neck, yanked him close, kissed his temple, and then let him go, so very pleased with him.

"Well now," Stone said hoarsely, clearing his throat. "Spontaneous affection. How very out of character for you."

It took another second for me to find my voice. "I can't help it. He's done something to me."

"To all of us," he rasped. "Such is the power of a true omega."

I turned to look at him. "What do you mean?"

"I don't remember much about our mother," he confessed, "but I do recall she was always so afraid, no confidence at all. Perhaps she feared some horror befalling father, and when it did, and the sky fell down around her, that's why she all but disintegrated. I don't know; I was so young."

"Yes, I remember that feeling." I was finding it difficult, suddenly, to speak around the lump in my throat. "Of being scared. And Dad would always tell me there was nothing to be afraid of, and to go and run."

He nodded. "I think whatever an omega is, either warm and confident and full of life, like Avery, or hesitant and fearful like our mother was, that sort of fills the house because, good or bad, when there's an omega in the home, they set the tone. I suspect that's where a lot of those horrible stories come from where an alpha and their entire family is plunged into ruin." He wasn't usually so thoughtful, and we never spoke about our mother. We were both being introspective. "It's probably not something an omega even does consciously, but is more their innate influence. It's fascinating, really."

It was.

Tomlinson delivered my scotch and water then, and brought a container I mistook for a pitcher at first, except it was covered and had a straw protruding from the top, to Avery. I had no idea that such an item even existed in my home.

"Mr. Davenport, your guests have arrived, sir."

I would have met them where I greeted all my announced visitors, at the entrance to the great room after my staff escorted them in, but I handed my drink to my brother and quickly crossed the room to my mate. When I reached him, I turned him gently to face me, and the wan smile was a concern. Instantly there was a jolt of panic that he was unwell, followed by my understanding of the issue; it was so clear and precise that it took me a moment to realize he hadn't spoken to me.

"You need to eat." I made sure my tone left no room for argument from him.

"I will," he soothed me, stepping close, into me, leaning. "I'm okay."

"You're not," I pronounced, trying for gentle but ending up growling instead. "We're going to the kitchen now."

"I don't want to ruin——"

"You won't ruin anything," I assured him, taking the huge water receptacle from him and passing it to Tomlinson before bending to lift him off his feet and start for the kitchen.

"I'm not helpless," he imparted, bumping his head against mine.

"Yes, I know. You're actually terribly capable, but at the moment you've used all your energy reserves in bed with me, you haven't hydrated enough, and you've had nothing to eat."

He made a noise, like murmured agreement, before his hand slipped around the side of my neck, his thumb sliding back and forth over the ruined left corner of my lips. "If we're gonna live together, you have to promise me some things."

If?

Was he mad?

As though all his clothes weren't already under my roof, as well as his cat. "Tell me what you need promised," I directed instead of explaining to him how he was never getting out of my home. *Our* home.

"I need to make changes to things without asking permission."

As though he hadn't already started. "Of course. It's your home now; you do as you please, as you see fit."

He nodded. "And you can't take it back."

"No, of course not," I assured him, annoyed that he thought I would. "If you make a change, I would never––"

"Not that," he whispered, changing position, turning into me, arms wrapped around my neck, squeezing tight.

I stopped walking, struck by what I thought he was saying to me. "Avery," I husked, rubbing his back, "lift your head and look at me."

Slowly, he eased back until he met my gaze.

"You are my other half; I insist you begin taking me for granted this instant."

My words were ridiculous, because I wanted him to worship me, crave me…love me. But what I wanted was not the important part. What was crucial was that he heard what I said, and that he smiled. The curl of his mouth was heart-stoppingly beautiful, and only then did I admit to myself that Avery Rhine, soon to be Avery Davenport, was my love. I would do anything he asked of me and more, just to see his eyes glow like quicksilver when he looked at me. He had me utterly enthralled, and I had no idea when I'd tripped down the rabbit hole.

"We will be together always; you have my solemn oath."

"Okay, that's it, you promised," he murmured, pressing his lips to mine.

And I would spend the rest of my life proving to him that I meant every word.

He sat at the island in the kitchen and ate some wedges of cheese, broccoli florets dipped in hummus, some crusty bread fresh from the oven, and was utterly dazzled when Francisca produced a fire-roasted artichoke for him.

I stood there, glowering, arms crossed until I finally barked at her. "I know we have cold cuts and leftover roast beef that would give him the protein he––"

She gasped.

Avery turned and looked at me uncertainly, squinting.

"What?" I grumbled at him, because he had me worried that he was going to pass out and die from lack of sustenance. I wanted all his energy back. Him looking peaked had frightened me more than I thought it would.

"Begging your pardon, sir"—Francisca scowled at me—"but you are aware that omegas don't eat meat, are you not?"

I looked at her, then him, then back at her. "I recall my mother sitting at the table and eating with my father," I snapped.

"Of course she would have," she assured me as though I had been sucked back in time and was a four-year-old again. "I've no doubt they took their meals together, but an omega could no more choke down a piece of any animal than you could eat the tires off your car. It's simply not possible. They're vegetarians."

I had no idea, and honestly, it was quite unobservant on my part. But in my defense, I didn't speak to the omegas of friends and acquaintances, and had certainly never noticed what they consumed during a meal. I'd assumed we were all eating the same dishes, partaking in all the same courses.

Avery squinted at me. "Right now you're rationalizing why you didn't know that, aren't you?"

How did he know?

"You don't like to be surprised," he alleged with a rakish grin, "or wrong."

"I——"

"Even eggs," Francisca informed me. "They don't eat them. I made this egg-free bread special for him, and I ordered a second set of utensils and pots and pans today, and another cabinet to go inside the pantry so there will be no cross-contamination during the preparation."

"I appreciate that," Avery told her, smiling.

"And I appreciate your mother's cook, Corvina, calling to give me some wonderful tips and insights."

"Tofu tacos sound gross, but I swear they're delicious," he assured her.

"I look forward to making them for you. And of course, pizza is easily done."

"I'm sure Corvie was a bit bossy on the phone; I apologize on her behalf."

"No, she was quite lovely. As I said, I enjoyed our chat, as well as her explaining that you're a bit of a handful."

"She lies a lot," he assured her.

I had never seen my cook, the woman I saw day in and day out, smile so fondly at another living person, other than her own children, who were both away at college. She hadn't known him an hour yet, and it was clear she already adored him. That's how it worked with omegas, though, that influence Stone and I were speaking of earlier, and Francisca was a beta, so she was susceptible to his charm. But still, it was something uniquely him too. I had no idea how every alpha who'd crossed his path before me had not demanded his contract immediately. What was even more amazing were those he'd slept with who, afterward, had allowed him to walk out of their lives. I was both overwhelmed with gratitude and homicidal at the same time. I wanted to kill every alpha who'd been with him, taken him for granted, treated him cheaply, and cast him aside. Though, for all I knew, Avery had been the one to walk away, since he'd tried to do that with me.

"There you are," Mrs. Huntington, Avery's mother, announced as she came into the room, rushing over to her son, who turned on his stool to open his arms.

She was there instantly, wrapping him up, hugging him tight, kissing his cheek before giving him one last squeeze and then stepping back.

"An early feast?" she teased him.

He groaned. "I missed a couple meals today."

"Avery," she gasped, glancing at Francisca, "how dare you not allow Francisca to take care of you. How thoughtless and rude."

"Begging your pardon, ma'am," Francisca chimed in, eyes on me, "it was the earl who did not bring your son immediately to the kitchen to be fed, nor did he call for a meal before you arrived."

Mrs. Huntington slowly turned to me until those eyes, eerily like her son's but darker, scarier, were looking through me. "I'm sure you know that omegas must eat on schedule, Mr. Davenport. Like clockwork. As a police officer, his meals are, of course, sporadic sometimes, but the moment he walks into this house, sir, I'm certain that you'll direct your staff to feed and water him as though he were the rarest of creatures, in need of constant care."

She was lecturing me while being quite careful not to appear to be doing so at the same time. It was impressively done.

I glanced at Francisca, then back at my mate's mother, then at him. His smile, all teeth, guilty and sheepish, let me know that yes, he'd screwed up, and yes, he was going to let me be thrown right under the bus of his mother's displeasure.

"I will endeavor to do better, madam," I promised, giving her a slight bow.

She didn't appear impressed.

11

AVERY

After I ate my before-dinner snack and my blood sugar balanced out, I felt better, stronger, and having slept, my mind returned immediately to the case. While I'd always raged against the machine that ran the lives of omegas, it was nice now that I was being ignored in the wedding preparations because, at the moment, I was trying to work through something in my head. There was a piece I was missing, and I had the weirdest feeling it was right in front of my face.

"Avery."

I turned quickly to my father, who'd spoken. "Yessir?"

"What do you think of next month? A December wedding, before the holidays?"

"I think that's too far away," I answered, looking across the table at Graeme, sitting between his brother and mine. "Don't you agree?"

"I do," Graeme murmured, and those warm mahogany eyes of his almost glowed as he stared at me. The laugh lines crinkling in the corners made my pulse quicken. The man had a strange effect on me, carnal and debauched and sheltering and grounding all at the same time. I wanted to fuck him and talk to him, have him hold me down and hold my hand in equal measure. It would be so wonderful if everyone went home.

"A Thanksgiving wedding, then," my mother suggested. "With a harvest theme, all gold and orange and wine."

"Yes, please," I baited her, "lots of wine."

I got pelted with olives and peas, and Graeme and Stone and Gigi were stunned at my family's behavior. They were also surprised when they arrived not in suits and ties, pantsuits or dresses, but just as I was, in clothes for relaxation. Or, more precisely, their individual versions of dressing down. My father looked good in his layers, a dark brown herringbone wool blazer and matching waistcoat, a denim shirt, vintage jeans, and tan wingtips. The newsboy cap was a final flourish, and I saw how my mother kept eyeing him and knew he'd worn it for her benefit. She loved him in hats.

My mother was in black trousers and a white dress shirt and shiny black lace-ups. Ambrose had on a sport coat over a dress shirt and jeans, his polished Chelsea boots catching the light when he took a seat on the couch. His wife was in chunky boots and leggings and a long off-the-shoulder sweater. Andrea looked good in four-inch leopard print heels that Gigi loved, and ankle jeans and a sweater that was as old as my cardigan. Her husband was in chinos and a cashmere sweater over a dress shirt, tucked and belted.

They all looked nice, comfy, while Graeme and his family looked like they were entertaining clients and brokering some high-powered deal.

"I wanted them to know how important this dinner was for me and my family," Graeme explained to me as we stood together in a corner. "But now they must think that we're all terribly pretentious, with Stone and I in suits and ties and Gigi in her couture."

I tipped my head at my father. "He likes to wear all those layers because my mom thinks he's hot," I teased my mate, who looked at me in absolute horror. "So when he gets a chance, he does. That's how he looks when they go out antiquing."

"Why are you telling me this?"

Leaning against him, he put his arm around my shoulders, tucking me into his side. "Because you don't ever have to impress them; they're your family now, and if you were in those lounge pants and T-shirt you had on when I showed up this afternoon, that would have been fine."

"I would never entertain in such casual attire," he informed me, sounding almost affronted. "What does that convey to one's guests?"

"To them, to my family, who are now yours as well, it says that you're comfortable with them because we're all just hanging out," I assured him with a snicker. "But that's not you, and that's okay. You're comfortable having dinner dressed in your suit and tie, but just know for next time that if you wanted to wear some jeans and a sweatshirt, that'd be okay too."

When he didn't say anything for a moment, I looked up at his face.

"I don't own either of those items," he deadpanned, the concern on his face evident.

I laughed and turned into him, wrapping my arms around his waist and squeezing tight.

At dinner, Ambrose told me about how upset Graeme was the night of the gathering, and how Graeme had lifted him off his feet and held him on the wall. "I knew then, he was crazy about you," he told the table, lifting his glass.

"Welcome to the family, Graeme, Stone, and Gigi. We're so happy to have you."

I was proud of my brother and got up and went around the table to hug him. He groaned like I was killing him, and everyone laughed.

Later, as was tradition, I showed everyone my mark, and they all took turns kissing it to give Graeme and I their blessing.

Because the wedding was still a couple weeks away, Graeme would host a party to announce our union the following Friday, but since the contract was signed, his house was now mine, and we were, per lupine law, bonded. He had a ring that resembled a signet but was more crudely fashioned, gold, chunky and heavy, an ancient piece made by hand, not from a mold, passed down through his family for generations. His father had worn it most recently, before it was placed in a safe and locked away. But it was Graeme's to bestow, and he wanted me to wear it, starting now, and so slid it onto the middle finger of my left hand, holding a spot there until the wedding, when he would give me a band of his own design. Everyone clapped when he lifted my chin and kissed me.

They wanted to see the house then, so Stone and Gigi, excited to share their home, our home—I had to get used to saying that—took my family on a tour, all except my mother, who stayed with me. She took me aside when Graeme excused himself to make a call, held my hands tight, and looked up into my eyes.

"Are you truly happy?"

Of course she would check. She was my mother. "Yeah," I told her, smiling. "You can't tell, 'cause you don't know him yet, but he's good. Like, down deep, all the way through. I know it in my heart," I whispered. "He's strong, and not just as an alpha or a *cyne*, but as a man. He's not gonna let me get away with anything, but he's not going to try and change me either." She nodded instead of crying, and I let go of her hands and eased her into my arms. "He's gonna love me someday, I know it. I can feel it."

"Foolish child," she chided me, kissing my cheek. "He loves you now."

"No, not yet. You wanna think so 'cause you're a romantic and—"

"He never takes his eyes off you," she interrupted before she took a step back to gaze up at my face. "He touches you constantly. It was physically difficult for him to sit across from you at dinner, and while you were staring at his father's ring when he put it on your finger, I was looking at him. The pride on that man's face nearly made me cry," she said, pulling a handkerchief from the pocket of her trousers and dabbing at her red, puffy eyes. "And my goodness, he's all but drowned you in his pheromones. I can barely find your woodsy scent under his."

Scent. Pheromones. Her puffy eyes. Something I should know.

"What?" I asked after a moment, trying to figure something out, thinking I needed to keep her talking. "Mom?"

"Your scent, love," she reiterated. "I can usually smell you easily. I can pick out all my kids, but not right now, which is, you know, normal. Once everyone knows that you belong to him, he'll stop pumping out those pheromones. It's a natural part of the process of mating."

"Yes," I agreed quickly, the spark in the darkness becoming clear. "Mom, I have a huge favor to ask."

Her eyes narrowed. "Of course."

. . .

I FOUND Graeme in his office, and even though I needed him to come with me, I couldn't help but take a moment to admire the way the cut of his suit accentuated his broad shoulders, narrow waist, and long legs. Even from across the room, I could feel the strength and power radiating off the man. He was breathtaking.

Standing near the double doors that led out onto yet another private balcony, he was framed in moonlight, and when he saw my reflection in the glass, he turned to look at me.

"I wanted to give you and your mother some privacy before I returned."

"Which is great, and thank you, but so ya know, she's crazy about you."

His eyebrows lifted. "Is she?"

"Yeah, my whole family is."

He crossed his arms as he gazed at me. "Your *whole* family?"

"Yep. Everyone. Especially me."

"Especially you?"

"Listen," I rushed out, because even though I wanted to stand there and flirt with him, I didn't have time. "The second we get home, I would love to come back into this room and have you fuck me against the glass door, but right now I need your nose."

Instant scowl. "You say the most confusing things at times, are you aware?"

"This won't be the most confusing, promise, but will you come with me please?"

"Of course," he agreed, striding toward me. "Let me call Izzy, and I'll have her bring––"

"No. I got it covered. My Jeep's right outside."

"You can't be serious," he deadpanned, looking horrified.

"C'mon, it'll be great. It'll be an adventure."

"And that's a good thing?"

Ten minutes later, I was thinking he might not be enjoying how fast I drove and took corners in the city. The deduction came from the fact that he had one hand on the dashboard and the other on the Jesus handle as I navigated us back to his cousin Remy's house in Highland Park. For most of the ride, he remained silent, unable, it seemed, when he felt his life was in peril, to banter with me. Finally, when we were almost there, he took a deep breath.

"Explain," he ordered, white knuckling the door handle as I took a tight corner. "For the love of—you're going to roll us."

"You're very preoccupied with my driving."

"Because I'd like to live long enough to marry you."

I scoffed. "You're not gonna die, and I'm not gonna flip my Jeep. The only car I've ever rolled was Ambrose's Porsche, and technically, it was more a jump than a roll anyway, since it landed in a tree."

It took a second. "Pardon me?"

"It's a long—see, it was a small tree, and there was a ramp, but that's not important," I explained. "The takeaway is that I lived, and so did Ambrose, so yanno, it's fine."

Slight whimper from him. "Who generally drives, you or Detective Massey?"

"We take turns."

"You lie," he accused me as I rolled to a stop in Remy's driveway. "He drives. I bet he even drives your car, doesn't he?"

I grunted and got out, not bothering to lock it, and walked around the front to wait for Graeme. "Can you hurry up?"

It took him a moment to stop clutching things, another

to unfold his long legs from the passenger seat, and he was a bit unsteady when he was finally on his feet beside my car. "I do believe I may very well vomit," he informed me, and I had to admit he did look a little green around the gills.

"I don't know anyone who can sound so imperious as they announce they're gonna spew in the driveway."

"As if I would void the contents of my stomach in a driveway," he snapped at me. "I would have the decency to do so in the bushes."

The man being flustered was crazy hot. He was so proper and polished and dignified, and here he was glowering at me and getting defensive about where he was going to puke. I could fall so unbelievably hard for him.

Rushing over, I took hold of the lapels of his Ralph Lauren Purple Label double-faced cashmere topcoat, lifted up on my toes, and kissed him.

It was quick, but I made sure he felt it, and he licked his lips when I broke the kiss to stare up into his eyes.

"That was awfully brave of you," he commented drolly.

"Yeah, well, I figured you weren't quite *that* nauseous."

He grunted, and I smiled, grabbed his hand, and tugged him after me toward the front door. Once there, I tore off the police tape, knowing at this point it was fully processed and the house had been cleared for Remy, or Remy and his vordr as it were, to retake possession. Opening the door, I pulled Graeme along behind me and headed directly for the living room, stopping for a moment to let my eyes adjust to the dark, as lupine eyes did.

"Tell me what we're doing here," he demanded, but gently, not letting go of my hand.

"There were a ton of smells in here, you remember?"

"Pardon?"

"The night of the murder," I reminded him, turning so

we were facing each other.

"You mean the omegas."

"Yeah. All their scents, piled on top of each other, made your eyes itchy like you were having an allergy attack."

He nodded.

"When you told me about all the smells messing with your nose, I thought it was from the party. Now I realize your senses were overwhelmed because Talmadge had all the omegas in and out of here, and I'm wondering, because you're an alpha, and even more so, a *cyne*, could you have deciphered individual scents?"

"Of course," he assured me.

"Yeah, see, that's what I thought." I squeezed his hand, excited to share this with him. "Graeme, pheromones can hang in the air a couple days, sometimes longer. It's one of the easy ways wolves can tell if they're being cheated on."

He squinted at me. "That's true, but why are we discussing—ah," he gasped in understanding. "You want me to walk around and see if I can pick up any lingering scents of people I might have met."

"Yes," I told him, pleased that he'd figured it out so quickly. Giving his hand a final squeeze, I let go and pulled out my phone, ready to take notes as he started moving around the living room.

There were smells he picked up—fresh peaches, the seashore, newly-mown grass—and, of course, all the chemicals—luminol and dusting powder, the coppery smell of blood and ozone from a camera flash. But there was nothing he could pick out specifically that triggered any memory in him or, through his description, in me.

We made our way to the bedroom where we'd talked and shared a kiss, and when I turned for the door, he was there, blocking my path.

"What're you doing?"

"I've failed you, and I'm sorry."

"You didn't fail me; it was a longshot."

He cupped my cheek, his thumb sliding over my chin before he tilted my head up so he could lean in close and kiss me.

I opened for him, just as I had that night, but instead of claiming my mouth he stepped back, taking rough hold of my biceps. "Graeme?"

"Your friend," he gasped, "the blond. The one who stood in line to meet me."

"Yeah? Bridget. What about her?"

"Her pheromones," he began, releasing his grip on me, rubbing my arms for a moment before letting go. "They smell like strawberries and vanilla and caramel. I remember distinctly because, as I told you, I didn't want to breathe hers in the night of the party and lose yours."

"Sure."

"Her scent was here that night; I can recall that with absolute clarity."

"But that doesn't make any sense," I apprised him. "Bridget doesn't need to be put into a mock heat; she's got suitors lined up for miles. Maybe you just picked up the scent here because you were carrying it in your nose."

He shook his head. "No. That's not possible because, not to be crude, but you and I--"

"Don't remind me. I'm sure my mother's holding on to the 'you screwed my son in the laundry room' card so she can play it when she wants something."

"These things only matter if the omega is not offered for. As I was not leaving that house without your contract in my hand, any and all breaches of protocol are forgiven."

"Not to her," I assured him. "You'll see. It's gonna be…

be...wait," I mumbled, working through what I just now figured out. "Shit."

"What?"

"You couldn't have carried Bridget's scent because we had sex in the laundry room."

He scowled at me. "Isn't that what I just said? I feel as though that was me who postulated––"

"So effectively, your palate was clean because you only had *my* scent on you after the laundry room, but when you smelled Bridget here that night, that would have to be fresh."

"Yes, I'm aware," he deadpanned, like I was restating facts for no good reason.

"I know Bridget was never here, but she wouldn't have to be," I acknowledged, turning to smile at him. "Because my platinum blond friend has a little sister."

I FELT BAD FOR WADE. It was a lot to have thrown at him since I woke him from a dead sleep when I used my key, unlocked the front door of his apartment, and turned off the alarm. He was confused when I made him wash his face and brush his teeth, change into a T-shirt and sweater, jeans and hiking boots, grab his gun, and follow me out into the cold. Graeme in the driver's seat as I slid into the passenger side, was hard to wrap his brain around. We stopped and got coffee at a diner close to his house, and I found out that Graeme drank tea, not coffee, and the discovery was endearing for no good reason other than it was his preference. I leaned sideways and kissed his cheek.

"What the fuck is going on?" Wade yelled, and it was loud in the interior of the car.

I opened my mouth to say something, but Graeme interrupted, glancing at Wade in the rearview mirror.

"He wanted to tell you," Graeme revealed to Wade, "but my preference was to wait. I apologize for that, but I'm a very private person. I didn't realize, until Avery explained it to me, how important you are in his life. Not just his work partner, but his best friend as well."

Wade nodded, holding Graeme's stare.

"Avery and I are to be married on Thanksgiving weekend."

"And how long've you guys been seeing each other?"

I cleared my throat. "That's not how it works for wolves. When you find your mate, that's it, you're done. It goes from zero to sixty in a day, or a night, or merely hours."

Wade huffed out a breath. "That seems crazy to me."

"But it's exceedingly normal for lupines," Graeme assured him.

"Huh."

"Hey."

Wade switched his focus to me as I turned around in my seat to face him. "I'd really like you to be my best man, if you would."

He crossed his arms, scowling. "Of course I'll be your best man. Who the hell else would you even ask?"

I nodded. "No one."

"That's right, no one," he grumbled, and then met Graeme's eyes again in the rearview mirror. "I need you to be okay going on double dates, 'cause I'm still looking for *my* mate."

"I will be more than happy to accompany Avery on double dates with you and however many women there turn out to be."

"That's the spirit." Wade smiled finally, pleased, it seemed, to be locking that part down. "It'll be fun."

"And I have private tables at many restaurants," Graeme added. "So even a last-minute rendezvous will still see us dining in style."

Wade glanced at me and smirked. "This is going be very good for my rep."

I groaned loudly.

"So how does it work for the stag party? Do you guys both come?"

I chuckled. "I like that you have your priorities in order."

"Well yeah," he grumbled, leaning forward to grip Graeme's shoulder. "You're a lucky guy. Avery Rhine is the best man I know."

Graeme giving Wade's hand a quick pat made me warm with happiness. For so long, the two halves of my life ran concurrently, but they never, ever, mingled. I was a cop, a friend, a colleague, and a human. Conversely, I was an omega, a son, a brother, and a wolf. I was both parts at the same time, but I had kept them separate and distinct, always, never trusting anyone enough, on either side, to fully accept the other. But now, having accepted that I did, in fact, want to be mated to Graeme, wanted to be loved by him, it seemed that both sides could finally function together and become one. I could become me.

Graeme was my bridge. A supportive mate who didn't want to change me, who would take me as I was, as a police detective, as an equal, was the only one who could work in my life, and somehow, defying all odds, I'd found him.

I wished I could somehow make the evening go quicker so I could get back to our room, to our bed, and tell him what it meant to me to have found the one man who had no desire to remake me or strip me of my freedom. I wanted to tell Graeme what a blessing and a gift he was.

I couldn't wait.

12

GRAEME

As a *cyne*, there were things I had the authority to do. For example, I could demand, by virtue of my title alone, that another alpha make any member of their *holt*—or if there was no *holt*, then their family—accessible to me. Only a *cyne* of equal power, with the same wealth and resources, could decline my request. As Jerome Mills, Bridget's father, was merely an alpha, I appeared at his front door with Wade and Avery and demanded an audience with his children, as was my right.

Detective Massey, who insisted I call him Wade, was amazed that Mr. Mills could neither turn us away nor demand that we return in possession of a warrant. He was, however, within his rights to remain during the questioning, though he was not permitted to interrupt or interfere in the interview.

After both women dressed, they came into the library to speak with us. When Mr. Mills declined his right to stay, to listen and offer emotional support to his first-born daughter, Bridget, and his second-born, Saoirse, both omegas, I was appalled.

"What the hell?" Wade asked the man's retreating back as he closed the library door, leaving us alone with them. "Don't they need a chaperone or something?"

"I appreciate your concern for my reputation, Detective," Bridget told Wade, smiling at him sadly, "but the fact is, if Mr. Davenport were inappropriate with either my sister or myself, that would be a boon for my father, as not just an alpha, but a *cyne*, would have to offer for our contracts."

Wade moved to sit down in front of Bridget on a heavy, ornately carved coffee table. "I think that's messed up, Miss Mills."

"Bridget, please."

"Bridget," he repeated. "Could you please tell us——"

"If you would hold that thought one moment, Detective," she imparted sweetly before she grabbed one of the throw pillows beside her and flung it at Avery's head. "We're friends, you asshole!" Bridget snarled at my mate, rising and quickly slipping around Wade, closing the distance between herself and Avery, lifting her hand as though to strike him.

I was about to interfere.

"You hit me, and I will hit you right fuckin' back," he snapped at Bridget, crossing his arms, glowering at her. "And you know I will."

She crossed her arms, mirroring him, staring daggers.

He pointed at Saoirse. "Nice dye job."

Bridget's eyes widened in the anger I could feel rippling around her. "You think that was my idea?"

Saoirse screamed then, standing up, hands clenched into fists, stomping around Wade as well, moving behind the couch so she could pace, and shrieked at my mate, "Avery, it's my turn!"

"Sit your ass down," Bridget demanded, spinning to face

Saoirse but not moving away from Avery. "This is all your fault!"

Saoirse lifted her fists and screamed again, whipping around the couch, ready to charge over to her sister.

"You will sit. Now," I commanded, compelling her with the strength in my voice and releasing just a trace of my pheromones.

Saoirse dropped into the closest chair, the one near the end of the coffee table, shivering with rage over her inability to defy me, her wolf submitting to my rank and power.

"What the hell?" Wade breathed out, glancing at Avery, who gave him a slight shake of his head.

"It's fine," Avery promised his partner before retuning his attention to Bridget. "You need to come clean right fuckin' now so I can protect you."

She pressed her lips together tight, as though she wanted to talk to him but was afraid to. She was visibly forcing herself to hold in the words she wanted to share.

"Listen to me," he urged her, "I know, sure as I'm standing here, that you have never gone to an alpha to have them put you in a mock heat, so what the hell, Bridge?"

She opened her mouth, then closed it, and then opened it again, like a fish gulping for air on dry land.

"It's not fair!" Saoirse cried, clearly distraught as she hid her face in her hands and began to sob. "It's my turn, Avery. You know it is. It's time, and it's not fair, and I'm sick of it!"

Wade stood up and looked, amazingly, to me and not Avery for answers. "Catch me up, please. He's total shit at explaining anything lupine related."

I cleared my throat. "When there is more than one unbonded omega in a family, the firstborn must secure a bonding before the second, or subsequent children, may do so."

Wade thought a moment. "So Bridget has to get married before Saoirse can."

"Yes." There was no reason to correct him, to clarify that omegas didn't get married, they were bonded...though here was Avery, for whom that rule did not apply.

"So your sister wanted to jump the line," Wade stated as he crossed the room to stand in front of Bridget, "and she was gonna do it by having Remy Talmadge put her into a fake heat."

"Yes," Bridget rasped, her eyes filling as she stared at the detective, reaching for him before she could stop herself.

He took her hand in both of his and stared into her welling eyes. "Tell us what you did," he prodded her gently.

Quick shuddering breath. "I sent my bodyguard to put the fear of God into Remy Talmadge, and to make sure he stayed away from any girls with platinum hair."

Wade eased her closer to him, glancing at Avery, who was nodding. The pieces came together quickly after that.

Lucas Grant, Bridget's loyal bodyguard, whom I had never met—but was assured by both Avery and Bridget was built like a brick wall—was the man bouncing my cousin off the sidewalk. He had delivered Bridget's threat with his fists, and on the night of the murder, had gone with Bridget to Remy's house to look for Saoirse after Bridget received a call from her mother reporting that her youngest had snuck out.

Lucas finished with Remy, grabbed Saoirse, her platinum curls dyed black, threw her over his shoulder, and carried her to the car, where he stuffed her into the back seat with her sister. The two of them had screamed at each other all the way home, and then Lucas had locked Saoirse in her room before he spent the rest of the night calming Bridget down.

"There's surveillance footage of our house you can look

at," Bridget informed Wade. "And it's all time-stamped. Our neighbors have cameras too, if you need more evidence, but none of us killed Trent Highmore. We had no reason to. Saoirse never got in the house, I had no idea Highmore was even there, and I can promise you Lucas didn't either."

"Where is Lucas?" Avery asked her.

She made a tsking noise of disapproval. "He needed a little extra cash this month to cover his brother Ray's gambling debts, so he's providing security at a sampling party downtown."

When Avery turned to look at his partner, probably to explain what that was, he must have noticed my disgusted expression. "Find sampling parties morally reprehensible, do you?" he baited me.

"Perhaps instead of trying to get a rise out of me, you might want to illuminate what a sampling party is for your partner."

I got a grunt before he turned to Wade. "Some omegas who debuted two or more years ago attend sampling parties, sex parties for alphas where everyone's allowed to screw without benefit of a contractual obligation."

"Wait now," Wade growled. "We were talking about this yesterday, or whenever the fuck it was at this point, and you said that an omega can't have sex with an alpha unless the alpha signs a contract first."

"That's the law, yes," Avery explained.

"Then what?"

"Between two consenting people, in secret, in a private setting, the law can be broken," I summed up.

Wade gestured at me. "Which I get, but a sampling party is a lot of people, in a lot of rooms, with, I assume, private security, so how does that even work?"

"It's by invitation only, so they have a head count and

then hire however many people they need, based on that number."

"You should go to those," Saoirse yelled at her sister, banging her fist on the arm of the chair. "You should go and whore yourself out and secure a fucking match!"

"Saoirse," Avery began, trying to soothe her. "You don't mean what you're––"

"She's been out twelve fucking years, Avery! How has she not made a match in *twelve fucking years*?"

I thought about Avery, who was thirty-two now, who had made his debut two years before Bridget, and his friend Linden, who I suspected was the same age as Avery. The richer, more beautiful, more desirable the omega, the longer it seemed to take to find a perfect match, as many of their families wanted to wait and see if there was a wealthier alpha just around the corner. Some were bonded quickly, of course. I'd seen beautiful male and female omegas debut at eighteen and bond in their first year.

Over the years, though, I'd seen a change. Alphas were waiting longer and longer to bond with omegas if they didn't find a true mate in a beta or gamma. Some, like me, were pushed to attend the parties because of our place in lupine society. It was necessary to produce an heir, to find an omega to make a home. But for non-*cynes* or alphas who weren't heads of extended families, those who were enjoying living their lives and being young and free, there was no hurry. As a result, more and more omegas were struggling. Many didn't have families who could support them indefinitely, so were thrown out into the workplace or, worse, the street, with no skills, as they'd been raised solely to be parents and homemakers. Of the lupines who were sex workers, the largest percentage of them were omegas who'd never been bonded.

The practice of parents raising their kids to be a certain way and then punishing them for turning out in that exact manner, had always been egregious in my eyes. Why weren't parents held responsible for that? Why wasn't there a penalty for parental ineptitude and failure to produce a "desirable" omega? Of course, the answer was simple. Money. Parents put into the omega the resources at their disposal, as the payoff when their child bonded could potentially be doubled. How could it be their fault if their child was not as beautiful as others, or as polished or poised? Was it the fault of the parents if the omega was an introvert and therefore not able to banter or engage in witty repartee? The problem was that nothing could be changed until laws were passed in regard to omega freedoms, education, and most of all, bonding. They had to be given the same rights as alphas, betas, and gammas, but until the council could be swayed, it was difficult to imagine a change. Perhaps them seeing my marriage to Avery, my mating instead of a bonding, would help. I could only hope so.

"It's not fair that just because no one wants her I'm not allowed to attend the gatherings to see if I could find an alpha of my own!" Saoirse's raving drew me from my thoughts.

"Saoirse--"

"I want to run a household," she choked out, shaking as she stared at Avery. "I want to have children and anything and everything else my heart desires, but because of *her*," she railed, and I could hear the hatred in her voice, poisoning every syllable, "I'm getting older and older while all the omegas my age, who I went to finishing school with, are already bonded. And soon I won't be able to compete with the new debutantes."

"Saoirse—"

"They're all so young and pretty. I see their pictures in the paper, and I don't even get to go to the parties and meet the girls taking away my dream."

"Listen," Avery advised her, "simple omegas, poor ones, those not as beautiful as your sister, some of them mate early, quickly, because their parents are so relieved that someone wants them they're willing to undervalue their contracts. Others jump at the first offer because what if, for whatever reason, they never get another one? You know that's how it works."

"Yes, but—"

"Those like your sister and you, cultured and educated, it can take years to make the right match. You know as well as I do that it's not Bridget's decision who she bonds with, it's your father's. If you want to be mad at someone, it should be him, not your sister."

"But he asks her," Saoirse revealed to Avery. "Our father goes through the offers with Bridget, and I hear her turn them down. It's obscene, Avery. She's not young anymore; she can't hope to compete with women my age and younger. She's past her prime, the bloom is off the rose, and she needs to accept an offer and settle."

Bridget's inhale was sharp. The scream that followed was ear-piercing. "You catty little bitch, how dare—"

"Your father would never allow that," Avery declared, cutting Bridget off and trying, I could tell, to get Saoirse to hear him and understand. "She's worth far too much to him."

I knew, of course, that Avery meant worth, as in love and caring, but the reality was, monetarily, Bridget was her father's most valuable asset.

"But it's my turn!" she screamed, picking up a glass wolf

from the table and hurling it across the room, where it fractured into a million pieces, each prism catching the light from the fire and projecting a chaotic rainbow of colors on the wall.

"You should call someone to clean that up," I suggested to Bridget.

She rushed to the door of the library, pulling her oversized sweater around her, and threw it open, charging out into the hall.

"No more outbursts," I warned Saoirse.

She nodded quickly.

Wade moved over near me, and when he spoke, it was low so Saoirse couldn't hear. "So even though you're not her alpha, she's just gonna listen to you?"

I tipped my head close to him. "I'm a *cyne*. I sit on the *Maion* council. There are only twelve of us here in the US. If she were to question my authority, I could annex her family, and all their assets would be forfeited to my *holt* for me to do with and invest as I see fit."

"What you're telling me is you're kind of a big deal."

"In some circles," I replied, "yes, I am."

He grunted. "For the record, I don't care who you are. If you don't make Avery happy, I'll figure out a way to make sure you aren't either."

"And I appreciate that, but rest assured, you'll never have cause to make good on that threat. I promise you."

He offered me his hand then, and we shook on our mutual love for Avery Rhine as the man himself squatted down beside Saoirse's chair, talking to her, soothing her. Even though I doubted it would help—she seemed furious at her sister, and I couldn't imagine that dissipating anytime soon—it was kind of him to try.

Avery asked Bridget, as soon as she returned with a

maid, if she'd seen Imogen Lowell when she was waiting for her sister and Lucas in the car.

"I'm not sure who that is," she informed him. "Why?"

"Just checking," he replied, not wanting to give anything away before returning his focus to Saoirse. "How about you? Did you see her?"

"I'm not sure who that is either," she reported, "but I think I saw a girl for a second before Lucas slung me over his shoulder. I mean, if anyone saw her, it was him."

"Okay," Avery acknowledged, standing from his crouch and walking a few steps away from the two women as Wade left me to join him.

Bridget slipped in beside me the second I was alone. "It's so kind of you to help Avery with his investigation," she admitted, putting her hand on my forearm as she gazed up into my eyes. "Where would he be without your gracious assistance?"

"Well," I replied, unable to keep the evil grin off my face, "you help your mate at any given opportunity, do you not?"

It took a second for my words to filter through, but when they did, her breath caught, her eyes went round, and her mouth dropped open.

"And yes," I husked, staring at the man as Saoirse leaned forward, pressed her face down into his shoulder, and sobbed, "I meant mate; I wasn't being fanciful or overly romantic. He was made for me, which is why he never made sense for anyone else."

Her eyes filled instantly. "I truly, truly…could not be happier for him. He's always been the best of us, and, my dear earl, may I say with absolute conviction that the cavernous scar across your face makes my stomach roil, but Avery's first words on the subject was that it didn't matter.

He easily saw past what made me, and I'm certain many others, physically ill."

It was an impressive comment, first praise for Avery and then a dig at how she found my appearance so horrifying as to make her sick. As if what she thought about Avery or I mattered in the least. The reality was that many would have accepted my suit, even her, based solely on my financial portfolio. Avery didn't care. He had his own job and a wonderful family for backup. What he did care about was me. The way he looked at me, responded to me, touched me, ached for me told me everything I needed to know. To most, I was repugnant. I'd been judgmental and cold before the accident, "difficult to get to know," people reported to my grandfather, both aloof and conceited. After the accident, many said the outside mirrored the inside, and finally everyone could see that. The only problem with writing me off was that I was worth so much damn money. Certainly a hideous countenance and an abrasive personality could be overlooked for billions of dollars.

I didn't trust anyone, least of all those who waxed poetic about how unimportant my looks were when I had such a great heart. I hated the ones who thought that because they were beautiful and I was a sideshow freak, they could wrap me around their finger. I much preferred those like Bridget, who saw only my disfigurement and knew, without question, that the only way past it was to be paid.

"How astute of you to recognize and acknowledge my mate's strong moral fiber. It's one of the things I admire most about him as well," I assured her, easing my arm free, repelled by her touch. "He does seem compelled to help everyone he can, even—" I paused for a beat, making sure I had her undivided attention. "—those who may not deserve his compassion and kindness. I remain exceedingly grateful he wants me, and that it matters not a whit to him who I am or what I have, only that I belong to him. I am humbled to be graced with that particular blessing."

She was staring again, thunderstruck and speechless, so I used that to my advantage. Excusing myself, I slipped by her and reached Avery, who was clearly ready to go as well. He took hold of my arm to get me moving, and then slipped a hand to the small of my back to keep me with him as we left the house side by side.

13

AVERY

Leaving Bridget and her seething sister, we drove downtown, toward the Loop, to find the sampling party so we could talk to Lucas. I warned Bridget and Saoirse before we left that if either of them called and gave Lucas a heads-up, for any reason, before I got a chance to speak to him, that one, or the pair of them, would be charged with interfering in or obstructing an ongoing homicide investigation.

"Don't test me," I warned one of my oldest friends and her little sister.

Both of them had nodded their agreement.

"Listen," I warned the other two occupants of the car as we made our way downtown. "I can't have you guys walking in there with me, so maybe you should wait outside."

Graeme scoffed. "I would never allow you to walk into a party like that alone."

"I can assure you I walked into much scarier situations than this on a regular Friday night when I was a patrol officer."

Wade nodded, backing me up. "There's no doubt."

"And now?" Graeme wanted to know, and I could see the flash of concern on his face.

"Now?" I grimaced. "It's so much worse."

"Let me understand," he murmured, and I could see how hard he was gripping the steering wheel. "Your life is in constant danger?"

"No, not constant danger," I assured him. "Police work is eighty percent watching, waiting, following up, and only twenty percent is bullets flying at your head."

"He wears a vest," Wade chimed in. "When he remembers," he finished unhelpfully. "But we work homicide, not vice or undercover or SWAT. As far as jobs go, we get shot at the least."

"This is ridiculous," Graeme began, his voice catching, "but somehow, having been there for parts of the investigation, seeing you two at work, I had an image in my mind that it was the drudgery of putting together leads, asking questions, and…the idea of people actively trying to do you harm hadn't entered my mind."

"It shouldn't," I assured him, patting his knee. "We're not paid-by-the-hour private investigators following cheating husbands. Even those guys get shot at more than us."

He didn't seem appeased, and I had a niggle of worry that I'd somehow pointed out a concern he hadn't thought about or been aware of before I turned his attention there.

Lucas's phone pinged a block away from where Graeme pulled over and parked the car. Before we got out, Wade and I hid our IDs, his stuffed into the shaft of his boot, mine in an inside pocket of Graeme's trench coat. Wade left his shoulder holster on since he was supposed to be Graeme's bodyguard, and I made certain my ankle holster was secure after we both checked that we had a full clip ready to go. It was always best to be prepared.

It was easy to find the place once we located the narrow alley between two buildings, but Graeme was not pleased about us separating. The problem was, I couldn't walk in with him. I knew myself too well; I'd be far to possessive and unable to leave his side, and that wasn't smart.

Gripping my arm, he walked me a few feet away from Wade, stopped, turned me to face him, and then took hold of my chin, tipping my head back so I had to look him in the eye.

"There will be suitors all over you, and you know, in a roomful of pheromones and adrenaline and --"

"Just wait and see." I leaned in close and inhaled his mossy, earthy scent. "That's all I ask."

The quick shake of his head spoke to my being deluded, but that was okay. Some things did have to be seen to be believed.

I went first, down the alley, reaching an open door and stepping across the threshold into a neon-purple-lit room. The bouncer asked for my invitation, and I explained I was a beta and had been invited by one of the omegas.

"They always forget who they fuckin' invite," he groused, gesturing me inside. "God, how much do I hate omegas?"

I suspected that a great many wolves who didn't know any omegas felt the same way; the general consensus was that omegas were useless. Unless you were a rich alpha, they were a burden, and lupine society would be better off without them. A sampling party was not designed to change the hearts and minds of regular alphas, betas, or gammas. All it did was perpetuate the stereotype that all omegas were good for was sex.

Grabbing a stool at the bar of the two-story club that had been rented out, I chatted up the bartender, who was appreciative of the fifty-dollar tip I gave him. Since I'd only ever heard about sampling parties, but had no idea how they worked, I asked him to explain.

The gist was that a group of omegas would get together, approach an alpha about a party, and he would then rent the space, shell out cash for the upfront costs—plenty of clean towels, security, and most importantly, the alcohol that needed to flow nonstop—and paid for the staff and the cleaning afterwards. When I inquired as to what the alpha who paid for the party received, I was told that he alone—or he and whoever else he chose—got to have sex with the participating omegas. That was the payment; the alpha got to put them into heat.

"Heat?" I asked the bartender, making a face. "Really?"

"Yeah, man, really. Wait'll you see it. It's fuckin' hot, until the fever breaks."

"Fever?"

"You know, not like an actual fever. I mean, when they're themselves again."

It was an act, and I was sure it was a good one, because he seemed sincere that it was amazing to see, but I wasn't buying it. There was no such thing as an omega completely losing themselves, and remembering what I'd experienced myself, how out of control I'd felt, but only for a short time, I knew I was right.

I saw Graeme and Wade walk in from where I was sitting at the bar, sipping on a Pepsi, and left quickly to grab an empty table. Wade detoured to the bar while Graeme crossed the room and took the chair beside me, not looking comfortable in the least.

I turned to him, one eyebrow lifted.

"At the moment, it seems as though you were right," he commented, deferring to me with a tip of his head. "I don't understand how, but there are many alphas milling around, and as far as I can tell, none of them have even glanced your way. They truly can't sense you're an omega."

"I told you."

"But down here, near the dance floor and the bar, that makes sense. Upstairs, where I suspect most of the omegas are on display, with blood and pheromones pumping, things might quickly change."

"I'll still smell the same as I do right now."

"Under different circumstances, though, they might discern that you are, in fact, an omega."

"Maybe, but consider, too, that I'm telling them I'm a beta. I'm presenting myself as one, and let's face it, a *cyne* like you has to spend a whole helluva lot of time in your wolf form settling disputes, accepting challenges, and defending the members of their *holt*. The more time you spend as a wolf, the more you trust your senses and not just your humanity."

He grunted. "That's quite insightful coming from you, since your mother informed me that you and your wolf are not close."

I groaned and leaned back in my chair.

"I'd like us to run together soon."

Rolling my head to the right, I smiled at him. "I'll run with you; I'd like that."

He didn't smile, but his eyes glinted as he stared at me.

"Did you have any trouble getting in?"

Instant scowl. "I'm a *cyne*, the man nearly pissed himself speaking to me. I didn't even have to bother explaining who Wade was."

I snorted. "Pissed himself, huh?"

He took hold of my chin. "I'm quite powerful, you know, even though you appear to be immune to my wolf."

I turned my head, kissing his palm, and then eased from

his grasp. "I'm not immune; I just don't feel any fear, only your dominance."

His jaw clenched as he breathed through his nose.

"And your dominance makes me wanna submit."

"Avery," he warned me.

"Roll over and beg you to--"

His growl cut me off. "If you want to remain here, I suggest you desist with your teasing."

"Who's teasing?"

"You're playing with fire."

I leaned sideways and kissed the side of his neck, nipping gently, and when I sat back, he was staring at me with his hand covering the bite. "Just know that I want you all the time, all right? You never have to wonder, 'Does Avery want me, crave me, ache for me?' because I do. I would like nothing better than to be home in bed with you, but I appreciate you coming here and being my backup."

He was quiet a second, like he was running through things in his head. "Of course I've never had a mate before, but beyond that, I've never been the object of someone's desire or affection. I've never been wanted for more than a few hours, a day at most. No one's ever looked at me like you do, with heat and longing and genuine warmth. I'm quite enamored of you."

"Enamored, huh?" I teased him, leaning into his space again and kissing his cheek. "I'll take it, for now, and hope the adjective gets better."

He huffed out a breath. "Do you prefer beguiled or enchanted?"

"Stop, you'll make me all verklempt."

He opened his mouth, probably to growl at me because I was driving him nuts, but Wade joined us and put a snifter of what I hoped was brandy down in front of Graeme before taking the chair across from me. He took a sip of his own drink and then put it down fast, making a face that made me snort.

"Not good?" I teased him.

"It's supposed to be a gin and tonic, but there is no *tonic* in that at all," he said, glancing around. "You know, this is much less Sodom and Gomorrah than I was expecting."

"Me too," I agreed.

"That's because the parts you're thinking about are upstairs," Graeme offered grimly.

Wade and I turned to him.

His sigh was both irritated and resigned. "When I was younger, before I knew I could say no to my friends, or if they were even friends or would respect my decisions, I was taken to more than one of these."

I grinned at him. "And did you participate?"

Instant scowl. "I'm sorry, but exhibitionism is *not* in my comfort zone, in case that was some sort of caveat for our mating."

I laughed and bumped him with my shoulder. "It's not a caveat, baby," I teased him.

He took a quick breath. "Shall we go up, then?"

The stairs were wide enough for four people to walk together, side by side, and there was a small balcony halfway up where one could stand and look down at the dance floor below. The top of the stairs led into a huge open space that was set up with various stations. It was crowded with people, unlike the first floor, but not so bad that we couldn't push our way through to get a glimpse of the displays.

There was one with a small orgy, six omegas—three women, three men—performing sexual acts on one another. In the next, a beautiful woman was strapped to a St. Andrew's Cross, and when Wade checked to see if she was all right, wasn't being forced in any way, she gave him an enthusiastic thumbs-up.

Walking the area, we eventually came across what appeared to be a semiprivate room separated from the rest of the space by a gauzy red curtain, and we slipped through. The dozens of people writhing naked on the floor...were far less interesting than Lucas Grant.

"Okay, guys, there's no picture taking or––Avery?"

As I stepped in beside him, he glanced at Graeme and then Wade. "Why do you have a human with you? He's not allowed to participate."

"We're not here to participate," I assured him. "We're here to talk to you."

He groaned but pulled his phone from the back pocket of his jeans, texted someone, and then waved across the room. I realized there were four guys in there, one in each corner, and the one he signaled walked around the outer edge of the floor to take his place.

Outside, Lucas rounded on me angrily, grabbing my arm to hold me still. "The fuck are you doing here?"

"I told you, we came to talk to––"

"You should be more careful," he barked, squeezing my bicep to help make his point. "You put yourself up for grabs by walking in here. Omegas have even fewer rights than usual when they come to these kinds of parties."

"Why the hell're you manhandling him?" Wade snapped at Lucas. "You need to get your––"

"He's safe," Graeme announced to Lucas, and I could feel the pulse of power from him, rolling over me, through me, and saw when it hit Lucas. Hard.

He jolted, and when he turned to face Graeme, he looked scared. From the slight shivering to the wariness in his eyes, Lucas Grant seemed poised to run. It was unnerving to witness.

"Do you know why he's safe? Would you care to guess?"

Lucas cleared his throat. "Your mate, sir. I apologize. Of course he's safe, both in your company and as he carries your mark."

"Holy shit," Wade gasped beside me.

Lucas Grant was a big man, covered in hard, heavy muscle, and he was tall as well, even taller than Graeme's own six feet four inches, but still, I knew if they fought, it would be no contest. If my mate wanted to, his innate power being so much greater than Lucas's, he could snap the bigger man in half.

After a long moment, Graeme gave Lucas the slightest tip of his head, and the relief on Lucas's face and in his posture was immediate. He trembled for a moment, as though shaking off the paralyzing fear, and then leaned back against the wall, like it was the only thing keeping him vertical. Then he turned to me, looking wrung out.

"I always considered us...maybe not friends, but not just acquaintances, and I know you were sincerely worried about me until you recognized my mate, so can we talk now?"

He nodded.

"We need to know if you saw Imogen Lowell when you grabbed Saoirse from Remy Talmadge's front porch."

"Who?" he asked, taking a breath and pushing away from the wall, having recovered from his fright, looking more like the confident beta I knew him to be.

"This girl," Wade chimed in, holding up his phone to show him a picture of Imogen from the society page.

Lucas took the phone, made the picture bigger, and I saw it on his face when recognition hit. "Yeah, I saw her with…what's his name, the alpha who was killed in that robbery?"

"What robbery?"

"I dunno. It was downtown, I guess. The only reason I know about it is because it was in the news this morning, and Bridget was reading about it on her tablet. She was surprised because he was one of the alphas who was in negotiations with Linden's father over his contract."

"Do you remember his name?"

"Of course, Colby Richter."

"Why do I know that name?" I asked Lucas.

"Probably because he was at your folks' party on Friday. He was there, courtin' Lin like regular. All those guys just need to cough up the cash already. If I wanted an omega, I wouldn't haggle; I'd pay whatever dowry the family was asking."

"As would I," Graeme agreed. "We're of the same mind."

Lucas gave him a slight smile.

"Your cousin doesn't have a gambling debt, does he?" Graeme pronounced. "You need money for something else altogether, do you not?"

I glanced from Lucas to Graeme and then back to Lucas.

He let his head fall back until it hit the wall. "Yes, sir, I do."

Reaching inside his coat, Graeme pulled out his gold business card holder, took out a card and handed it to Lucas. "I'm always in need of good people to assist with various business pursuits. Do give me a call, and we can discuss your situation."

Lucas hesitated, then took the card, stared at it, and slowly lifted his head to meet Graeme's gaze. "I don't know that I have any skills you would—"

"I'm a *cyne*, Mr. Grant," Graeme informed him, his voice

deceptively mild. "I suspect you're not privy to the extent of the various skill sets I might make use of."

"Yes, sir," he said, and his smile was wide and real. "Thank you, sir."

"Now, would you be so kind," Graeme directed him, "as to give us a timeline of your evening on Friday."

"Sure," Lucas replied quickly. "Uhm, Bridget got a call from her mother that Saoirse had left the house without permission, and since we both knew where she had to be going—back to that sleazebag Talmadge's—we jumped in the car and headed up to Highland Park."

"Sleazebag though he may be, Mr. Talmadge is my cousin, so I'll thank you not to elaborate on his character and stick to the pertinent details, please."

"Sure," Lucas agreed.

"So you went to Talmadge's because you knew Saoirse tried to go before."

"Yeah."

His story corroborated Bridget's. When they arrived, Lucas spotted Saoirse, with her terrible dye job, about to go in the house. He told Bridget to stay in the car, got out, snuck up behind Saoirse, and when the front door opened, he grabbed Talmadge, gave him a quick, brutal beat down, and then scooped up Saoirse and delivered her to Bridget. He happened to turn back toward the house, and that's when he saw Imogen standing with Colby in Remy's living room.

Later that evening, according to the police report Wade pulled up on his phone, Colby was robbed and killed two blocks away from where Imogen's body was found. Unlike Imogen, however, Colby's death did not seem at all lupine related. He was killed by two gunshot wounds, one to the chest and one to the head. The police report concluded it was a robbery gone wrong, as his watch, wallet, and an expensive pinky ring were stolen.

"Thank you," Wade acknowledged Lucas after we confirmed Colby's death.

Lucas nodded, shook Graeme's hand when he offered it, gave me a smile, and then slipped back inside the room.

"What was all that about with Lucas?"

"Don't you know?" he asked me, one eyebrow arched.

"If I knew, I wouldn't be—oh," I breathed out, realizing what Lucas needed to buy that he didn't want to haggle over. "That's never gonna—you realize even if you pay him a million dollars to do nothing, and even if he saves enough to buy her contract, plus the dowry, Bridget herself would never agree to it."

"I do realize that, yes."

"She's not looking for someone to pay her father so she can go off and live in a little house in Brookfield or, you know what I mean. She's looking for the fairy tale. She's looking for you."

"I'm aware," he soothed me, cupping my chin in his hand. "But I'm already spoken for."

"Yes, you are," I husked, not caring what Wade was probably thinking about me having a moment with my mate in the middle of an investigation.

Graeme smiled at me and let his hand drop away. "Unfortunately, Mr. Grant has been led to believe that if he buys Miss Mills' contract, she will be his. She's either in love with him and has agreed to wait until he's saved the needed funds, which could account for the twelve years of being unbonded, or he's made his desires known and she's never corrected him. Either way, he believes her to be his, which makes me wonder about her statement."

"Why?" Wade asked.

"Because Bridget told us that after they returned home and Lucas put Saoirse in her room, he spent the rest of the night calming her down."

I nodded. "And you think she sleeps with Lucas under her father's roof all the time."

"I suspect so, yes. Her pheromones are all over him, her scent is in his lungs, and under his shirt he's carrying some kind of marks that are still healing."

"You can smell all that?" Wade prodded Graeme. "Even in here with all these people?"

"Yes," he informed my partner. "Bridget, like most wolves, uses her claws when she has sex, and I noticed a small amount of dried blood under her fingernails when you took her hand."

"Seriously?" Wade questioned him.

"If she's using him, then it's a horrible betrayal. If she's not, it's terrible to do to her sister, and if Saoirse is aware, then perhaps that's fueling her anger. Because we've overlooked one rather important detail. While Lucas was with Bridget calming her down, can Saoirse's whereabouts be substantiated?"

I looked at Wade, who crossed his arms and stared at Graeme, and then I gave my mate my undivided attention as well.

"Why are you both staring at me?"

"That was some nice detective work there."

He dismissed us both with a wave. "May we leave now? I believe we should return to Bridget's home and watch the surveillance tape she spoke of."

"Yes, sir," Wade teased him. "Let's go."

Walking back downstairs and toward the front of the club, we made our way through a small crowd and emerged through an opening, where we suddenly found ourselves standing with a large group of people, all watching a man on his knees, face to the floor, hands cuffed behind his back, ass lifted, pants rucked to his knees, crying and begging and gibbering as he was fucked from behind. It was startling to be confronted by such a needy, desperate, unscripted, seemingly unscheduled sex act.

The stations, those were obviously staged and expected, the alphas milling around them and reacting, yelling out encouragement and profanities, though they weren't riveted and appeared almost bored.

That wasn't at all the reaction to the scene before us.

Everyone here was spellbound, not moving, barely breathing. This act was shocking, striking, because the omega taking the pounding from the alpha seemed utterly lost in the sensation. For his part, the alpha doing the fucking had only loosened his pants enough to free his cock.

It didn't last long, the alpha came, bucking inside the omega before another alpha yanked him off, still dripping, and took his place behind the omega, plunged his hand into the bucket of lube beside him, slathered his dick, and then shoved inside, to the hilt, in a single fluid motion.

The first alpha was still collapsed on the floor as a server brought him a bar towel that he used to clean himself up. As I watched, alphas began to line up even as the one who was currently screwing the omega grabbed his hair in what appeared to be a painfully tight hold and slammed into him over and over. When he finished, the next one took his place, not bothering to use the lube, crowing that he was slick enough, much to the clapping and whistling of the men in the line, as well as the crowd.

I couldn't stop staring at the omega's face. He wasn't in pain. He wasn't screaming at anyone to stop or get off him. In fact, the only word he uttered, over and over, was yes.

It was terrifying. My vision tunneled down to the omega's face and the ecstasy on it, the tears and the mewling whimpers. Everything I thought I knew, what I'd spoken to other omegas about with such conviction, with such hubris in my certainty, was obliterated by what I was seeing—an omega completely lost to his heat.

"Avery," Graeme spoke my name gently, reverently, stepping in front of me, which allowed me to get my bearings as he became the only thing I could see or smell.

"What the hell," Wade gasped beside me, taking a step toward the men.

Graeme put his hand out to keep him there. "That's an omega in full heat, and you'll hurt him if you stop it."

"There's no way," Wade choked out, and Graeme moved aside, as I wasn't the only one who needed him. He had to make sure Wade stayed put as the third alpha finished, was handed a bar towel by a server, and another took his place, passing his drink to a friend so he could open his fly, scoop out some lube, and coat his shaft before shoving inside of the omega. "He can't know what he's doing. We have to stop this."

"We don't have the right," Graeme stated, while a few feet away, a woman went to her hands and knees near the male omega, an alpha behind her, throwing up the back of her dress, dragging down her panties as a stack of bar towels and another bucket of lube was carried over by a server and set down beside the woman. The alpha unzipped, pulled out his already fully erect penis, grabbed some lube, slicked himself, and then spread the omega's legs and pushed inside of her.

"This is wrong," Wade rasped angrily. Graeme turned him around so his back was to both the omegas.

"This is what these parties are about," Graeme

explained, his voice flat but still commanding. "I know it's horrifying to you, because this isn't done at the clubs you frequent, but the displays, the different people having sex, the girl on the cross, for example, those are warmups. Those are to make sure whoever shows up has something to look at, and stays. Meanwhile, several omegas are having sex with the alpha who's paying for all this, and as soon as they're done, and he doesn't mark them, they go into heat, at which point they stumble out here to the main area and have sex with whoever wants them."

"You're serious."

"Yes," Graeme assured him, turning him around. "Look at them."

I had been watching my mate as he spoke to Wade, and when I turned back to the two omegas, I was stunned to see six more, all with the stack of towels next to them, the bucket of lube.

"This is actually happening," Wade gasped before Graeme flipped him around again.

"When an omega goes into real heat, not the mock heat Remy perpetrated, they are calling for an alpha to bond with. The small amount of pheromones produced during *les fausses chaleurs* is nothing in comparison to what an omega in a full, real heat is capable of. Only an alpha who's truly mated can withstand the call."

Which meant that all the alphas bonded to omegas would succumb, as none of those were true.

Graeme turned to make eye contact with me. "Your brother, your father, my brother, your brother-in-law, hell, my grandfather, all of them could be here, just as I am now, and not feel the pull to go over there and get in line."

I couldn't find my voice. Before he and I, I'd never heard of a mating between an alpha and an omega. And if it wasn't real, if he wanted what he could get from me but didn't want *me*, then everything I'd been, even for such a short time, building on and counting on, could be taken away. But that was crazy. My family had kissed my mark, ours was a true mating, and I knew that, my wolf knew that, and I felt it when we'd been in bed together, that it was a true joining, like we were one thing. But now, faced with what I'd never even credited as being real, the doubt was gutting me.

"Wade, I need you to excuse us for just a moment," Graeme announced before he released him and grabbed me, pulling me after him through the crowd and out the other side where it was quiet and cooler, near the windows that looked out on the city.

Manhandling me roughly, he spun me around to face him, both his hands on my hips as he stared down into my eyes. "Listen now."

I couldn't do anything else.

"Your mind is reeling, but even if you question everything else, you can never question the promise between us, our union."

I nodded, trying to swallow around the lump in my throat.

"It's human to doubt, to worry and wonder, but the truth lies with your wolf."

Yes, it did. My wolf knew I belonged to Graeme. I was given a mark, and that was forever and always. It was a vow, made in flesh, irrevocable.

"You are mine, I am yours, and that's all."

My eyes filled before I was even aware the tears were welling up. As quickly as I tried to brush them away, they returned.

"You didn't believe omegas went into heat like this," he told me.

"No," I choked out, shaking my head.

"And now you're thinking to yourself, *that could've been me, because I've slept with a lot of alphas and none of them gave me their mark, so why didn't I succumb to the heat?*"

"Yes," I whispered the confession. "How did I—why didn't I...do that?"

"Some of it, I believe," he replied, grinning with a huff of resignation, "is your mother, actually."

"My mother?"

He nodded. "Yes. She told me that first night she didn't raise an omega, she only raised alphas."

"Yes, but nature is––"

"You, my mate, were raised with the same confidence that your mother instilled in both your brother and sister. You wanted to be a police officer, and you became one. You know who you are, and that sense of self is not defined by someone else, so how could any alpha you didn't choose possibly make a claim on you?"

I couldn't help myself and leaned into him, wrapping my arms around his waist, pressing my face into his chest.

"Your mother assured me that you would not, under any circumstances, go into heat. I thought her naïve, and she is, a bit, as she based her belief solely on how you were raised when the other reason, the most important part, in my estimation, is that you are *not* a bonded omega."

Leaning back but not letting go, I lifted my head to meet his gaze. "I'm sorry—what?"

He took my face in his hands. "I've seen hundreds of omegas in heat in my lifetime, which was why I was so worried about you being alone that first night, as I thought you would succumb. Now I realize, of course, that you were never going to go into heat, because of what you are," he explained. "You're a mated omega, *not* a bonded one."

It couldn't be that simple.

"You were raised, just as every alpha, beta, and gamma is, with the potential to be a true mate. Heaven knows we don't all find them, but the possibility for you was there. Because of that, you weren't going to accept a mark from any alpha but your true one, me, and so sleeping with other alphas posed no danger to you of bringing on a heat."

"But I was in pain the other night after we——"

"I know," he interrupted me, not wanting, I was sure, to go back over the laundry room incident where he had shed all his inhibitions. "I was the same. I was supposed to put my mark on you then, so of course, when I didn't, it was difficult for both of us."

"So you're thinking that was all normal?"

"I do." His smile was lazy and sexy, and he brought his hands to my shoulders. "I think, after the blessing that was finding our true mate, we were supposed to stay together."

"Probably," I mumbled, leaning into him again, loving the heat rolling off his body, the smell of him, leather, and musk from the fur of his wolf, crisp pine and smokey sandalwood. "I should have stayed. I knew it was wrong when I was leaving."

"But see, now I understand the reason you did, and could. You have a very important job, and your wolf knew, even if you didn't, that leaving me might be difficult, but it wasn't forever because I'm your mate, and you'd be in my den at some point."

I chuckled. "Your den, huh?"

"Don't tease your alpha," he warned me playfully as he rubbed his chin in my hair, the scent marking important since we were surrounded by so many alphas.

I wrapped my arms around him and squeezed tight. "I kinda like teasing you, though."

"Going forward, what I hope," he rumbled into my hair, "is now that you're mated you'll stop fighting your nature every day."

"I don't fight my--"

"You're strong and capable, but at heart, you're still an omega," he intoned, his voice low and gravelly. "True mate or bonded, you still need to nurture others and be part of a home."

"I'm not going to quit my job and--"

He snorted, and my head snapped up so I could meet his gaze, which was surprisingly warm, as was the rakish grin that made my knees go weak. "Love, I know you're not quitting your job. I just mean that I volunteer to be lavished with all the love and nurturing until you're ready to start a family with me."

I was stunned. "You think I'm father material?"

"Without question," he stated, and then gathered me in his arms and kissed me.

Amazing how everything unfurled in my chest, all the fear, all the doubt, all the questioning, everything that had been solid, then bent but not, as it turned out, broken and was now, suddenly, reinforced.

"You called me *love*," I murmured when he lifted his mouth from mine but before he eased back so I was still breathing his air. "Did you know you did that?"

"Did you know you called me *baby*?"

"I did?"

He grunted.

"Well, you are."

"As are you," he whispered, "my love."

I grabbed him; I couldn't help it. I wrapped my arms around his neck and kissed him with everything I had, and when he kissed me back, and chuckled as he wiped away my tears, I knew I was done with anything but being all-in.

He knew me. Really knew me already, like my family did. He knew when to laugh, when to call me on my bullshit, and knew when I was *this close* to falling apart.

I loved him kissing me, I needed him hugging me. He was careful, but not too careful, because he recognized I wouldn't break, and that was amazing. Tender and gentle, but he grabbed and manhandled me too, like he saw the two distinct parts of me no one understood before him. He got me, and it was so fast, scary-fast, hit-by-lightning fast, but that was how true mates worked. And even if I didn't believe it, even if I had never seen it happen to my brother, and then my sister, it wouldn't matter because this I grasped, this I could feel.

"I can't believe I'm gonna tell you this right here," I ground out. "This is the worst--"

"It's not. It makes sense that here, in contrast to the nature of omegas all around us, you would give me your nurturing self."

The words had never passed my lips to anyone I wasn't related to.

"Now," he insisted. "Tell me now. It'll be all right. I'll catch you."

Big breath, deep breath. "I love you, Graeme."

His smile was luminous, but the fierce look in his eyes turned it into more of a glare. "And I love you back, you vexing creature. How dare you doubt our mating at the first test of--"

"Yeah, good, kiss me now."

And he did.

14

GRAEME

It was difficult for us to leave the club because Wade was torn. He heard Avery when he assured him the omegas weren't being hurt, and he heard me when I reiterated the same sentiment, but believing it was another story. He needed to be guided outside, not quite forcefully but nearly so. I understood. His oath to serve and protect was at war with what he'd just witnessed. He felt as though he was leaving the scene of a crime, and I appreciated, as he paced in front of me, his need to grasp the entire picture.

"So if you're an omega, and you have sex with an alpha, and he doesn't mark you, then *wham*, heat."

"Normally, yes," I replied, prepared to work everything through with him.

"How long does a true heat last?"

"No more than twenty-four hours, sometimes less, and then it abates," I answered irritably, realizing I needed to get to the heart of the matter. "What's your concern?"

"It's barbaric," Wade declared adamantly.

"Not the heat, correct?" I needed to clarify. "The practice

of alphas putting omegas into heat and not marking them, that's what you find offensive."

"Yes—I, of course. The heat is natural and organic, it's that spectacle that's horrific."

"It's antiquated," I corrected him, "but culturally accepted, as so many rituals and laws that pertain specifically to omegas are. And that's why I'm working with others, albeit slowly, to change legislation where omegas are concerned."

"You are?" Avery asked, looking up from his phone, texting with Peck, who, along with his partner, Ness, was at Bridget's home, after midnight on a very early Sunday, to look at and acquire, if needed, the surveillance tape from Friday night.

"I am, but it's going to take time, as many of the people speaking out against changing laws for omegas are omegas themselves. Many of them don't want the same rights as alphas and betas and gammas, because then so much more will be required of them and remove them from their traditional roles."

"That's all well and good," Wade told me, "but right this second, how can those omegas be safe in there?"

"It's the omega's *choice* to be put into heat and then exhibit themselves," I declared, well beyond tired of discussing it and turning toward Avery, wanting, needing to be closer. I understood it was shocking and appalling to Wade, but he wasn't a wolf, so it was unreasonable of me to expect it to make sense to him.

"Wait," he barked, moving to face me, blocking me from stepping closer to Avery.

Instantly, because the drive was primal, I went still.

"Shit," he gasped, backpedaling, staring at me. "What the hell?"

"It's fine, it's fine," Avery soothed him, moving between us and into my space, hands slipping under my trench coat and my suit jacket to my sides, sliding over my ribs as he bumped his head on my chest. "Just take one more step back, Wade."

He was wary, his gaze flicking from my face to Avery's and back before returning to me. "What happened? Your eyes did a weird thing, like when a cat's eyes glow in the dark."

"That's eyeshine, lupines call it wolf eyes," Avery replied gently. "It's just a reflective layer behind the pupil of our eyes. No big deal."

"Yeah, but why?" Wade addressed his question to my mate.

"Our mating is brand new," he informed his partner, still using a soothing, calming tone, soft, gentle, like he was talking to a wild animal. "Graeme and I haven't spent any prolonged time together, and because of that, as my alpha, he's very protective of me and my space, and of *his* position in relation to mine."

"I don't under—"

"You walked between us," Avery apprised him. "That's Wolf 101 at the academy."

Wade stared at him for a long moment, and then a look of both resignation and annoyance crossed his handsome features. "Shit," he groaned, upset with himself for making such a rookie mistake. He took another step back and gestured at me. "Graeme, I know better than that, and we're just getting to know each other, and...man, I'm so sorry. Forgive me."

I was stunned. I'd never had a human apologize for missing the social cues of being a wolf. There were things one observed in the areas of business and law enforcement across cultures, and the list for lupines was as accessible as any other, but more often than not, simple things—like don't wear heavy perfume to a deposition with your lupine attorney—were ignored. But Wade made immediate amends once his misstep was pointed out. "Of course," I replied sincerely.

His smile was tentative. "My TO, when I was a rookie, told me that you never step between an alpha and their mate. She said it's not only rude, but if the lupines in question are newly mated, it's extremely fuckin' dangerous."

It was. Even potentially lethal.

"I swear I'll be more careful in the future. I'm usually the guy that's on top of this kinda stuff. I wouldn't want you stepping between me and my wife someday, so yeah, I get it. And look, I know you're sick of answering questions about the omegas, but that whole scene is really eating at me."

"Right now you're worried the omegas have no choice in their current state."

"Yes."

"To an extent, you're right, but only insofar as, once they begin, they can't stop until the heat is over."

"But what if something goes wrong and nobody helps them or—"

"Oh, I see," I rushed out, as annoyed at myself as he'd been moments ago, because I had missed something too. "I understand the source of your concern now. You're worried that scene might devolve into something—"

"Like rape, or a gang rape," Wade croaked out. "I'm thinking about, what if the omegas want to stop and no one will listen, and I don't see how I can leave, knowing I could prevent something like that from happening."

"I apologize for the disconnect," I apprised him. "I was attempting to explain to you what will happen based on pheromones, et cetera, and your concern is with their physical safety."

"Yes." His shoulders relaxed, and he exhaled in obvious relief that we'd finally got to the heart of his concerns.

"Then let me ease your mind and tell you that by lupine law, the alpha who agreed to throw the sampling party is *personally* responsible for the safety of every single one of those omegas. He may take on the fun of putting them into heat, but he'll pay with his life if anything nonconsensual were to occur."

Wade's eyebrows lifted in surprise as he stared at me. "Really?"

"I give you my word. As I'm sure Avery explained to you, if an alpha has sex with an omega without benefit of a contract, that's considered theft. The alpha in this case has had sex, or allowed another to have sex by proxy, with all the omegas in that club. That was done without benefit of a bonding, and that's irrefutable, as they're all clearly in heat. One can only conclude that if ruining one omega can have you sanctioned and reported to the *Maion* council, then more than one...you forfeit your life."

"And the alpha is aware of that?"

"It's what he agrees to when he accepts the request to throw the sampling party."

"Then why would anyone ever agree to do that? As a *cyne*, you could just walk in there and bust them, and that would be it for that alpha, right?"

"But it's understood that it's what the omegas want."

"That seems shady," Wade replied. "An alpha who's with an omega, one on one, things get outta control and they end up having sex; if that alpha says it was just for fun, he's screwed. He has to make an offer for that omega or he's sanctioned."

"Yes."

"But the alpha who throws a sampling party, he gets to have sex with all the omegas and he just skates by?" Wade was squinting at me. "Explain the logic to me in that."

"In your example, the alpha chose the omega he wanted to spend time with, and then, when they were alone, he and the omega had sex. The difference with these sampling parties is that the alpha doesn't choose. A number of omegas come to him, mostly those who made their debut years ago, and ask him to host the function. Typically, the alpha has had no previous contact with any of the omegas, and so there's no issue that, beyond being approached, the alpha has done anything wrong."

"That's really thin," Wade assured me. "There's no way that stands up in court."

"These parties have been happening for centuries," I explained to him. "Mistresses were chosen this way, pleasure slaves, all so the omega would not be left to die in the street."

"Well, tell me this; is the alpha who sponsored the party in there somewhere, or does he just leave when the festivities start?"

"As I told you, he's responsible for the health and life of every omega at the party. Wouldn't you stay if your life was on the line?"

"Hell yeah I would," Wade admitted.

"So the omegas choose to be there, no one forces them —outside of familial duty, and that's a discussion for another day—but in many respects, they are physically safer at a sampling party than in a variety of other circumstances."

"Okay, point taken," he replied, squinting, still

concerned I could tell. "And what if a female omega gets pregnant?"

"As lupine females enter a cycle of fertility only once a year, much like their wolf counterparts in the wild, avoiding an unwanted pregnancy is a simple matter of forethought and planning."

"Yeah but--"

"Also, to be allowed to participate, female omegas must sign a contract stating they're not in their breeding cycle."

"I see," Wade said, exhaling a deep breath.

"Now then," I stated gently, "beyond your own personal distaste, over which I have no control, I believe that covers it."

"It does, yes." He gave me a hint of a smile. "Thank you for your patience with me."

"Your concern for others is an admirable trait."

He grunted. "Avery and I get in trouble for worrying so much about people, victims, when we're supposed to have moved on."

I could see that about them. Avery was made to nurture others, and Wade was a knight. They probably got in a *lot* of trouble.

"All right," I announced, and both men turned to me. "Are we to adjourn to Bridget's home to meet Detectives Peck and Ness?"

"No," Avery told me. "We're done for the night."

My heart leapt. "We're going home?"

Avery smiled at me and nodded. "Yeah, we're going home."

"I'm gonna take a cab," Wade told us, yawning. "Marcie's place is--"

"Meggie," Avery corrected him sharply.

"Hah, I was just testing you."

Avery scowled at him. "You were not. You've said it wrong enough times now it's stuck in your head like that."

Wade grimaced as though, yes, perhaps. I liked watching their interaction quite a bit.

"Shit," Wade groused, "I think my phone is in the back seat of the Jeep."

"I'll go get the car and drive back and pick you up." Avery leaned up for a kiss, which I gladly gave him; then I passed him the keys and he bolted down the street, turning the corner a moment later.

"I sincerely do appreciate you explaining the omega thing to me," Wade admitted, putting a hand on my arm. "And for the record, I know he's an omega. I'm not stupid. All the parties he's gotta go to, I know what that's about. I just didn't want him to think I thought any less of him because of it. He's kinda weird about anything having to do with being a wolf."

I nodded. "He is, but I hope to work on that with him."

Then we talked about real estate and how he wanted to buy a house, but his apartment was so easy to take care of, and centrally located. We talked about a couple restaurants I wanted to try, and a Korean place that he and Avery loved.

"Can I ask you a question?"

"Certainly."

"You're a *cyne*, and that's above an ordinary alpha, right?"

"Correct."

"But what does that mean?"

"It means I lead a *holt*."

"Which isn't a wolf pack."

I nodded. "Natural wolves have packs; lupines do not."

"You have families, like Avery's dad is the alpha of his family."

I nodded.

"And *holts*, which is several families, right?"

"Exactly."

"But how does that work?"

"It's like a vassal system. I take care of large numbers of people who, collectively, make small payments to me that I then disperse at my discretion, based on need."

"So like, if my kid needs college tuition."

"Yes."

"But what if one family doesn't have kids?"

"There are other factors. Consider medical bills, retirement, buying a home," I replied, and then smiled. "Buying a home in Paris or Tahiti."

Wade grinned at me then, and I liked that we were getting along. He was important to Avery and so to me as well.

"There are businesses that might need a bailout: farms, law firms, restaurants. Or a doctor who wants to open their own practice, a mechanic who wants their own garage. There are a million things people need, but instead of going to a bank, or some other financial institution, I take care of it. Or, I should say, my brother, my sister-in-law, and I, along with a whole team of talented, qualified people, take care of that."

"You *are* like a lord in a castle taking care of all your vassals, all your people," he agreed, ruminating on everything I'd just said. "That's impressive."

"That's what a degree in contract law and finance gets you," I conceded, smiling at him. "I'm the CEO of Davenport Limited, and I'm the Earl of Wakefield and Muir, and I own land that, combined, is bigger than the state of Alaska. I'm telling you this not to brag but to answer your question."

"Can people leave the *holt*?"

"Most certainly."

He grunted. "But why would they?"

"Why indeed," I agreed, knowing I sounded smug, but I was a good leader, and I took excellent care of all the people who put their faith in me.

We were quiet for a moment, both of us realizing that we'd been talking for a bit.

"What the hell?" Wade grumbled, rubbing his arms. "Did he take a detour to a pet store for more cat toys?"

"Does he do that?" I was beyond amused by the mere suggestion.

"Hell yeah. I can't tell you how many stakeouts we've been on that by the time he gets back with my coffee, it's ice cold because he saw a special spider toy that can climb up walls."

I chuckled, imagining Avery's face lighting up with happiness over the discovery of something for his beloved feline. "Let's walk toward the car and see what he might have diverted for."

But there were no open stores on our way to the Jeep, only dark streets, and when we turned the last corner, we both saw the Jeep where we'd left it, parked in front of a closed dry cleaner. I jogged toward the car and then stopped suddenly.

"Graeme?"

"Wade, I—" Turning, I inhaled deeply, spun around and faced him. "He never even got this far."

Wade made a call, and the streets were swarming with police officers no more than ten minutes later. I was somewhat comforted by the fact that whichever way I looked there were flashing lights, men and women questioning bystanders, entering buildings, and searching alleys, all in pursuit of Avery.

I was worried, yes, but I also had great faith in Avery. He'd been a police detective for quite some time, he was both capable and smart, and more than anything, me succumbing to fear, wouldn't help matters in the least.

No one wanted me to move, not understanding that I was the best person to look for my mate, but there was protocol, and even with Wade arguing on my behalf with someone downtown, I was to either go home and wait for word or remain with Wade at the staging area. If I moved, they would restrain me. As Avery was a police officer, that superseded him being lupine, meaning I had no more rights than an average person, *cyne* or not.

I called Kat to let her know what was going on and alert her to the possibility that, as Wade eventually informed me, I would be able to shift once the scene was transferred from the district we were currently in to the eighteenth, where Wade and Avery worked.

"It's not necessary for you to wait. I——"

"Kat," I stopped her, my voice breaking, "I'll do anything to find my——"

"Your mate, yes. But I put GPS trackers in all his shoes before Iz informed me you can't do that with a police officer. I'll take the others out tomorrow, but at the moment——"

"You know where he is," I gasped.

"Yes, I know where he is," she informed me.

I really needed to stop interrupting her when she was talking.

After explaining to Wade the brilliance of my assistant, and before he could tell me the trackers had to be removed, I assured him she would do so the following day. Wade couldn't tell the site commander that Avery had an illegal tracking device on him, but he didn't want to waste the time of his fellow officers by having them continue to search for him either, so he lied and told the commander he'd heard from Avery, and that he had seen something sketchy and left to check it out. The commander was annoyed, but pleased Avery was in no danger, and shut down the search. On our way back to the Jeep, Peck and Ness showed up, and Wade and I got in the back of their Chevy Suburban.

I explained about the GPS, and Ness, who was driving, hit the gas as I directed him.

"You know you can't put tracking devices in his shoes, Mr. Davenport," Peck explained, being diplomatic but adamant at the same time. "That's against our department policies, and—"

"I'm well aware, Detective, and they will be removed tomorrow, but in the interim—" I directed his partner to take a left at the end of the street, "—let's find him."

"Hey, listen," Ness began, "we got the surveillance footage from Mr. Mills' cloud, but turns out it was exactly like Bridget Mills said. No one went back out after they all got home."

With the flashing light coming from the grill of the car and the siren blaring, people were pulling over to get out of our way. I liked his driving much better than Avery's. It was fast, but without the cornering and lane switching that made me nauseous.

"I'm surprised," Wade stated. "I was sure Saoirse was involved."

I suspected that we all had.

Once I told Ness we were a block away from where Avery was, he turned off the lights and siren, and we pulled over.

"You should stay back," Wade cautioned me, concerned, I was certain, about my safety. "We can take it from here."

"I think not," I assured him, striding forward quickly.

When we reached the Pilsen neighborhood and what appeared to be an abandoned house, given the boarded-up windows, Peck and Ness went around the back while Wade and I took the front door.

"I know I'm probably wasting my breath, but I'm going to insist again that you stay here," he whispered, lifting his gun in both hands, the weapon light illuminating the way. "The three of us are armed; you're not. I'd rather not lose my job because you caught a bullet."

There was protocol to follow, and I knew Avery would want me to respect his partner.

"I'll give you five minutes to call me, and then I'm coming in."

"Ten," he countered. We'd already exchanged numbers earlier in the night, so without another word, he slipped into the shadows of the house.

A man of my word, I waited eleven minutes before I followed in Wade's footsteps and slipped inside. The cloying scents of damp mold, stale cigarette smoke, and old blood seeped from every pore of the place, assaulting my enhanced sense of smell, so I breathed through my mouth as I got my bearings and waited for my wolf's eyes to adjust to the dark.

There was a crash then, like shattering glass, and I heard gunshots, and then Avery yelled, "No!" So I made my way toward the back of the house, following the sound of my mate's voice, quiet, as only a predator could be, as I crept down the hallway toward a door at the end, where I could see light shining through the gaps around its frame.

And then the assaulting scent of fresh blood and something else, something familiar, hit me.

Roses.

The scent was of graveyard roses left out to rot after a squall. It was Linden, Avery's friend, but instead of his smell being vibrant and alluring, it was fading, and I suspected, so was he. I had to reach him because, more likely than not, he was with my mate.

There was no way to get down the steep basement stairs without being seen unless I could stay in the shadows and leap from the small landing rather than take the last flight to the bottom. Stripping fast, I left my shoes and clothes in a mound, shifted to my wolf, which was not small, and crept down the stairs, then shot off the landing. It was far too cluttered to make no noise at all.

"The hell was that?" a woman asked.

I heard a man answer, "It's probably rats," and I moved quickly, so when he charged over near where I was, kicking things out of the way, I slipped around the other side, camouflaged in the shadows, and stepped under the stairs, staring out into the room.

I saw him instantly.

Avery was sitting on the end of a faded floral-print couch. There was dried blood on his face, and his arms were restrained behind his back, probably with the same rope that was around his ankles. On the opposite end of the couch was Wade, who was restrained the same way, except he was unconscious. Peck and Ness were on a large rug in front of the couch, not tied up but knocked out as well.

Pacing in front of the rug was Bridget; sitting in an armchair holding a gun was her sister Saoirse; and on the floor, bleeding, was Linden. He looked like he'd been beaten repeatedly, his right eye swollen shut, and there were bones broken in his once beautiful face. I suspected that his whimpering was not from the pain alone, but over Lucas Grant, who was lying beside him in a pool of blood.

A man walked by the stairs, over to Linden, and kicked him hard in the chest, which sent him rolling into a puddle of Lucas's blood.

"Shut the fuck up," he yelled, crouching beside Linden, grabbing hold of his rose-gold mane and lifting his head so their gazes met. "If you don't want to be chained in my punishment room instead of sleeping in my bed every night, you better figure out where your loyalties lie."

He shoved Linden's face back down into the blood, rubbing it there until he was coated in gore.

"For fuck's sake, Daw," Bridget yelled at him, "leave him alone. What kind of a bonding do you ever hope to have if you terrorize him right now?"

"How dare you speak to me like that," he chided her. "He's a possession, mine to do with as I like, fuck when I want, beat when I want, share when I want, just as you'll be when Gansey signs your contract, you stupid sow."

"And you're certain he's going to see my father tomorrow?" she asked hopefully.

He shook his head. "Even after everything, it's still all you care about. I swear to God, is there anything as useless and pathetic as an omega."

"Why kill Trent and Imogen?" Avery asked, and both Daw and Bridget turned to him. "And why kill Colby?"

"I killed Colby because he was outbidding me for Lin's contract," Daw explained to him. "I followed him, used a gun so it wouldn't look like it had anything to do with wolves, but imagine my surprise when I walked to Colby's car and found Imogen Lowell and the omega I've wanted since I first saw him at the gathering party at Gansey Runyon's home."

Avery turned to look over at Linden. "You and Colby went to Remy Talmadge's place to pick up Imogen. Why?"

"She was a family friend," Linden replied softly. Clearly it hurt him to speak. "Her family—her father—is nearly bankrupt. She needed a match now, this year, to keep her family in their home and off the streets. She has two little sisters, both omegas."

"But this whore was there too," Bridget shrieked at Saoirse, walking over to her and backhanding her hard.

Saoirse absorbed the blow, made no sound, didn't speak a word, and then turned her head as though nothing had occurred. It was only then I noticed how dead her eyes were, how broken she appeared, and wondered who, precisely, had shot Lucas Grant.

"You killed Highmore," Avery accused Bridget. "You killed him because you thought he was Talmadge, and you didn't want him putting any more omegas into *les fausses chaleurs*. Why? This is what I don't get. You're ten times more beautiful and elegant and smart and funny and--"

"I'm getting old, Avery!" she yelled at him. "I'm thirty years old. All the alphas my age are looking for new and fresh, and the young alphas all think I'm the same age as their mothers! The only alphas interested in me are ones the same age as my father, who already have their own children, who want nothing more than a companion they can fuck when they feel like it."

"You could've come to me and--"

"And what? You would have helped me find a *job*?" Her voice dripped with derision, and her eyes were hard and cold as she glared at him. "Jesus Christ, Avery, just because you never wanted the life that Lin and I did doesn't mean you get to look down on us."

"I never looked——"

"And the irony of all this is that you, who is the least deserving of all of us to bond with a *cyne*, is the one he wants," she announced with a laugh that held no humor. "Could life be any less fair? I mean, he's gay, so I had no chance, but to want you over Lin? That's astounding; it's *insane*. I can't even fathom such thing."

"Stop talking," Daw snarled at her as Wade opened his eyes, looking around wildly. "We need to kill them all and dump their——"

"It's his fault," Saoirse shrieked, and I was moving even before she stood and pointed the gun at Avery.

Wade screamed behind the tape over his mouth, and I saw, peripherally, Daw raise his hand. If he had a gun, I'd be dead, but I had to reach Avery.

"Saoirse!" Bridget cried as her little sister put three bullets in my mate.

15

AVERY

The moon was out, and that was weird, because when I was dragged into the house, it was raining. But now it was clear, everything bathed in blue tones, and the long grass to the right of the meadow I was in fluttered in the crisp breeze. I could smell the earth, fresh moss, balsam and cedar, and even a campfire in the distance. It was soothing, and I wanted to curl up beside one of the trees and close my eyes.

I needed to rest.

The problem was, something was moving at the edge of the field. I wasn't alone, and so instead of just dropping to the ground like every muscle in my body told me to, I moved toward the sound, lifting my muzzle to scent the air, trying to catch a whiff to identify the presence.

I was stunned when an enormous dire wolf, gray and black with traces of silver in his thick coat and on the tips of his ears, stepped from the tree line. He stared at me a long moment and then bolted toward me.

Running would be a mistake. He was bigger, stronger,

faster; he'd be on me in seconds and take me down if I did anything but stand my ground. Growling, threatening him, would also be a mistake. To try and make myself small but not vulnerable, capable but not antagonistic, seemed like the best answer.

When he veered off at the last second, running by me, crashing into the long grass and disappearing out of sight, I was surprised. I could hear him charging around, doing zoomies like my stupid cat did at three in the morning, and when he popped out a second time, just his head before he was gone again, I realized that perhaps he was mad.

Wolves didn't play with others they found in their territory; they killed them. So what was with him circling me in the grass but not attacking?

When he shot out of the grass again, running by me, he hit me. He didn't do it hard, he didn't hurt me, but the force was enough to tumble me to the ground.

Getting up, I growled, and when he flew by again, he nipped my ear and then tugged on my tail. The next time, I shot away from him, because he was fast, but I was agile, could turn faster, and so dove forward and nipped his back leg.

His balance upset, he rolled into the grass, out of sight, but then shot right back out to face me.

I snarled.

He crouched down, and when I took a step forward, he lunged and caught my nose with his wet tongue.

Stunned, I stood there frozen as he got closer, nuzzled his nose into my ear, under my neck, and then moved so he rubbed up against me, and waited.

When he took a step back, I mirrored his movement, stepping forward, wanting, for whatever reason, to stay close. I would not be separated, though I didn't understand why, so even when he turned and sped away, I ran too. After only moments, I was keeping pace with him, running at his side.

We ran fast over the forest floor, crushing fallen leaves under our paws, crossed through small streams, the shadows that would have normally made me wary causing no hint of concern because this beautiful, fearsome creature was with me.

When we found a second meadow, smaller and covered in thick, sweet grass, he veered into me, knocking me off my feet, rolling me over and over until I came to a stop, lying on my back, paws in the air, staring up at the stars.

He flopped down beside me, head on his paws, staring at me.

Rolling to my side, I stared back at him, and he lifted his head, amber gaze holding mine as his pheromones engulfed me and I breathed in his incredible scent.

Oh. Yes. That was why. This was the reason I couldn't be separated.

My mate. I was staring at my mate.

Rolling over, whimpering, I crawled forward and rolled again to my back, offering him my throat, crying for him.

Biting my neck, he kept me still for a moment before he nudged me forward, wanting me to run. But I was so tired, and I just wanted to rest.

He rose to leave me, running forward and then circling back, and when he did it a second time I got up, even though it was hard. Everything hurt, my body was so heavy I could barely lift my paws but...I had to follow. I had to be with him.

Whining for him to stop only made him run faster, and I

fell, a lot, and it was hard to get back up, but he waited only a moment, so I had to catch up. I felt as though I were running through mud, and I slowed, but he was there, just ahead, so I pushed on, needing us to stay together. It was strange, but he smelled like a promise. He smelled like a warm den, and I had to keep going so I could curl up beside him when we got there.

It felt like we ran for days, and gradually my paws weren't sticking in mud anymore. I could lift them easier, I had traction, and I felt a surge of speed, and he called for me, and I ran and ran. And flying forward, I leaped from the forest floor and dropped—

"Avery!"

There were lights everywhere, and my chest was on fire, and I screamed and flailed because I was terrified. It had been quiet and dark and serene and—where was my mate?

"Stop!"

The yell was like thunder, and everyone froze, no one touching me as Graeme was hovering over me, looking terrible and beautiful at the same time.

"Turn off the light," he ordered, and with a click, everything muted, got quiet again. "There, love, calm down, just breathe for me."

I concentrated on in and out, looking up at his puffy red eyes, wondering what in the world was going on.

There was a nurse, I saw her out of the corner of my eye as my head rolled, and I saw an IV bag and all the monitors before I turned my head to see Graeme again.

"Come sleep with me in the den."

Yes, somehow that seemed imperative, such a simple request that called to something primitive in me. I didn't even care if anyone heard my whimper, I just wanted to curl up beside my mate. When he bent down and hugged me, I could finally breathe.

MY EYES FLUTTERED, and it took me a second of blinking to realize I was looking at a window with rain beating against the glass. Beneath the window was what looked like a wide padded shelf, and stretched out on that was my mother. There was a crocheted blanket covering her—one my grandmother had made—and she was fully dressed, except for her Duck boots on the floor near her.

Closer, sitting in a recliner, was my mate, head back, eyes closed, holding my hand even in sleep. He looked so good, so warm, so strong, so much like home that I rolled sideways so I could stare at him.

Turning my head, I saw Kat at the end of my bed. "You have a light step," I told her, because I'd had no idea there was anyone else in the room. It wasn't that I just hadn't noticed her at first; I had missed her completely.

She nodded. "So I've been told."

I noted her expression, how soft it was when she looked at Graeme, and then harder when she met my gaze. "You have something to say."

"I do."

"Please."

"There has to be a compromise."

"Of?"

With a quick tip of her head, she indicated Graeme. "You want to keep all the freedom you've always enjoyed even now that you've found your mate," she apprised me coolly. "That's impossible."

I'd been thinking about that myself.

"He, being an alpha, would prefer complete submission."

"Yes."

"Equally impossible."

"Agreed."

"He's a smart man. He knows, logically, that it is precisely your independence he finds so attractive."

I took a breath. "What do you think?"

Slight smile from her. "I appreciate you asking me instead of telling me to go to hell."

"It's concessions, isn't it?" I asked her. "On both sides. I have to impose my own limits on myself and be mindful of how I'd feel if the roles were reversed."

"Yes."

"And he?"

"He will understand," Graeme said, and I gasped and turned to him, finding him standing now beside my bed, "when you cannot call in the middle of a situation, and will try not to lose his mind. He will work at having faith."

I lifted my arms, and he bent and filled them, hugging me, but not nearly tight enough. "I won't break," I husked into the side of his neck.

"That has not yet been validated," he assured me. "You were shot once in the shoulder and twice in the chest."

I was? "How long ago?"

"Two days ago."

Jolting in his arms, not wanting to let go, afraid to ask more questions but needing to, I took a breath. "Wade?"

"Everyone is alive."

"Not Lucas." I would grieve his loss.

He scoffed.

Letting my hands fall from around his neck, I tipped my head back and looked up at his face. "Graeme?"

"Lucas was gravely injured, and he lost quite a bit of blood, but once he shifted to his wolf and then back, just as you did once the bullets were removed, the healing could begin."

"How did he have the will to shift with so much damage?" I baited him, because of course I knew. There could be only one answer.

"Because I'm so happy to see you, I'm not even going to yell."

I leaned forward and wrapped my arms around him. "You saved Lucas by ordering him to shift for you."

"It was done for you," he replied flatly. "I knew it was what you would want."

"You knew it was the right thing to do because you're such a good man," I murmured happily, loving his hand in my hair and the other rubbing circles on my back, and the kiss on my forehead. "Now, tell me everything from the beginning."

"I will," he mumbled, hugging me before he collapsed back down onto the recliner, put his head back, and closed his eyes. "As soon as I can think again."

I turned to look at Kat.

"He has not left your side once in two days. Three hours ago your doctor came in and pronounced you healed. We just had to wait for you to wake up. Then, and only then, did he close his eyes."

"Don't make me sound like a saint," Graeme groused at her. "I'm not...that...good."

His breathing was slow and even in seconds.

"He is now, and has always been, one of the very best men."

"I know," I assured her. "He saved me, didn't he?"

She nodded. "Only your mate, your true mate, could

have. Only they can find the wolf inside your mind. I'm told it's quite something."

"I hope you find your true mate someday," I said, turning to look at the unconscious alpha beside my bed. "Because yeah, it is quite something."

My mother, who awoke moments after Graeme passed out, had all the information about how everyone was. Kat took a seat on the padded shelf my mother had been lying on, on her phone, not about to leave her boss sleeping and vulnerable in my hospital room.

All my fellow detectives were well, and the fact that I'd kept Wade Massey from my mother for so many years was, I was told, nearly unforgivable. They'd seemingly talked almost nonstop the entire first day, and he was invited to the engagement party. She was also having him in to speak to her seventh and eighth graders in the next two weeks. She had, in essence, annexed him, and I wasn't surprised in the least. When he came into my room an hour later, he hugged her before he hugged me.

"Why do you smell like toasted pumpkin?" I asked him.

"I have no idea," he grumbled.

"You've been with Linden."

"Uh"—he smiled sheepishly, which I'd never seen him do in three years—"yeah."

Huh.

"Tell me from the beginning."

After my mother excused herself, she and Kat went to get coffee, as Wade could be counted on to protect not only me but my mate as well. They gave each other a nod.

"You and Kat buddies now?" I teased him.

He squinted at me. "Are you kidding? That woman is

badass. After you were shot and Graeme knocked Saoirse down, it took all his focus to keep you alive. Saoirse got up, and she's got a gun, and that guy, Daw Abernathy, he's got a gun, and all I could do was yell into the duct tape over my mouth…and then Kat—Jesus."

She had put a bullet in Saoirse's right shoulder, put one in Daw's leg, disarmed them both, zip-tied them both, and kept Bridget from leaving the basement with a punch to the face that knocked her out cold.

"She's a fuckin' ninja. I'd marry her if she liked guys."

"Tell me the story."

He nodded slowly.

Bridget had planned to have Lucas kill Remy Talmadge to stop him from putting the omegas younger than her into a mock heat. She had left the party with Lucas, and together they headed to Talmadge's place. Once there, Lucas ordered Bridget to stay in the car. When he discovered Saoirse at the front door arguing with Talmadge, Lucas beat the crap out of him and then carried Bridget's little sister back to the car. But when he got there, he discovered Bridget was gone, so he locked Saoirse in the trunk and went back to the house, thinking that was the most logical place for Bridget to go.

Bridget had snuck out of the car while Lucas was distracted, hid, and while he was busy stuffing Saoirse into the trunk, Bridget walked into the house, ran into Highmore, and he escorted her up to the bedroom, thinking she was there to be put into mock heat. He told her he could take care of her immediately, as Imogen, who was very young, had swooned.

Bridget saw Imogen passed out on the bed, smelled all that had gone on in the room, and snapped. Her fear, her jealousy, her anger, all of it was unleashed in a wave of lunacy and rage that crashed over Trent Highmore. Bridget, who had always been an incredibly fast shifter, was a wolf in seconds, and the alpha didn't even have time to run. Sometimes speed superseded strength, and the murder had been one of those instances. In short, it was a classic crime of passion.

Lucas must have heard the mauling, because he quickly located Bridget in Talmadge's bedroom murdering Highmore, but hid when he noticed Talmadge fleeing down the hall toward the panic room. Seconds later, he saw Imogen running toward the front door. Keeping a cool head, he went into the bedroom, found and grabbed the camera, and then moved things around in the room to throw off anyone who might be looking for the recording device.

Bridget had shifted back to human by the time he'd finished, so Lucas carried her and the camera back to the car, got Saoirse out of the trunk, put both sisters in the back seat, and headed home. On the way, he told Bridget about seeing Colby and Linden.

"Lucas lied when he told us he saw Colby earlier that night in the house." Wade made sure I had every last detail. "The first time he saw Colby was in the driver's seat of his sports car, idling in the street outside Talmadge's house, while he and Linden were waiting for Imogen."

Linden had left the gathering party with Colby and had him drive up to Talmadge's house to collect Imogen when she'd called him, begging for a ride. Bridget had then called Linden, ostensibly to chat. When he told her that he and Colby were stopping to score before taking a friend home, she called Daw—an old family friend—and gave him a heads-up.

"Colby wanted drugs, and since there's only a few places to get stuff strong enough for lupines, Daw knew where to go. So, seeing a chance to get rid of his rival for

Linden, namely Colby, he waited until the other alpha was on his way back out from scoring, killed him, robbed him, and then found Colby's car with Imogen and Linden inside."

"So who killed Imogen?"

"Daw," Wade told me. "He was going to rape her and tear her apart. That's his confession he gave to his father and Peck. You know wolves can't lie in the presence of their alphas; the alphas can tell."

I nodded.

"So yeah, I guess it was going to be brutal, and he was going to do it in the alley, to make it *special* for her first time, but Linden got out when Daw yanked her from the back seat and put himself between them so she could run."

My breath froze in my chest. Linny tried to save her?"

Wade nodded. "But Daw threw him into a wall and went after Imogen."

I winced, waiting for the end.

"I guess when he landed on top of her, from what he confessed to his alpha, he accidentally snapped her neck."

"And it made him so mad that he couldn't rape and torture her, he spent time desecrating her body."

"Yeah."

I nodded. "Then what?"

"Linden ran, made it home, and an hour later, Daw showed up. He made arrangements with his father for Linden's contract, and as a show of good faith, paid his father a quarter of a million dollars to take Linden with him for no more than two nights."

So not only did my friend have to see Imogen die, but then he was forced to leave the safety of his home with Daw. He was, at heart, a gentle soul, and to be betrayed and brutalized... my heart hurt, thinking about him.

"He begged his father not to force him to go, but to no avail."

I couldn't even imagine.

"From what he said, his father's been pimping him out for a long time, since before he was of age, and he's been through several heats."

And I'd told him for years that he was crazy, that there was no such thing, while the whole time he was going through them because his father saw him as a whore.

I had to own that my denial of an omega's heat, of my own heat, had more to do with my dismissal of everything wolf-related than anything else. I had never wanted to believe it, and because all I'd ever dreamed of was to be a police officer, and to live my life as a human and nothing more, I had gone out of my way to prove to myself, and others, that it didn't exist.

But everything changed when Graeme came into my life. I had a safety net in him. He loved being a wolf, embraced his wolf wholly, and I needed to learn that piece from him, trust in the part of me I had always raged against. I had immersed myself in being human, in being the same as Wade and the majority of my friends. Now, with Graeme's help, it was time to do the opposite and embrace the feral part of my nature that, if I was being honest, had shaped who I was just as much as anything else. It was time to make peace with my wolf.

"Avery?"

"Sorry," I choked out, hurting for Linny and hoping that it wasn't too late for him and me. I had to start with an apology and hope we could build from there. "I'm surprised Linny told you all that about his life."

"Why?"

"He's always been a bit more secretive than that," I

answered, saddened that we'd been friends since childhood, but Wade was the one he chose to confide in. I took a breath. "Did Daw rape him?"

Several emotions crossed Wade's face before he answered my question. Knowing him as well as I knew myself, I suspected chief among them was something like a virulent, righteous fury. "Yes." His voice was flat when he continued. "Brutally. Daw shifted into a wolf and tortured him, and then shifted back into a man and violated him."

"Okay."

"It was vicious, what Daw did to him," Wade rasped, squinting to ensure that no tears fell. "If Linden were human, he would have needed stitches. Do you understand?"

"I do," I managed to get out. "How long did he have him?"

"From Friday night through Saturday and into Sunday morning, when he was in the basement with us."

Clearing my throat, I met Wade's gaze. "Where is he now?"

"He's down the hall."

"What, uh...what's going to happen to him?"

"I don't know, but it's no longer up to his father."

"I'm sorry?"

"Your mate there, he bought Linden's contract from his father and sent movers to the house and packed up all his belongings. Apparently he's been moved into your old room in your parents' house."

"Graeme moved Lin in with my parents?"

"He did, yes. Originally, he was going to have him live with you guys, but your mother insisted that he move in with her and your father and the rest of your family instead.

She wants to, and I quote, 'Smother him with affection and make up for lost time.'"

I smiled at him.

"She made it sound like she's been wanting him to be hers for, well, forever."

I nodded. "Yes, she has."

I could remember when I was little and she would hug me, and how her heart would break when Linny looked up at her with his big eyes full of longing, biting his bottom lip and asking if maybe she might want to hug him too. I was certain she would lavish him with affection now that there was no one standing in her way.

"Well, I've only known your mother a couple days—which we're both pissed about, by the way—but I suspect she's a person who gets her way."

That was putting it mildly.

"So Graeme gave in, and Linny is in your old room, and your mother's thrilled."

I glanced over at Graeme, who was breathing heavily but not quite snoring. He was not waking up anytime soon.

"Do my parents know that Linny tried to save Imogen?"

"Yes."

"Okay. Do Imogen's parents know that Linden tried to save her?"

"They do."

"Do they blame him for her death?"

"That I don't know, but I don't see how they could. They know Daw's an alpha, and they know he had a gun; he was stronger than both of them."

"Bridget killed an alpha," I reminded him.

"She did," he agreed, "and she was pumped up on adrenaline. I've seen the video, so I know that she shifted before Trent Highmore even knew he was in danger. She had the element of surprise on her side. He looks drugged in the video too, probably hopped up on all the pheromones, right?"

"Probably, yes."

"Totally different situation than Linny and Imogen sitting in the car like lobsters in a tank waiting to die."

"What's going to happen to Imogen's family? Do you know?"

"Your mate's brother...Stone, is that right?"

"Yeah."

"Okay, so Stone went to see Imogen's folks, and he put together some sort of financial plan that involves him taking over the selling of their home and giving them a small loan until that occurs, and then realigning assets. The important part is that Imogen's parents will be able to live and take care of their other daughters, though they will no longer be members of the... *jarl*? Am I saying that right?"

"Yes."

"So yeah, your fiancé, he's like, you know, a scary black ops fixer guy. He goes around saving people and rearranging their lives like it was never bad in the first place."

"And Bridget and the others?"

"Daw has a younger brother, so since his father has another heir, Daw's being castrated."

I could only stare at my partner.

"I think that might be the exact same face I made when I was informed of Mr. Abernathy's punishment for his first-born son."

"Holy shit."

"I had no idea that wolves were so—I mean, it's stunning to me that his own father could just order that done."

"Wolves take honor and their position in the hierarchy very seriously."

"Yeah. I would say so."

"What else with Daw?"

"Well, after he loses his balls, he gets to go live on a piece of property his family owns in Lucerne, under guard, until he dies of natural causes, a long fuckin' time from now."

"Switzerland is beautiful."

"Nowhere is beautiful if you're a prisoner for the rest of your life."

"It's better than he deserves."

"No argument."

"And Bridget and Saoirse?"

"Bridget's contract was given to a friend of her father's who's a widower, and she's going to live with him in a small town in Wyoming. I couldn't tell you which one."

She'd drink herself to death in a year, I had no doubt.

"And Saoirse's contract was purchased at half the asking price by that alpha Daw was screaming about to Bridget, Gansey Runyon. He's moving them to Sioux Falls, South Dakota. I guess he felt Saoirse had more childbearing years left in her than good ole Bridget."

"Jesus Christ."

"It's horrifying to me, even with what those two women did, that they can be treated like nothing. Like a possession. Kat thinks that with this latest horror Graeme will get even more support for his push for omega rights."

"I hope so."

He took a breath, as though girding himself.

"What?"

"I told Graeme, but now I'm telling you; I know you're an omega. I'm not stupid. I just don't get why you didn't tell me."

I took a breath. "It's weird. I didn't tell you when I first should have, because people have an idea about omegas. I mean, look at Bridget and Linden, and...I just never wanted you to think of me as weak. And then, by the time you knew me and I could have told you, it just seemed like you might feel betrayed that I didn't tell you in the first place, and it was just a mess in my head."

He nodded. "You should always tell me everything because I know you Avery. I know the kind of man you are and I know all about your heart."

Yes, he did.

"So don't hide anything else."

"No, sir."

He grunted.

"And Lucas?"

"Lucas is the only one Mr. Mills was pleased with, and as a result, he's being sent to work for his brother in Los Angeles, who has two sons, both omegas, who need a bodyguard."

I shook my head. "What a mess."

"Lucas could be brought up on charges of obstruction and tampering with evidence in a murder case, not to mention assaulting Remy Talmadge, but all of this amounts to lupine-on-lupine crime. Highmore's family wants nothing to do with this case; they just want to grieve alone. Graeme said his cousin won't be charging Lucas with anything, so...we're done."

We certainly were.

"There is punishment for the guilty, but not how I thought. I hope that Graeme can push for that legislation for omega rights. None of this would have happened if they had a voice and options and could make their own choices."

He wasn't wrong.

"You said you watched the video of Bridget attacking Highmore?"

"Yeah. Lucas turned over the footage."

"I'm sorry you had to watch that by yourself."

"We don't have to have all the same nightmares, buddy."

No, we did not.

LATER, leaving Graeme in the room under Kat's watchful care, my mother and I went down the hall to Linden's room. Slipping inside, we found him facing a mountain of food, and Corvina fluffing a pillow behind him. Wade was asleep in a recliner beside the bed.

"You think you have enough food?" I asked as my mother hugged and kissed Linden, leaning back to brush his long strawberry blond hair out of his face.

"It's not my fault that Corvie thinks I'm thin," he assured me, as surly as ever.

"You're far more than just thin," Corvina assured him as she walked around the end of the bed and cupped my cheek. "And so are you, love, but Francisca will make sure you're fed, and you're the only one who will eat her food without whining about it."

Moving in close beside Linden, I waited several moments while he ate before he finally turned and looked at me.

"Yes?" he snapped in that high-handed manner he had.

I was quiet, studying the bruises on his face that, even after two days, were still healing, and realized I was in better shape than him, even being shot three times, only because of my mate. Graeme was the only reason I was alive.

I was so blessed.

"Either speak or get out." Linny clipped the words.

I could go home at any time; him, they were still keeping

for observation. For the attack to still be showing on him, it had to have been savage. I couldn't help sucking in a breath.

"Do you want me to say thank you? Is that what you expect?"

His pride was something, but that was probably good.

Leaning in, I kissed his cheek.

He looked away from me, and I noted how he quickly brushed under each eye with the knuckle of his right index finger before slowly turning his head back to regard me. "Your mother's having your room redone completely, so I hope you're not sentimental about anything in there."

I bumped him gently with my shoulder.

"Owww," he uttered, scowling at me. "You're such a brute."

I glanced over at Wade and then back to him.

"Yes, I noticed him too. Hard to miss such a beautiful man, but why is he in here? Did he get lost on the way to your room?"

"My room?"

"Yes, I understand he's your partner. That's what he told me."

I nodded.

"Well, collect him, for goodness' sake. Don't leave him in here."

"He must be worried about you."

He grunted.

"Did he carry you out of the house?"

"I don't recall," he assured me, sniffling.

He had Wade's scent all over him, so I was guessing Wade had not only carried him but had not moved far from his bedside for long.

"Okay, then, I'll wake him up and get him out of here," I

told Linden, moving away from his side to walk around the chair.

"You know what?" Linden began, clearing his throat softly. "Perhaps just let him sleep."

He wasn't fooling me one bit. He'd been brutalized, and the second Wade was out of his bindings, he'd gone to Linden's side and been there ever since. Wade made me feel safe when we walked down the street together, so it had to be the same for Linden, having Wade right there, like a sleeping, but vigilant lion. It had to be the safest Linden had felt in years.

"Of course."

Quick cough. "My, uhm, mother came by to bring me my grandmother's jewels; she bequeathed them to me in her will. Before my mother handed them to me, she felt the need to remind me that a spoiled, unbonded omega was perhaps not the person to inherit Daniella Van Doren's jewels, especially not the Queen's Lament."

"That's the pearl-and-diamond necklace, right?"

"It is, yes," he spoke quickly, his voice pitching.

"Was Wade in here?" I asked, smiling.

"Yes. Yes, he was."

"How'd that go?"

"Well, he"—Linden took a breath and tipped his head at the intricately carved onyx-and-gold-inlay box that was sitting on a shelf next to the window—"grabbed the box and sent her on her way."

"Yeah," I whispered, smiling, "he can get loud."

Linden nodded.

"Okay," I murmured, taking hold of his hand, "I expect you at the party we're hosting to announce my mating this coming Saturday. Don't even think about trying to get out of it."

"Oh no, Avery, you can't want—"

"In fact, you'll maybe wanna come early so I don't end up in jeans or something."

The horror on his face, the way his mouth dropped open, and how he was staring, wide-eyed and thoroughly scandalized, was pretty funny.

"Maybe I should iron, ya think?" I threw that one out, glancing at my mother and Corvina, both appearing equally as horrified as Linden.

It was fun to mess with my family.

16

GRAEME

Bringing Avery home from the hospital, eating dinner with him, joined by his family, his parents, his siblings and their mates, my brother and Gigi, was so comforting that I had a bit of trouble holding myself together.

I had called my grandfather and woke him from a sound sleep while the doctors fought to save my true mate, to tell him I was terrified Avery was dying, that his body was shutting down, and I didn't know how to reach him through our link, the covenant vow that only true mates shared. He told me, quite sensibly, to shut up and listen.

"Go in there, get everyone else out, hold him as tight as you can, and clear your mind. Use what you know, where you think he'd *want* to be, what he'd *want* to be doing, and then think about what you, and only you, can give him. A true mate is the other half, the opposite side of the same coin. They provide what you don't have, what you can't create for yourself, and vice versa." He took a deep breath. "You have to think about the one thing Avery can only find in you. Only you, Graeme."

"Yessir."

"Your grandmother and I will be there soon, son," he promised, and hung up.

I knew why they were coming. Either my mate would die and I'd need them, or my mate would live and they'd want to meet him.

Charging back into the room, I made everyone stand back against the walls and leaned over, lifted Avery up off the bed, and wrapped him in my arms. At first I was afraid; I didn't want to hurt him, but he made a noise when I pressed him gently to my chest, a soft whimper of need, and when I clutched him tighter, his moan startled everyone, as was evidenced from their gasps. His breath on the side of my neck told me that he needed me, his mate, more than anything else.

It terrified me to think I could fail. I had no idea what I was doing; I was going in blind, without a map. I was always prepared, always confident, always in control…except with Avery. I had never expected him, and so was blindsided by this beautiful man who walked into my life and brought the sun with him.

But he had everything he needed, there was nothing he was lacking, and nothing that I alone could…could…

Home.

I was his home.

While he was unconscious, he was reduced to his most primal state, his wolf. Home was a complex idea, but a den, that he would understand. That he would need. The warmth and safety that only I could provide, because I was his mate.

Letting my mind drift, I imagined him running outside, somewhere safe, somewhere cool and lush, a forest that would shelter and protect him. This primal daydream led me to a hill, where I looked out over a valley, ripe and bursting with a riot of color. It was stunning, this Technicolor dream-state, and so perceptible it felt real as I ran down into the meadow.

The scene changed then, and his scent brought me up short. I saw him in the moonlight, a beautiful wolf, white except for the black marking on the tip of his tail, like it had been dipped in ink and used for a paintbrush. Small, delicate, his paws were tiny compared to mine, but I was a dire wolf, as all *cynes* were, nature seeing nothing to improve on as dire wolves remained unchanged since before the first ice age.

I wasn't sure what to do, how to engage his wolf; we'd never run together, but my mate was funny, had a sense of humor, so I teased him. I was playful, tugged on his tail, nipped at his ears until, frustrated, he snapped back. Once he decided I wouldn't hurt him and came closer, I released my pheromones so he'd know who I was. If the bond wasn't strong enough, he'd run and I'd lose him, both in the dream and in reality. He could easily die without our connection.

When he whimpered and whined, wanting to be close to me, I howled my happiness to the stars. He had to run with me, followed me all the way back to his body, cradled there in my arms, and it was slow, rough going, a slog, but then he picked up speed, and I felt him getting stronger. Then he leapt home, tethered by the astral cord, into his body, eyes open, flailing, the machines chirping, letting me know he was alive and breathing. And the blood, his blood that had needed replenishing, he had regenerated that himself.

My mate would live, and I cried softly into his hair as, even in sleep, he clung to me.

. . .

I COULD BARELY KEEP my eyes open at the dinner table. When I nodded off, Avery helped me to my feet, making our excuses to our family, and walked me to our bedroom. It had been redecorated: black and white with deep maroon, forest green, and sapphire blue accents. He stripped me quickly, and I crawled, naked, into the warm bed, cocooning myself under the new cotton sheets and heavy quilts. He tucked me in, kissed my forehead—no one smelled like him—and promised to be right back. And so, happy but emotionally and physically exhausted, my brain shut down, and I was out.

And I dreamed.

I was falling. I was freezing and wet, pelted with hail as I dropped. When I hit the water, a cold, roiling sea, I opened my eyes as I sank. I could see a room in the deep, and then there was blood and a knife, a white wolf sitting in a pool of blood, staring at me with dead eyes. Avery was swimming toward me, reaching, but the current kept pulling him away, no matter how hard I swam.

I was sinking, drowning but still kicking as hard as I could, trying to rise from the darkening water. I was drowning, and my lungs screamed for air. I needed to break the surface—

"Graeme!" Avery yelled, and I heard him even though he was hoarse, like he'd been yelling for a bit.

"Avery!" I howled, scrambling to sit up, everything spasming at once, my entire body a rictus of pain, and then he was there, on me, his warm body covering mine.

"It's okay, it's okay," he soothed, hugging me tight, his weight on top of me so welcome, so calming, so settling that I inhaled deeply, making sure my lungs were working.

"You're okay, baby," he crooned, kissing the side of my

neck. "You're here with me, and everything's okay. I'm all right, you're all right, and everything turned out fine."

Had I ever had any idea how much I would enjoy being called *baby*?

"It was just a bad dream, and sometimes, a dream is just a dream."

Yes.

He cupped one side of my neck with his hand, pressed hot kisses to the other, and I realized, after a moment, that I was naked and so was he.

When I wrapped my arms around him, he shuddered, and I rolled us so we faced each other, chest pressed against chest, close but not on top of him so I could look deep into his eyes, that were shrouded with dread.

"What's wrong?" I asked, using my thumb to wipe away his tears. "What happened? You were scared, and I felt your panic like it was mine."

"I'm sorry," he husked, "I didn't mean to--"

"Tell me," I demanded, needing to know, needing to protect him, whenever possible, from all things that could cause him pain. "I could almost taste your fear."

His hands were all over me, couldn't stop stroking up over my ribs, my chest, down my sides, mapping my skin with every graze of his palms.

"Avery?"

"I read Wade's report, and Daw had a gun too, and...if Kat hadn't been there, he could...he could have...killed you," he said gruffly, swallowing hard.

"It was scary for both of us," I murmured, my hand in his hair, savoring the feel of the silky strands on my skin. "But we came through. We both did."

He laid his head down on my chest.

"Avery, I--"

"Shh," he hushed me.

I smiled over how serious he'd sounded. "What are you doing?" I whispered.

"I'm listening to your heart," he murmured. "It's steady and it calms me and I like to be close to you."

"I like being close to you as well," I croaked out, my voice faltering with his nearness. "No great secret there."

"You're warm too," he moaned softly.

His sleek skin was hot, which was terribly distracting, but I needed to extract a promise. "You must take greater care with yourself, as your life is now more than your own."

"I promise to be more careful," he said, wiggling out from under me, pushing me over on my back, bending to kiss the side of my neck. I turned my head to give him better access, luxuriating in the feel of his hot mouth on my skin. "And you promise too."

It was hard to concentrate with his kisses, his tongue and his teeth licking and nipping at my skin. When his hand slipped around my slowly thickening cock, it was all I could do not to arch up off the bed.

"You were amazing in our shared dream," he almost moaned, his voice silky and hoarse as he reached under his pillow. "I loved us running together, and I haven't been able to get it out of my head. I never choose to be in my shifted form, I never want to be a wolf, but Graeme, I can't wait to run with you in the forest for real."

My heart swelled just thinking of us together, running side by side. It was my place as alpha to show Avery the beauty of his wolf, and this was progress.

"Promise me after the party on Saturday that we can go away, just the two of us, for a few days. Stone said you guys have a cabin that backs up to Matthiessen State Park where you can run at night. Tell me we can go."

The pleading in his voice between kisses, the desire, the way he was looking at me, and his hand on my cock brought a whimper up from my chest I would have been embarrassed by if it was anyone but Avery who'd heard it.

"It's your cabin too," I assured him, barely getting the words out but needing that to be clear. "Everything that's mine is yours."

"Then I want the two of us to go to *our* cabin, alone," he husked into my ear.

"Yes," I promised him. It sounded like heaven.

There was the snap of the bottle lid, and then I was slicked from balls to head, once and then again. I shuddered as he moved over me, clutching a hand towel, and the fact that he'd thought to get both, because he wanted me as soon as I was able, brought his name to my lips on a choked whine.

"I've got you," he crooned, lifting up, pressing the head of my cock to his entrance. "I couldn't wait to have you. Watching you sleep was agony."

He wanted me, and it was there, the truth of it in his blown pupils, the way he bit his lip, and the catch of his breath. I was what he craved.

"I don't want to"--my breath caught as he pushed down, taking me inside a fraction--"hurt you. Avery," I cried out, because the velvet vise of his ass engulfing me, squeezing slowly, in sweet increments, was hard to wait for. I wanted to be buried inside of him, and everything I was, man and wolf, screamed at me to take him.

"You feel so good, baby," he murmured, and the gruff, smoky sound of him as he took all of me, his ass flush with my groin, his hands gripping my chest, leaning forward to kiss me as I slid out a fraction, was so close to opening the door to the animal I was.

He'd been hurt, and I'd helped him heal the damage, but my beast was there, still so close to the surface, and he craved his mate with tooth and claw.

I breathed through the hunger, and it was heaven, the way he rode me, forward and back, deep, and I filled him to the hilt. Then he eased away, ravaging my mouth as his muscles rippled around me.

When he hooked his hand around my back, I did as he wanted and sat up, wrapping those long, beautiful legs of his around me, his knees bent over my elbows so I could yank him forward, hard, onto me, over and over, thrusting each time, no liquid roll but abrupt and hammering.

Both hands clamped around my neck, and he resisted when I tried to hammer inside again, and when my hands turned to claws, piercing his skin, where others had been fearful in the past, his smile was wicked and debauched, ready to play.

He wasn't afraid. He craved all of me.

It happened so fast, the flicker from man to beast.

My teeth gnashed toward his mark, and he scrambled free, but he didn't run; instead, he went facedown on the bed, ass in the air, in the same position as all the omegas had been at the club that night.

"Come, my alpha," he whispered raggedly. "Show me your power."

I was the nightmare that only alphas became—head of a wolf, claws where hands should have been, the penultimate moment before all that was left of me was the animal.

My jaws closed around the back of his neck, holding him down, still, as I shoved my length inside of him, plunging home, needing him stretched and filled, writhing on the end of my cock. My teeth ground down, tasted blood, and then I lifted up, claws buried in his hips as I rammed into him, making him buck forward with the rutting.

Grabbing the back of his head, seeing my claws in his hair, I lifted him to his hands and knees and then bit down into this warm, sleek skin, chasing the red rivulets with my tongue, licking them roughly even as I drove deep, needing more of his submission, his delicious scent, and his blood.

When he turned his head, looking over his shoulder, and I heard the mewling cries welling up from his throat, I curled over him, licking his mouth, and when his tongue rubbed over mine, I wanted to claim my mate as the man I was and no longer remain in my shifted state.

"Please," he moaned as I slid free and rolled him to his back in the middle of the bed, curling over him, shoving a pillow under his hips, draping his legs over my shoulders as I took hold of his cock and stroked him to the same tempo as my pounding.

"Graeme," he rasped, and I felt his muscles clamp down around me, spasming as he came over my hand and abdomen, arching under me, mouth open, head back, panting hard.

I buried myself inside him, pushing, pressing, trying to get even a fraction deeper, coming hard, pumping into his body before I collapsed on top of him, never wanting to move, to be parted, happy to lie between his thighs for the rest of my life.

My mate, my husband, my omega...my love. And God, he was. Never a doubt, no question, not from the beginning, from the first kiss, first smile, first touch of his hand.

Everything had been spinning for so long. I was in a million pieces, together on the outside but never within.

But now, the man whose arms and legs I was wrapped in as he panted into the side of my neck, chuckling, kissing, nibbling with his sharp teeth, had gathered me up so tight that I knew I would be whole always, from now on. It was easy to believe when you found your other half.

THE PARTY at my home was a zoo. The house was filled with the *jarl*; even those who'd never deigned to appear at functions before came to wish me the very best on my mating and assure me they were, of course, looking forward to the wedding. I chuckled quietly, because there was no way in hell my grandfather was allowing half of these people at my wedding; they simply weren't important enough to him.

As expected, Graeme Davenport the Third had insisted that Avery call him *Grandfather*, just as he'd directed Gigi to do when she and Stone were mated. He was in heaven, introducing Avery to the people who mattered, not, as he called them, the rabble. Richest didn't matter at all to him. Character, a loving family, sound judgment, both ethically and financially, that was the ticket. He already adored Avery's mother, and had made certain her hand had not left his arm.

My grandmother had taken Linden under her wing the instant she spotted him. Always a fan of flawless, cultivated taste, she found a confidant in him. He could spot a piece of fake jewelry from across the room, and so could she. Avery told me Linden had been worried that people would talk about him behind his back, but with Joan Follet Davenport holding his arm, no one dared. If she didn't like you, God help you; she could destroy social standing with a squint in your direction, and Linden was her new favorite, after Avery.

My new mate had stepped in and hugged her, squeezing a slight grunt from her she found enchanting. I hadn't been worried. The man was far too charming for anyone not to be spellbound.

There was food, dancing, rivers of cold champagne, a full bar, and since we were using the gold-plated flatware, Izzy had her team watching it like a hawk. No fork was going in anyone's clutch on her watch. When Kat relieved her, Izzy and her husband, Michael, one of the top accountants in the finance department—a quiet, bookish man with curly red hair and more freckles than I'd ever seen on anyone in my life, who could trip over a crack in the sidewalk—were dancing. Somehow, when he was with his wife, she made him look like Fred Astaire. The power of love was never to be underestimated.

Wade arrived, looking resplendent in an Armani tuxedo that fit him like a glove. It was fun to watch all the heads turn when the gorgeous man walked by. I enjoyed seeing Linden spot Wade and try and duck behind a giant arrangement of wisteria. Wade walking around behind his quarry as Linden slowly lifted his head, and then squealed in surprise when Wade tapped him on the shoulder, was the best thing that happened all night. I had no idea what was going on with those two, but my grandmother liked Wade just fine, and when she collected Linden, she took hold of Avery's partner as well.

Gigi, Andrea, and Avery's sister-in-law, Dove, were talking business in one corner; Stone, Ambrose, and Andrea's husband, Crawford, were discussing basketball in another, and I was ready to go. We'd made the announcement, there had been applause, Avery and I shared a dance that was only not horrible because my mate glided over the floor, and even though I was leading, much like Izzy did for her husband, he made me look good.

Afterwards, I was swarmed with people wanting to talk

to me, and I complied because it was the right thing to do, and Avery was bringing out a different side of me, a warmer side, and people were responding to that.

"To be a strong, respected leader is an excellent asset," my grandfather told me, "but now they realize that you're a man who can be loved, and...well now," he husked, smiling at me through brimming eyes, "I'm so proud of you."

Our hug was long. It was an uncharacteristic interaction for us, and I had only one person to thank.

THE NIGHT WORE ON, and I ducked into the library for just a moment and found Linden sitting on one of the couches, bent forward, with Wade sitting beside him, rubbing his back. Only Wade noticed me, and when he lifted his head, he mouthed the words *panic attack*.

I nodded quickly and was about to leave when Linden looked up.

"Oh," he gasped, and tried to get up, struggling for a moment until Wade placed his hand on Linden's shoulder, gentling him with the simple touch.

I watched as Linden's eyes fluttered with the careful display of dominance.

"He feels like he didn't say thank you enough," Wade blurted out.

"The words seem so inadequate, sir," Linden muttered with an exhale. He was mortified, and that was evident from the way he couldn't meet my gaze.

"Linden," I murmured, and his eyes flicked up to my face. "My grandmother desperately enjoys finding new talent and sponsoring shows at different galleries all over the world. She used to host quite a few when she traveled more, but as she's gotten older, she's cut back. She's particularly concerned that she's let down my home city of Chicago, and mentioned she'd like to talk to you about perhaps taking that over for her."

The way he gulped in air, he looked like a fish on dry land.

"You'll speak to her, won't you?" I made certain he heard the order in my voice so he could not mistake my intentions. This was not kindness; it was going to be a job. "And do as she asks. She so rarely makes requests of me; I would hate to disappoint her."

"Of course," he whispered. "It would be my pleasure."

"Excellent," I replied crisply, glancing at Wade, who I couldn't read, other than his eyes never left my face. "Have a shot of scotch, just a small one," I instructed Linny. "That always gets me breathing again."

I left them then, but as I walked away, I heard Linny ask Wade if he had lost his mind.

"I dunno. Maybe."

It sounded quite promising.

IT TOOK ME SOME TIME, going from room to room, to realize that my mate was missing. He was no longer with my grandfather, or with Wade's parents, or any of our family. I was getting nervous when my phone chirped. Pulling it from the breast pocket of my black velvet Ralph Lauren Purple Label tuxedo, I saw that I had a text from my mate. The words made me smile, "Meet me in the alley. We're running away," and I immediately slipped out of the room.

I pulled on my trench coat and left my house, which I now shared not only with my brother and his mate, but with my mate as well. There was something so comforting about that.

Slipping out the side gate, I walked around the corner to where Avery's Jeep was parked. When I was almost to the vehicle, his head lifted a bit above the dash, and when he spotted me, his smile was incandescent.

Earlier, when he'd come down the stairs to meet me in his brown tuxedo, hair slicked back, shaved, and wearing eyeliner that was Linden's doing, I nearly swallowed my tongue. He was gorgeous, and I couldn't stop staring at him. As we received people, he was kind, engaging, oozing charm and sex appeal, and with a smile that lit his face, his dimples wicked, I soon realized that everyone else reacted to him as I had. They'd never seen *this* Avery Rhine, the magnetic creature with the low, seductive chuckle who remembered their names, something random about them that to each was a surprise, and told them how pleased he was they were there. People appeared dazed, and I could tell, easily, which alphas he'd been with from their stunned expressions. What a mistake they'd made. He was luminous, and he came from a bedrock lupine family that was absolutely rolling in money. How had they not used the fact that he'd slept with them to their advantage, and pressed for a bonding? My scowl made them scurry even as I watched them look back at him in wonder.

But I was there beside him, and he leaned close to me constantly, planted dozens of kisses under my jaw, and held my hand when we walked into the ballroom together. Only I saw him clearly, just as he alone saw me. People had looked at me oddly as well. It seemed when I was smiling and happy, I wasn't quite as scary.

Now he sat up in the driver's seat and gestured at me. I jogged down the street to the car, and he got out and ran around to the passenger side and got in. I slipped in behind the steering wheel.

Gone was his tuxedo, and I was looking at a sweater under a fitted distressed leather jacket I found terribly sexy.

"Why am I driving?" I asked, making my voice work even though it was difficult.

"Only because you know where you're going," he assured me, grinning, "and not because I'm a bad driver and you almost threw up last time."

I nodded. "I see." I chortled and started the car.

"Are you comfortable? I brought you different clothes, so you can change if you want, or at least take off the trench and your tuxedo jacket. I can't drive with a ton of stuff on."

I let him help me take things off, and when I was down to my white shirt, I rolled up my sleeves, exposing my forearms, and he leaned in, kissed me, and told me to get going already.

Being ordered around by my mate was never going to be a problem for me.

"Come on," he groused when we reached the little cabin in the woods with the gravel parking area, a bridge over the stream that led to the front door, and a deck big enough to host a wedding reception. "Are you kidding?"

"What? We're really going to be roughing it."

His groan was loud, and for once *I* was laughing at *him*.

We made it inside, and he strolled to the living area, where he put our two small duffel bags down on one of the enormous sectionals and took in the view out the wall of floor-to-ceiling windows.

"Lucky I told Kat to have the place stocked before we got here or we'd be in big trouble. I could run down to the wine cellar and grab a bottle if you—"

Shaking his head, he opened the doors out onto the

back deck, which was just as spacious as the front, and started to strip.

"What do you think you're doing?" I barked at him.

He turned, waggled his eyebrows at me, took off my father's signet ring and put it on the railing, got naked fast, and then shifted fluidly with a seamless roll that I had only seen in other alphas.

"That's your shift?" I gasped, shaking my head. "Is there anything you're not good at?"

He tipped his head, and I laughed because his expressions were the same, man or beast; he was a smartass.

Just as in the dream-space we'd shared, he was a smaller wolf. I went down on my knees, then leaned back, folding my legs behind me, and he trotted over and nuzzled under my jaw. I touched his ears and his nose, rubbed under his chin, held one of his small paws, and then looked at his paintbrush tail. When he licked my nose, I stood and stripped.

My shift was much faster than his, and to watch a wolf's jaw drop was a lot of fun. I darted for the stairs, and he was right with me, following me as I ran from the cabin and deep into the woods. It felt primordial, like we were the only creatures in the cold, dark world, with only each other to keep warm.

We ran for hours, and then I headed for the cabin, wanting nothing more than to lie in front of the fire on warm blankets with my mate. My plan was to have him there, take my time and make him scream my name, but once we were back, he asked if I was hungry, and I realized that neither of us had eaten a thing at our own party.

Rather than put on the clothes we'd stripped out of before our run, we got comfortable instead. I took a shower and put on the fleece pajama bottoms, heavy socks, and T-shirt he'd packed for me, which made me smile. I found my mate in the kitchen, dressed much the same way, except he had on a zip-up Foo Fighters hoodie. Taking a seat at the island, I watched as he made me a simple ham-and-cheese omelet and, in another pan, an eggless omelet, with spinach, mushrooms, peppers and cheese, for himself.

"I like peppers," I chimed in, and he smiled and added them to mine.

"I didn't know you could cook."

"My mother taught us all. She was a short-order cook; that's how she put herself through college," he explained to me.

"I thought your mother came from a wealthy family as well."

"No," he assured me, "my mother was in foster care when she was young; both her folks were killed in a car accident when she was little, and her aunt, her mother's sister, didn't want her."

"I'm so sorry."

He snickered. "After she married my dad, people came from everywhere to claim her as family, but she wasn't havin' it. She always said all she'd ever needed were her own parents when she was little, and then my dad's folks later on."

"I bet your dad's parents adore your mother."

He scoffed. "To say the least."

My omelet was amazing, and I told him so, and got a kiss for the compliment.

"My grandparents both adore you, as do Stone and Gigi," I made clear, wanting him to know he was as loved by my family as his own.

"Same," he assured me, leaning over the island for another kiss.

Afterwards, cleaning up together and having a cup of chamomile tea in front of the fire before snuggling up and talking was, I realized, what I craved more than anything. Time alone with my mate.

"I've always put the wolf part of me second," he confessed, sliding his hand over mine, pressing our palms together, then turning it over and interweaving our fingers, over and over, and I realized how much I savored the relaxed, unhurried touching. "But I want you to help me love that part as much as the human side. I want to trust my wolf."

"I'll help you with that," I promised as he climbed into my lap, turning into me and coiling his arms around my neck. "We'll run together often."

"I love running with you," he whispered, kissing the side of my neck. "I can't wait to do it again."

Sitting there, telling him my stories, listening to his, I was so content I wasn't sure when I slipped from awake to dreaming. When I woke in the middle of the night, warm and cozy in front of the fire, all the lights off, I opened my eyes to find Avery snuggled into my chest.

"I love you," I whispered into his hair, clutching him tight.

"I love you back," he murmured with a yawn. "Now go to sleep."

He was bossy, but I loved that, and so did as I was told.

A NOTE FROM THE AUTHOR

∽

Thank you so much for reading **Muscle and Bone**. I hope you enjoyed Avery and Graeme learning how to blend their lives, and become more than fated mates, but true ones. If you did, please consider leaving a review on Amazon. Reviews help so much with a book's visibility and kind words are always appreciated.

If you enjoy shifters and action, please check out my **L'Ange** series.

Be sure to **follow me on Amazon** to stay up to date on new releases and don't forget to sign up for my newsletter **here.**

Please pop by my **website** or visit me on social media to stay in touch. I have some really cute pics of my furry ninja on Instagram. And if you like to listen to your books as well, you can find me on **Audible** as well.

I hope to see you soon!

ALSO BY MARY CALMES

∾

By Mary Calmes

WARDERS

His Hearth (Warders #1)

Tooth & Nail (Warders #2)

Heart In Hand (Warders #3)

Sinnerman (Warders #4)

Nexus (Warders #5)

Cherish Your Name (Warders #6)

L'ANGE

Old Loyalty, New Love

Fighting Instinct

Chosen Pride

Winter's Knight

HOUSE OF MAEDOC

His Consort

His Prince

MARSHALS

All Kinds of Tied Down

Fit To Be Tied

Tied Up in Knots

Twisted and Tied

TORUS INTERCESSION

No Quick Fix

In A Fix

Fix It Up

THE VAULT

A Day Makes

Late In The Day

More Than Life

Stand In Place

Published by **DREAMSPINNER PRESS**

www.dreamspinnerpress.comAcrobat

Again

Any Closer

Floodgates

Frog

The Guardian

Heart of the Race

Ice Around the Edges

Judgment

Just Desserts

Kairos

Lay It Down

Mine

Romanus * Chevalier

The Servant

Steamroller

Still

Three Fates

What Can Be

Where You Lead

You Never Know

CHANGE OF HEART

Change of Heart

Trusted Bond

Honored Vow

Crucible of Fate

Forging the Future

MANGROVE STORIES

Blue Days

Quiet Nights

Sultry Sunset

Easy Evenings

Sleeping 'til Sunrise

A MATTER OF TIME

A Matter of Time Vol.1

A Matter of Time Vol. 2

Bulletproof

But For You

Parting Shot

Piece of Cake

TIMING

Timing

After the Sunset

When the Dust Settles

ABOUT THE AUTHOR

Mary Calmes believes in romance, happily ever afters, and the faith it takes for her characters to get there. She bleeds coffee, thinks chocolate should be its own food group, and currently lives in Kentucky with a five-pound furry ninja that protects her from baby birds, spiders and the neighbor's dogs. To stay up to date on her ponderings and pandemonium (as well as the adventures of the ninja) follow her on Twitter Facebook, Instagram and subscribe to her newsletter.

- facebook.com/marycalmesbooks
- twitter.com/marycalmes
- instagram.com/marysninja
- amazon.com/mary-calmes/e/B00EJKMHDA
- bookbub.com/authors/mary-calmes

Made in the USA
Middletown, DE
07 April 2021